RETIEF AND THE RASCALS

KEITH LAUMER

BAEN

RETIEF AND THE RASCALS

Copyright © 1993 by Keith Laumer

A Baen Books Original

Baen Publishing Enterprises
P.O. Box 1403
Riverdale, N.Y. 10471

ISBN: 0-671-72168-2

Cover art by Gary Ruddell

First printing, May 1993

Distributed by
SIMON & SCHUSTER
1230 Avenue of the Americas
New York, N.Y. 10020

Printed in the United States of America

"THAT'S TELLING HIM, BEN!"

Retief called over the heads of the half-dozen assorted thugs crowding around the entrance to the cul-de-sac. "Run for it, Ben!" Retief called.

Magnan fled into the darkness, three of the Bloorians baying at his heels. Retief gave chase. He overtook and tripped Gugly Eye, a loafer he'd often seen hanging around the motor pool. Eye was the last in line. Retief moved up to grab Jum Derk by the collar and dump him sideways. Jumping over the still rolling Unspeakable, he overtook the front-runner and knocked him down, Wim's bellow and Shinth's faint voice shouting behind him. Retief called to Magnan, was ignored, and followed his fleeing supervisor along the echoing corridor.

"That did it!" Shinth hissed. "Close the passage, Wim!" Retief skidded to a halt and charged back toward the Groaci and his hirelings, but the Bloorian strong-arm squad had already rolled an immense, rail-mounted steel slab in place, sealing off the passage.

Magnan, noticing nothing, continued to flee, unpursued. He reached a narrowing in the passage, where a great bool-wood door stood half-open. He grabbed it in passing and slammed it, in Retief's face. The latch *clack*led decisively. Retief skidded to a halt and tried the knob. It was fixed as solidly as the wall of living stone beside him. Before he could move, an explosion threw him back against the opposite wall and down into a bottomless pit. . . .

Baen Books By Keith Laumer

Chapter 1

A noisy, jostling crowd of slightly mutated Terran-descended inhabitants of the planet Bloor filled the broad avenue, lined with the formerly imposing facades of Embassy Row. First Secretary Magnan, Econ Officer of the Terran Mission, accompanied by Jame Retief, two grades his junior, but six inches taller, were returning from a trip to the port to meet a newly-assigned colleague.

The purplish sun of the frontier world was casting ocher shadows across the noisy mob filling the Easiest Way, the primary avenue of the capital. The lone Terran-built ground-car with the armorial bearings of the CDT crept through the dense throng and pulled to the curb. In the front seat beside Ralph, the gloomy driver, Herb Lunchwell, the newly-arrived Econ Officer to the Terran Mission, dabbed at his forehead with a large floral-patterned hanky.

"My goodness, Ben," he addressed the senior officer present. "What's the cause of the riot? Won't they attack us as soon as we step out of the car?"

"What riot was that, Herb?" Magnan inquired interestedly. "If you're referring to the admittedly rather

high-spirited locals, actually this is rather a quiet afternoon. They're uninhibited, you see, and perceiving
their lots in life to be less desirable than could be
desired, they freely express their natural resentments,
but it's all quite harmless. They've no weapons, thanks
to enlightened Terran policy, and they'll soon disperse,
all friends again, and retire to the nearby bistros to
get roaring drunk. You'll get used to their noisy ways,
Herb, we all do. Isn't that right, Retief?" Magnan
turned to his junior for confirmation. Retief nodded.

"They're a little extra-excited today because this is
Distribution Day, Mr. Lunchwell," Magnan added.

"Oh, you're referring to the formal alotments of
rations and so on under the Goodies For Undesirables
Program, eh?" Herb responded. "By the way, Ben,
congrats on your appointment as Counselor of Embassy
for GFU Affairs; a plum, indeed—but you'll have to
be careful," he went on. "Every recipient will want to
be sure he's getting his fair share."

"And clearly," Magnan amplified, nodding, "each
one is already convinced he's being cheated. Odd," he
mused on. "We owe them nothing, yet we distribute
free gifts, and they complain it's not enough."

Ralph twisted to look back at his VIP passengers.
"Say, Ben," he offered, "OK if I just ease into the
alley up ahead?" He winced as a large, well-rotted
stench-cabbage impacted on the windshield directly
before him. "See, these guys here are mostly of the
Objectionable Clan; in town fer the annual rumble
with the Reprehensibles; they don't—I mean, I ain't—
well, you see, Ben, there's some guy from the Reprehensibles expecting—I mean, a guy could get hurt if
he din't do what—"

"Ralphie!" Magnan chided, "you *haven't* been trafficking with the lawless element again! Not after last
time!"

"Well, Ben, you see . . ." Ralph nudged the car

another ten feet through the tight rank of yelling Bloorian males and netted ugly looks, shaken fists, and a shower of small missiles. He was scrooched down in the seat in instinctive response to the barrage of stones, bottles, and dead animals raining down on the car, but he persevered, easing the heavy vehicle through the loafers, too lazy to riot, who crowded the sidewalk, past the plain gray stucco facade of the Groacian Embassy and the narrow front of the bonded warehouse, inching toward the brightly-lit portico of the Embassy of Terra. Then he braked to a halt as he encountered a solid rank of locals standing with linked arms, facing the Embassy car.

"End o' the line, gents," Ralph declared. "Them boys ain't moving."

"Where are the women and children?" Herb wanted to know as he peered anxiously out at the all-male mob.

"Oh," Magnan explained, "they have their own riots—no, a slip of the tongue, 'joyous expressions of high spirits,' as His Excellency insists we call them— on alternate days. Tomorrow is Ladies' Day."

Retief opened the door against pressure and stepped out, nudging a few locals aside to make room for Magnan and Herb, who emerged cautiously, muttering precautionary apologies to the displaced locals.

As they were passing the warehouse side-entrance between the two Chanceries, Magnan plucked at Retief's sleeve. "Really, Jim," he confided in an anxious tone, "I think we should have had Ralph force his way through and drop us on the doorstep. I fear the looks these xenophobic fellows are casting our way aren't all that friendly, in spite of our generosity toward their backward world." He shuffled forward, pushed by the mob.

"What's that 'backward'?" demanded a typically large, hawk-faced, horny-handed local dressed in the shabby bib overalls favored by the Bloorians. The big fellow stepped out from the warehouse doorway to deliberately block the walk, rolling his impressive shoulders in a truculent way. His grin was less than reassuring. As Magnan was forced against the unmoving bulk, the local doubled a right fist like a ham-shaped paving stone and drew it back, shifting his weight in preparation for putting all two hundred eighty pounds behind a low right jab.

"You tryna start sumpin wit' Slum Dob, a chief of one hunhert?" he demanded.

"*Do* excuse me, sir," Magnan twittered. "I regret my clumsiness, but could you just scroonch over a teentsy bit, say to your left, and allow us to pass? You see we're late for the ceremonies at our Embassy."

"Hey, all youse Objectionables," the lout called over Magnan's head. "Youse hear that? This here nance is tryna order me outa duh way! Are we gonna take dat?" He set himself and drove the cocked fist toward Magnan's semiformal early mid-evening dickey, but the blow impacted the palm of Retief's hand instead of Magnan's short ribs.

"Get behind me, Mr. Magnan," Retief suggested. Slum Dob looked puzzled, then yelped as Retief's fingers closed around his hamlike fist and began to squeeze; he uttered a louder yell and his left arm came around in a roundhouse swipe aimed at Retief's head. Magnan uttered a bleat and seized the arm with both hands as it jerked him from his feet. He hung on and was slammed against the wall of the shabby warehouse sandwiched between the elegant Embassies of Groac and Terra.

"Fellers," the Bloorian again appealed to the crowd, "I'm Slum Dob, working outa local Three-oh-one o' duh United Miscreants, an' I'm pretty big in duh Reprehensible Tribe and clan Objectionable, as well. An' dis mug, or I meana say dese *two* mugs, is tryna strip me o my civil rights an all! All you Reps and Regs and Micks and Obbies oughta rally to my pertekshin onna double!" As Slum Dob concluded his appeal, he lunged suddenly in an attempt to free his hand, but Retief braced his feet and yanked him back to a face-to-face stance.

"Come on, pal," Slum appealed, twisting his gargoyle-like features into what Retief decided was an attempt at an ingratiating smirk. "Lemme go before duh boys catch wise and get duh idea I'm losing my stuff, OK?" He tried a snap-kick to the shin, but instead his own shin impacted the edge of Retief's boot. He howled and recoiled, slamming Magnan against the wall.

"Jim," Magnan bleated. "Force this ruffian to release me at once!"

"Just let go, Ben," Retief suggested. "It's you that's holding on to him. Thanks for the assist."

Magnan released his frantic clutch and fell underfoot. Slum tried a left to Retief's jaw and found that fist imprisoned like the other. As his knuckles were ground together, he screwed up his face and snarled.

"Yuh better lemme be, Terry, if yuh know what's good fer yuh!"

"Tell me, Dob, what's good for me?" Retief inquired interestedly.

"Yuh know," Dob pled, "a smart guy wudda went wid duh flow, like us: stuff happens, so why get caught in duh wheels?"

"You mean if I were smart I'd be like you?" Retief prompted.

"Now yer getting duh sketch, Pal," Dob approved. "Say, yuh wanna kinda leggo my fistes?"

"I heard you appeal to the Objectionables to lend assistance," Retief commented. "I've heard of the Objectionables, but who are they and how did they get their name?" Retief gave Slum's hands a final twist and let them go.

"Well," Slum started, in a relieved tone, "inna olden time our poor ignernt ancestors and all useta work alla time: dey liked it, see? Hundin' and diggin' and hoein' spuds and puttin' in crops and all dat. But fin'ly *my* high-class tribe, dey useta call us 'duh Busies,' we were duh foist group to figger if we could let duh udder mug do duh hard labor and den strong-arm duh like produck of his labors, dat'd be a lot easier dan doing our own woik. See? So dat's why dey dubbed us duh Objectionables, get it? Dey objected, see, when we harvested dere crops fer em, duh Spoilsports, which we're hereditary enemies now. Smart! Right? But did duh udder clans appreciate dem kine o' smarts? Naw!" Slum made a throwing-away gesture with his newly released hand. "Dey was envious an' all at foist. Den dey trieda pull duh same stuff on *us*! Duh lousy bums! Now get dis part, Terry: while our ancestors was sleeping off a hard day hunding rock-goats in duh foothills—it was a habit, see? Anyway dese sneaky Unspeakables—dat's what duh tribal council called 'em, an duh moniker stuck—snuck in an' taken all duh goat meat after *we* done alla woik! Can you top dat for unspeakable? Dey were the nex' bunch to try duh scam, and pretty soon nobody was hunding no rock-goats no more, when dey could get duh eats free, and pretty soon alla tribes tipped wise to duh technique, and dat's duh basis o' duh Bloorian economy to dis day."

"No wonder they all call each other 'Scoundrels' and 'Hatefuls' and 'Unimaginables' and so on," Magnan mused.

"I see," Retief encouraged. "You boys were contentedly taking in each other's washing until we Terries came along and started handing out the equivalent of goat meat, and spoiled all the fun."

"Dat's it, chum," Slum confided. "Say, you got a good head on youse, fer a foreigner, I mean, and dat left hook ain't too bad, neither. Roont duh whole basis o' our culture, is what youse boys done! It ain't hardly to be borne!" Slum knuckled an eye in demonstration of his emotional distress. "O' course," he added, "we still got duh poor dumb peasants-like, duh B-9's, dat keep duh chickens and made duh bread and all—fer fun, see? Dey *like* woik! Some kinda throwbacks, I guess; it's lucky at dat: hamboigers don't grow onna trees, you know."

"I hadn't heard about the B-9's," Retief commented.

"Naw, dey keep to duh hills mostly." Dob grunted. "We don't mess wid 'em an' dey got smarts enough dey don't mess wid *us*."

"Great Heavens, Retief!" Magnan spoke up. "I'd never considered the Goodies For Undesirables program in that light! Why, we may have done irreparable harm to this lively emergent, ah, backward, or developing, that is to say inferior society, all in the name of Benign Dispensation!"

"Yeah," Slum confirmed. "Dat's duh trouble wit' you do-gooders, you go aroun do-gooding fer yer own kicks, and don't give no consideration to what yuh might be doing to hallowed local values an' all!"

He paused to grieve silently, while Magnan fought to restrain his emotion. "Goodness gracious me," he whimpered. "How can we—and in particular, I, make it up to them?"

"You could start by belting that Unthinkable who's lifting your wallet," Retief suggested. Magnan looked amazed, then jumped, clapped a hand over the pocket where he kept his credit coder and found himself eyeball-to-eyeball with a stubby seven-foot local. He yipped and jabbed forked fingers at the pickpocket's bleary eyes, a move that sent the fellow reeling back, yelling, and striking out randomly at the nearest bystanders among the clot of the idle curious who had fallen out of the free-for-all to observe the fate of the foreigners who had been cornered by Slum Dob, a proven Champion of One Hundred.

Noting their hero's distress, the mass of Bloorians advanced in a solid wave of brandished fists and snarling faces. While Retief battered an opening, Ralph and Herb made a run for it. Magnan was thrust back against the unmarked door, which collapsed under the avalanche. Retief felled a persistent Incorrigible as he reached for Ben, and urged Magnan through the opening. Inside, Magnan had shrunk back against the wall and was blinking in the dim gloom of the bonded warehouse, while recovering his breath.

"Good Lord, Jim," he commented between gasps. "It appears security is more lax than I had dreamed. Why, that door isn't even on the Schedule! I'd no idea—and now we're trapped down here! The security doors will be locked tight! Why does it smell so bad in here? There's nothing in bond right now except the remaining GFU supplies from the last shipment."

"Just a moment," Retief cut in. "I want to take a look over here." He went along the wall to the corner, where a flimsy construction of plywood partitioned off a cramped space. Through the gaping joints, dim light revealed brooms and mops.

"Retief!" Magnan yipped. "It's—that must be the storage closet used by the custodial personnel. Difficult chaps, those sweepers! Just last week the Admin Officer called the Boss Boy in to tell him he was raising their pay. The insolent fellow replied that it wasn't enough!"

"You have to remember the locals lose face if they're detected doing anything useful," Retief reminded his chief.

"Scant danger!" Magnan snapped. "That gang of loafers spend their on-duty hours playing Bliff in the back corridor. They don't even bother anymore to rub the used motor oil on the phones to make them shine!"

Retief eased through the open joint into the broom closet and invited Magnan to follow. Pushing past the mops and buckets, he eased the closet door open and the two stepped out into the brilliant light and bustle of the boisterous crowd filling the Embassy lobby.

"We hardly look presentable, Jim," Magnan carped. "We can't attend the gala in this state of disarray!"

"We'll have to, Ben," Retief countered. "Come on; no one will notice, after we've pushed our way through this mob."

"Heavens!" Magnan squeaked. "I'd no idea Hy had invited so many uncouth locals to attend the banquet! I doubt we can serve so many—and they look like big eaters, too!" He clutched Retief's arm. "Imagine the expression on Freddie Underknuckle's face when I tell him of the gross flaw in his security!"

"That's nothing to what Randy O'Rourke is going to tell his gyrenes when *he* finds out," Retief pointed out.

Retief led the way, forcing a passage through the noisy Bloorians of every caste, tribe, clan, union, service club, and fraternity, all argumentatively determined to be first to reach the banquet hall.

"It was awkward," Magnan was telling Retief breathlessly, "just to entice the members of so many of the local factions to foregather peacefully here tonight, suppressing for a while their innate instinct to attack everyone in sight!"

"With these boys," Retief replied, ducking under a roundhouse swing as he delivered a stiff right to the attacking Nasty's broad torso, "it's hard to tell peace from war."

"True," Magnan murmured judiciously. "Still, it appears that so far the paramedics have been able to evacuate the wounded at a rate which slightly exceeds the rate of mayhem. So we've no actual accumulation of casualties with which to deal."

"Jim," Magnan raised his voice to make himself heard over the hubbub, enlivened by a number of brisk fist- and knife-fights among the members of traditionally hostile guest-groups, "regarding the broomcloset, how did you know—or suspect—"

"Yesterday I saw three sweepers go into the broom closet and nobody came out," Retief explained.

"Oh, so it was after all quite obvious," Magnan sighed. "Pity Sergeant Randy O'Rourke didn't notice."

"It's not so strange," Retief pointed out. "After all, His Ex has failed to notice that the mob-leader to whom he's about to award the Legion Third Class is a dope-smuggling child molester."

"Retief! Remember it's Child Molester Pride Week!"

"I guess I had it confused with Rapist Pride Month," Retief confessed, as they forged ahead toward the receiving line.

"Now, Retief," Counselor Magnan cautioned as he trailed his tall, powerfully built assistant to the ornate double door where Marv Lacklustre waited, shaking hands and murmuring to each arrival. "We mustn't take it upon ourselves," Magnan cautioned, "to be adversely critical of His Excellency's choice as recipient of the Longspoon Award. It's quite true that Minister of Internal Chaos Bam Slang *had* acquired a somewhat unsavory popular reputation as a thieving, murderous leader of a dacoit mob, prior to our arrival, but since the CDT has recognized that he in fact embodies his people's legitimate aspirations for self-determination, we must acknowledge that he and his band of patriots were in fact, merely requisitioning supplies, albeit in an informal manner, to carry on the good fight against colonialism."

"Sure, Ben," Retief reminded his senior. "He had to kill all the women and children so as to 'emphasize the determination of the people to achieve democracy'; I read Hy's press handout. But why did he have to burn down the schools and hospitals we'd built and sell the relief supplies we sent in after the flood, then buy a solid gold bed? I admit I'm a little hazy on that part."

"As to that," Magnan evaded, "we should, of course, have provided the gold bed directly. And we have only the unsupported reports of the putative 'victims' to suggest that atrocities did in fact take place."

"That, and all the corpses," Retief agreed.

"Tush," Magnan chided. "You must learn to curb your tendency toward *ad hoc* cynicism. Remember: Bam Slang is the Fred Hiesenwhacker of Bloor, or, more precisely, of the Bloorish people."

"That's too mild an encominum," Retief suggested. "Hiesenwhacker only burned down the Legislature, with all the legislators and insurance company bagmen inside. Bam has wiped out the entire governmental apparatus."

"Still, the parallel is undeniable," Magnan insisted, "once one squarely faces the fact that any and all governmental meddling with the individual is innately criminal." Magnan fell silent as they entered the banquet hall, already crowded with Corps dignitaries and local bigshots, all wearing their gaudiest garb, including shrunken human—well, almost—heads dangling from the belts of the most august local chieftains. Brightly colored banners flanked the GFU logo adorning the center of the far wall, above the ranks of linen-, silver-, and crystal-decked tables. Some of the less sophisticated or hungrier local politicos had already seated themselves and were digging heartily into the tureens of gourmet viands simmering on the hotplates between places.

"Some of them are even using the spoons and

forks!" Magnan pointed out, with the pride of an animal-trainer.

The Terran flag, Retief noted, while prominently displayed in the decorative scheme, was always placed well below that of Bloor.

"Do you think," he inquired of Magnan, "that putting the flag in a subordinate position will actually convince the locals that they're as powerful as Terra?"

"Of course not." Magnan sniffed. "But it will encourage them to speak up forthrightly in defense of their traditional freedoms in the negotiations, or at least so Ambassador Swinepearl has determined."

"The locals aren't snotty enough for him?" Retief asked. "I thought he was quite impressed by the way they invaded his last tea-and-croquet party with armored cars and machetes and stole all the balls and dumped the tea in the fountain."

"Oh, yes, he was of course delighted at their show of high-spiritedness," Magnan assured Retief. "The Information Service was, too. 'All Bloor Rejoices!' the headlines proclaimed. 'Diplomatic Breakthrough' was the mildest encomium I heard! So valuable in building the Image! I shouldn't wonder if Hy Felix nets a promotion from the affair! The Agency is more responsive to individual initiative than the Corps, the more especially as regards those of us privileged to serve with the Goodies for Undesirables Program."

Young Marvin Lacklustre had been dragooned for the task of running the receiving line: after consulting his seating chart, he directed Magnan to a place near the Ambassador's thronelike seat, and shunted Retief to a spot opposite a gorilloid Bloor Ward-boss, who was busy saucering and blowing a plate of *consommé au beurre blanc*.

The local glanced up as Retief took his chair, and grunted. "Bloody good soup, pal, onney it ain't even got no barf-bug heads in," he commented.

"Pity," Retief commiserated. "I guess George forgot."

"Hah!" the Bloorish politico grunted. "Duh dough dey pay dem chef guys, dey shunt oughta fergit stuff. If dis George was on *my* staff," he added with a suggestive glint in his piggy eye, "I'd bend duh sucker plendy. Look at dis stuff!" He displayed a spoon brimming with the delicately seasoned fluid. "Nothin'! Just soup, is all!" He swallowed the offending provender with an audible *gulp!* "Tas'e OK, I gotta give it dat," he acknowledged. "Hey, throw the punk over dis way, pal!" he called to the Terran seated opposite.

The dignified First Secretary of Embassy of Terra thus addressed obligingly passed the wicker basket of hard rolls, one of which Bam seized and attempted to saw in half with a butter knife. He tossed the utensil aside and tried to bite the roll.

"Jeez!" he exclaimed. "A guy could bust a tooth on dat!" He dropped the superb bun on the floor, and leaned forward confidentially. "Ain't dey got no Wonder Bread aroun'?" he whispered. "A guy could put a liddle peaner budder and jelly on, and, man! That's chow!"

"No Wonder Bread," Retief reported. "We vowed to give it up for the Memorial Millennium, along with the peaner budder."

"What's dat millinery—what you said?" Bam demanded, swallowing more soup, which he had discovered he could get down more quickly if he picked up the bowl and poured it directly down his throat.

"In honor of the thousandth anniversary of Terran-Bloorish relations," Retief explained.

"Yeah, that's when youse Terries first come snooping aroun' good old Bloor inderfering wit duh, like, legitimate aspirations of us Detestables, right, which we was onney tryna get duh like B-9 peasants and all shaped up to get out duh vote and all," Bam mourned.

"According to the record," Retief told him, "the

Survey Team landed in the middle of a massacre in which thousands of the local citizens had already been slaughtered by the State Police, and the carnage continued until put down by the armed recon cars the Team had along."

"Oh, yeah, duh boys was busy cleaning up on the Bad Guys, you know, duh bums hadda crazy idear *they* ought to be running the massacree. Otherwise, see, duh bad guys woulda been massacreeing duh good guys and all."

"And just how did the bad guys differ from the good guys?" Retief queried. His informant frowned, then brightened. "Dat's easy, pal," he confided. "Duh good guys was on *our* side, an duh bad guys—"

"I get the idea," Retief cut in. "Very practical approach."

"And see," Bam continued, "duh present-day Good Guys party, udderwise knowed as duh Detestables, inherited duh, like, mandle o' leadership and all from dem oily Patriots which dey was on'y cleaning out duh reactionary element and all."

"A noble genealogy," Retief conceded. "I take it that's why your present Chief of State is intent on eliminating all dissident elements in a direct fashion, by burial alive."

"Sure; dem like free elections Mr. Ambluster made us hold was a big help. Identified alla Bad Guys voted wrong. We gotta bury 'em alive where you Terries won't let us have a few deadly weapons to kill 'em wid."

Just then Retief noticed that Magnan, two tables away, was flapping his napkin while keeping his eyes fixed on Retief. He was mouthing words as he signaled.

"Looks like one o' your boys is having a attact," Bam noted. "See? Duh skinny one at duh V. I. of P. table."

"I'd better go over," Retief said, and did so.

"Retief!" Magnan burst out in a stage whisper as Retief came up. "You'd best change seats, at once. Marvin can just change his chart. There's been—that is, there could be—I fear—the Ambassador will be furious! We must avert bloodshed at all cost! Quickly, now!"

"What's it all about, Ben?" Retief asked. "You forgot to say."

"Oh, yes, to be sure," Magnan gobbled. "No time to waste. It's his Ferocity! He's decided to rush things along by collecting reparations at once, rather than waiting until he's won the war, with Terran assistance! Clearly, he has no grasp of the proper protocols in such matters!"

As he spoke, Magnan was eyeing the resplendently robed seven-foot-six Wim Dit, Grand Inquisitor of Bloor, who, arriving late, had spilled a number of top-ranking Terry diplomats from their chairs so as to take one to the position of honor at the head of the table, on which he had dropped a freshly-killed three-pound ulsio, a hairless, muskratlike animal which had been kept as a pet by Wes Spradley, the Econ Officer, who was hovering nearby, complaining in a diplomatic yell.

"The Honorable Wim Dit is upset by Wes's attempt to protect his protégé," Magnan explained.

"Called me a 'big, ugly ape,'" Wim mourned, cuffing aside Marvin Lacklustre as the young fellow attempted to soothe him.

"Now all youse fancy-pants can clear outa my way, and pack alla eats down here where I don't hafta reach none!" Wim ordered.

"Magnan!" the treble voice of His Excellency the Ambassador Extraordinary and Minister Plenipotentiary of Terra squeaked, directly behind Magnan, causing him to leap and look around wildly, failing to notice the stubby A.E. and M.P. standing so close to him.

"I thought I heard the Ambassador!" Magnan yelped, his gaze passing above the short, plump Chief of Mission. "Where *is* the little devil? I mean," he amended as he belatedly noticed his boss wringing his hands in Distress, Deep, Ceremonial Occasions, for use on (1072-C). "I mean," he improvised, "Yes, indeed, Mr. Ambassador, how can I be of service?"

"I *heard* that, Ben!" Swinepearl squeaked. " 'Little devil,' you said. I'm not too little to write an ER on you, sir, that will freeze your career like the Riss glaciation! 'What can you do?' you inquire! It is precisely to answer such questions that the Corps had dispatched you here as my Chief of Political Section! So, what are you going to do about it?"

"About what, sir?" Magnan croaked. "I see His Ferocity laying about him with that dreadful great sword, almost nicked at Sitzfleisch with that one— good thing Nat's been limbering up in the gym lately, and—"

"Never mind that, Ben!" Swinepearl's shrill voice cut through Magnan's chatter. "Take the necessary action! At once!"

"Sure, sir," Magnan rattled. "But you forgot to say what the necessary action is, sir."

"As you know, Ben," His Ex stated stonily, "it is not my policy to meddle in the internal workings of my Sections, by issuing excessively detailed instructions. This outrage must cease at once, before some of the opposition dignitaries I've coaxed here revert to type and reply in kind to Wim's truculence! So get cracking!" Magnan nodded and went over to stand beside Retief.

"Well, Retief," he addressed the younger man, "this is it, I guess. His Ex demands I *do* something! I may as well bite on the bullet at once!" Attempting to appear inconspicuous to Lord Dit, Magnan stepped off determinedly toward the slightly less burly Bloorian Prime Minister, Gad Buy, also Commander in Chief and Cub Scout leader.

"We've had some high times, Retief," Magnan stated over his shoulder. "Who'd've thought it would end like this?" Retief overtook Magnan just as a late-arriving guest hooked a chair out with his foot, causing the slender Econ chief to trip and fall heavily into the lap of His Ferocity, who rose, grabbing Magnan by his neck and the seat of his purple pants and raising him overhead.

"Mum Dug," the immense Bloorian addressed the Minister of Staff seated beside him. "You seen dis here ruffian assault me wid yer own eyes!"

"You got me wrong, Chief," Mum objected stoutly. "I di'n't let duh sucker use *my* eyes to jump yuh wit! I'm true blue, Boss, yuh know dat!"

"Don't tell me what I know!" the Grand Inquisitor bellowed. "If I di'n't have dis here Terry on my hands, I'd—"

"My dear Mr. Grand Inquisitor." Ambassador Swinepearl's mellow tenor spoke up before the rising hubbub made communication impossible. "I must insist: put Ben Magnan down at once!" His Excellency the Terran A.E. and M.P. sat down with a defiant *thump!*, ignoring the fact that His Ferocity had failed to respond to his command. The background murmur was taking on an ugly note, punctuated with cries of "Get Terry!" and "T'row the rascals out!"

"Dear me," Magnan bleated from his position above Wim's lumpy head. "I *do* hope nothing is going to happen to spoil our nice beginning!"

Retief came up to the Grand Inquisitor, who loomed two feet above him. He poked the behemoth in his armored ribs. "Put him down, gently," he ordered. The giant looked down with an expression of wonderment.

"Who you telling to 'put him down'?" he inquired. "Yuh want to get squashed, liddle feller?" He rubbed the spot Retief had jabbed. "Got a broke rib," he moaned.

"Not yet," Retief replied. "I just want you to put Mr. Magnan down, very carefully, and not in the hot soup."

Wim scowled and made no move.

Retief looked up at Magnan's expression of Urgent Appeal (a masterful 3-b) and said, "Get set, Ben; there might be a slight jolt." With that, he drove a pile-driver left hook to the same spot he had poked earlier. It felt like socking a stuffed crocodile, he noticed. He felt the costals collapse, and Wim dropped Magnan, who landed nimbly on his feet on the linen, missing the big tureen almost completely, while Wim uttered a howl like a gutted dire-beast. He collapsed into his ornate chair, and made an attempt to shove Retief into the one hastily vacated by Mum Dug, whom Retief threw under the table, before sitting in his chair.

"Dis midget done hitten me!" Wim grieved loudly, staring around at his loyal Vile Party colleagues, all of whom were shifting uneasily in their chairs and making threatening gestures at the nearest Terry, but making no move to attack—yet.

"Youse mugs gonna set and let him get away wid socking yer boss inna gut?" the Grand Inquisitor yelled.

"Shut up," Retief told him curtly. Magnan, on all fours on the table, was *shush!*ing him frantically. "Retief!" he hissed, "you must remember to whom it is you're addressing!"

"Yuh got yer syntax scrambled, Ben," Wim grunted. "Dis ain't no time to lapse into like incomprehensibility!"

"Sure not," Magnan gobbled. "Retief didn't mean, I mean, it was just a slip, and if, in your magnanimity, that of a great leader, you'd overlook it just this once, why, I'm sure posterity would honor you!"

"Skip all that," Wim cut in on Magnan's babbling. He fixed his ocher eyes on Retief. "As fer yuh, Shorty," he growled, drawing from his foot-wide tump-hide belt a frog-sticker that would have made Jim Bowie blush with shame, "Try dat again and I'll cut yer heart out!" A hush had fallen. All eyes were fixed on the huge knife in Wim's fist. Swinepearl moaned and slid from his chair in a faint.

"Really?" Retief replied in a tone of Deep Interest, Synthetic (1045-c). He took a needle-pointed dagger from its sheath on the side of his boot and put its point under Wim's clifflike chin.

"And just how do you plan to cut my heart out before I can slit your dirty neck?" he asked harshly, noting from the corner of his eye that the Ambassador had been helped back into his chair.

"Retief!" Swinepearl's yell cut through a rising clamor, which fell abruptly back to dead silence.

"Don't do it, my boy!" His Ex choked. "Not after I've secured His Ferocity's agreement to accept a twenty-five-million-guck no-strings grant from GFU, the first great triumph of my assignment. Ben, dissuade him, and your temporary appointment as Counselor of Embassy for GFU Affairs is confirmed tomorrow morning! My word on it!"

"Retief!" Magnan gasped, attempting to shrug off the grip of a large ward-boss who had, in defense of his boss, taken a grip on the First Secretary's slender neck.

Retief switched targets, and prodded the boss's arm with the stiletto. The arm at once withdrew, letting Magnan's face fall perilously close to the *consommé*.

"Get up, Ben," Retief suggested. "Climb down here beside me, and watch for knives."

Magnan made gulping noises and complied.

"Now," Retief addressed Wim. "You take your gang and march out of here and back to your kennels. We'll send some Peace Enforcers around in the morning to round up the ringleaders."

"You hurted my favorite rib," Wim complained. He fingered his hurtie and winced, miming the agony occasioned by the injury. "OK, Dug," he barked. "Get dese slobs shaped up and don't fergit duh doggie-bags." He emphasized the suggestion with a blow to Mum Dug's jaw that would have knocked the ascending ramus off an ox's mandible. Mum gave him a resentful glance and set off, yelling commands.

"Drat!" Swinepearl carped, casting a regretful glance at the departing silverware, including the big platinum serving tureens, which the enterprising locals had scooped up in bags improvised from the heavy linen tablecloths. "My moment of triumph has turned into a fiasco! As for you, Hy," he switched targets to the excitable TIA rep, "not a word of this in the media, do you understand!"

"Sure, Chief." Hy nodded in agreement. "But how am I gonna stop the local yellow press from reporting how Ben Magnan roughed up the local Chief of Government, huh?"

"That, Mr. Felix," His Ex responded coldly, "is precisely the challenge to meet which the Agency has dispatched you here for! As for you, Ben, I'm surprised at you! From my seat, some six feet distant, I clearly heard the *whap!* when you actually assaulted an honored guest!" He gave Magnan a final glare and sat down to a final buzz of "Huzza!" and "Well said, sir." Retief put away his dagger and threw Wim's larger blade into a handy waste receptacle. His Ferocity settled back in his chair and looked around threateningly.

"Whom, I, sir?" Magnan gobbled, struggling to restore normal respiration. "But you said, that is, I understood His Excellency to suggest that I put an end to the provocation occasioned by His Ferocity's intransigence! No offense, sir," he added, with a glance at Wim, who frowned.

"I never said about that 'intransigents,' " the Ambassador exclaimed. "Anyways, knock off the Cheyne-Stokes breathing and get this mess cleaned up in time for the Award ceremonies, which I'm postponing 'em to nine A.M. tomorrow morning!" He threw himself back into his chair, brushing aside the attempts of his loyal staff to commiserate with him in his moment of trial.

Magnan turned to Retief. "Well, you've done it this time, Jim," he stated in Tones of Doom (3-c). "How'll we ever get 'em back together in time for the Awards?" He looked appealingly at Wim, who was glowering as he fingered the pricked spot under his jaw, where a drop of purple blood was forming.

"Maybe we ought to reconsider the Awards," Retief suggested. "Spending the Terran taxpayers' money to give solid silver potties to local hoodlums might not be in the best interest of Galactic Peace after all."

"Retief, what a gross remark!" Magnan chided. "You know as well as I it's traditional to single out the most notorious local troublemakers to hail as Enlightened Liberators of the People and jump them up until they begin to believe it themselves—or at least moderate their most antisocial tendencies so as to assuage Enlightened Galactic Opinion! Supplying the commodes was merely symbolic of our determination to provide the basic necessities."

"Certainly," Retief acknowledged. "But perhaps, just this once, a touch of the non-traditional would be in order, to pacify these gangsters before they've murdered the entire electorate. And maybe thunderjugs *will* remind them not to crap on the carpets."

"A radical notion, Jim," Magnan carped. "After all,

we've His Excellency's very own guidance in the matter. Tomorrow the Platinum halo, *with* bladder, will be handed to Wim Dit, elevating him to the pantheon of the Arm's great Liberators, thus changing forever the role of Bloor in interplanetary affairs! Their fleets will be converted to pleasure boats to accommodate the hordes of holiday-makers flocking here to the newest tourist attraction in six lights! The annual revenues from landing tax alone will exceed the sums extorted by Wim's protection rackets over the past decade! Can we allow all this to be lost merely because of a trifling misunderstanding?"

"What's to misunderstand?" Wim demanded. "Duh mug hit me, and stabbed me, too." He displayed a purple-stained fingertip in proof of the latter charge. "I guess I got a right to some reparations, eh? How about a private pleasure-planetoid like duh one I see about onna tube, you CDT boys built fer dat Yub duh Unspeakable over Hangdog Tree, he shun't invade no more like inoffensive smaller powers an' all?"

"Forget it," Swinepearl suggested crisply. "After all, Your Ferocity," His Ex continued from his throne, "you haven't yet run up a record of murder and pillage to qualify for the same league with Yub! You'll be lucky if I let you have a six-hundred-bed funhouse, including six hundred prime broads (local, of course)!"

"Nix," Wim dismissed the offer. "I get tired o' duh same ol' hoors. Let's have some new hookers, fresh in from Terra. I'll see about staging a few raids to like beef up duh old rep."

"Heavens!" Magnan murmured to Retief as the two resumed their chairs at the festive board. "One less sophisticated than ourselves might almost receive the impression His Excellency was encouraging pillage and rapine."

"Hey, Ben," Hy Felix called in the near-silence which followed the exchange. "How's this sound?

'Terry A.E. and M.P. Offers Reward to Local Hoodlum to Encourage Increase in,' uh—"

"Pillage and Rapine," Wim suggested.

"That's it!" Hy exulted. "There's a lead that'll stir up the City Room back at Sector!"

"Don't you dare, Hyman!" Magnan barked. "You know very well it was merely an unfortunate turn of phrase! Why, His Ferocity would never dream of taking it literally!"

"Say, Ben," Wim interrupted, giving Magnan a rib-cracking nudge with his elbow. "Did I get that right? Old Swinepearl is offering me six hunnert Terry hoors if I step up duh old pillage and rapine, right?"

"Hardly!" Magnan rejected the idea indignantly. "He only meant—I mean, he meant Corps funds can hardly be expended to rid the Galaxy of a plague too minor to have captured the attention of Enlightened Galactic Opinion! It's merely a matter of proper PR. You've done enough! Be reasonable, Wim!" Magnan's voice faded with his realization of the futility of his efforts. "One can hardly expect the public to condone the award of Class One perks to a mere neophyte in the world of planetary rape!" he argued, reasonably enough. "It would mean upgrading the entire schedule of Goodies, at fantastic cost to the electorate! Actually," he continued more confidently to Wim Dit, "you people barely qualify as Undesirable under the charter of GFU! Indeed, I note that among the epithets you people have applied to each other, 'Undesirables,' while appropriate, is notable by its absence! Let well enough alone! GFU will provide a modest funhouse with banquet synthesizer at the least, and possibly an Imperial model comfort station, just like His Excellency's!"

"Modest is fer loosers," Wim Dit grunted. "You boys'll hafta excuse me." He rose ponderously. "I gotta go—to see to duh maintenance o' law and order, I mean, before word gets out duh conference is falling apart. Got some unsavory elements here in Bloortown might wanna take a'vantage and all. Also, I got a distribution o' good honest graft to supervise. Ta."

"The wretch!" Magnan spat when Wim was well out of earshot. "After accepting a no-strings grant of twenty-five million guck—the highlight of His Ex's Embassy to Bloor—he callously refers to it as 'graft'!"

"But he *did* say 'honest' graft," Retief pointed out.

"Of course!" Magnan rejected the rationalization. "All was carried out in strict agreement with GFU policy as well as Sector Regs!"

"You can't really blame an unsophisticated ward politician for getting confused," Retief suggested. "It's exactly the way he's been operating since the first time he delivered the vote from a two-block sector of Bloor City in return for control of the choice paper routes."

"There are of course parallels between interplanetary do-gooding and crooked politics," Magnan conceded. "But after all, the basic Laws of Nature are 'Dog eat smaller dog,' and 'What's in it for me?' "

One of the larger local ward-heelers, timing his move carefully, shoved his chair back suddenly. He had been miming preoccupation with bending spoons into circles with which to play quoits, employing a silver candlestick as target. Magnan tripped over the abruptly intrusive furniture and uttered a sharp, "Ow! That hurt, you damned clumsy boor! Or, excuse me, sir, did I disturb your vandalism—oops!—I mean your jolly game?" Then recovering his élan: "Pray proceed and I'll get out of your way."

"Damn right," the hulking lout muttered. "Yer spoiling my aim. Cull and I got duh punchbowl bet on dis round!" He elbowed Magnan sharply, not *quite* breaking a rib, as the X-rays later attested, and wrapped a long soup-spoon around his ankle-like wrist.

"Not bad," he conceded, admiring the shiny bracelet.

"Guess I'll just incorporate duh bauble inna my already preddy gaudy, I gotta admit, lifestyle. Par me, Cull, I gotta go and be sure old Wim cuts me in fer a full share. Hang loose, and don't let no lousy scruples louse up yer career."

"Did you hear what he said?" Magnan inquired of Retief. " 'No lousy scruples,' he said, and do you know, Jim, I think perhaps that's exactly what's been retarding my career development! Could it be ... ? 'Out of the mouths of babes,' you know." After a moment's thought he resumed:

"I might cite the present fiasco as an example; rather than treacherously encourage Hy, quite *sub rosa*, of course, to broadcast His Ex's folly in not only recognizing the local mob leader as *de facto* government here on Bloor, but in going to press for *de jure* recognition, and thus to pressure Sector to recognize the regime as qualified under GFU, thus to initiate the shipment of solid gold bedsteads on a scale unheard of since the post–Persian Gulf era! I abetted His Ex's extravagant idiocy, by keeping mum, thereby sharing his culpability! I stand astonished at my own nobility. I could have scored points at Sector, and even at the Department itself, had I exposed the folly and offered in its place a carefully tailored program of spot-subornation to eliminate the scourge fattening itself on the inoffensive Bloorian electorate!"

"Certainly you could have," Retief agreed. "But you'd have been unable to live with yourself if you'd advanced your career at the expense of saving the Terran taxpayer a few zillion guck and preserving the lives of twenty million Bloorian peasants."

"True," Magnan murmured. "One can hardly break with tradition so grossly, without suffering grave internal distress, which might almost—almost, I say—impel one to take umbrage at the grosser incivilities offered one." He paused to thrust out a foot to hook the oversized brogan of the second-string politico who had tripped him, precipitating that worthy face first into one of the few remaining platinum serving-bowls.

"Oops," he said casually. "Don't count that one, Jim." As the local thug wiped cheese dip from his eyes, the Terrans departed.

Chapter 2

Leaving the festive banquet hall, the two diplomats stepped out into the Easiest Way, and turned toward the better-lit sections across the open sewer known as the Glue Danube, partly for its consistency and partly for its aroma of rendered animal carcasses.

As they approached the bonded warehouse, a lone figure, tall and long-armed, separated itself from a stone pier and stepped out into their path.

"Retief!" Magnan gasped. "That fellow—I have a feeling . . . !"

"Just carry on, Ben," Retief advised. As they came closer they could see that the fellow facing them had the slime-greenish pigmentation associated with the high-ranking Bloorian Unspeakable tribe. The big fellow was standing loosely, his arms slightly spread, blocking the way.

"Goodness, not again!" Magnan choked.

At ten feet, Retief stopped and spoke casually to Magnan. "Do you want this one, Mr. Magnan, or may I have him?"

"Why, you go right ahead," Magnan blurted. "One doesn't like to hog *all* the fun."

27

The tall Unspeakable fixed his gaze on Magnan and opened his mouth as if about to speak, but Retief took a quick step and snap-kicked him just below the left kneecap; the injured leg buckled, and the mugger fell forward with a yell. His jaw accidentally intersected Retief's knuckles with a discouraging sound between *crunch!* and *splat!* His face impacted the oily cobbles and his left leg kicked once before he became utterly still.

"Gracious!" Magnan yelped. "You've killed him!"

" 'Fraid not," Retief countered, and gave the fellow a light kick in the ribs.

At once the downed Bloorian's hand shot out, the foot-long knife in its grasp missing Retief's ankle by half an inch. Magnan stamped hard on the big-knuckled grasping member and exclaimed, "Why, the sneaky rogue! He'd have waited until we passed, then jumped up and assaulted us from behind!" He stamped on the knife hand again and caught up the weapon.

"Nix, pal," a gravelly voice issued from the cobble-dented mouth. The fellow wiped a hand across his face and sat up. He then extended the snot-and-blood-smeared hand to Magnan.

"Gimme a hand up, chum," he ordered.

"*Au contraire,*" Magnan told the dazed local sternly. "If you attempt to rise, I shall be forced to fell you yet again." Suddenly changing targets, he blurted, "Retief! Where's the car? I distinctly told Ralphie to wait close by!"

"I heard," Retief told him. "I suppose by now the limousine is in the nearest chop-shop."

"What about Ralph?"

"Oh, Mr. Magnan!" Ralph's voice came from the gutter ahead. "Sir," he went on, "I was just sitting quietly looking at my komix, when some ruffian reached in and dragged me right out through the window! Then they took the car, and . . . and—"

"Never mind, Ralphie," Magnan encouraged the battered, barely recognizable rag-clad figure who tottered toward him from the shadows. "We can requisition a new limo. And I shall get off a sharp Note to His Ferocity, protesting the incident."

"Yeah, that's cool," Ralphie conceded. "But what about my front teeth, and the back ones, too, some of 'em?"

"I'm sure Sector will authorize the best quality implants available," Magnan soothed the battered chauffeur.

"How about me?" the fallen Bloorian demanded. "I guess youse loosened up a few o' my favorite molars, too, which he clobbered me when I wasn't expecting—"

"Calmly, my man," Magnan urged, taking out his pocket recorder. "What was that name again?"

"Yer want my mob moniker, my borned name, my legal designation, my class tag, my CD handle, or what?" Magnan's new client demanded. "Just put me down as Dock Noun; dat's my secret sobriquet, on'y don't tell nobody."

" 'Anybody,' " Magnan corrected sharply. "Very well, Mr. Noun, I shan't. As for your implants, I suppose I could squeeze them in under GFU."

"Put me down fer a set o' dem new prosthetic limbs I heard about in *Trivia Today*, May issue, too," Dock added to his shopping list.

"But there's nothing wrong with your limbs!" Magnan gasped. "In fact, they seem unusually sturdy!"

"Up till when I got savaged but now," Noun corrected. "Got dis bad hand. You accident'ly step on it, pal. Anyways, I make duh nex' rumble wid five arms working, I'm a sensation. Maybe six, OK?"

"Ridiculous!" Magnan dismissed the plea. "The CDT, and even GFU, is hardly in the business of bestowing supernumary limbs on intransigent locals who have yet to produce His Ex's throne-car!"

"You want it back?" Noun inquired in a tone of surprise. "Ain't going to do his Ex a whole lotta good—withouten duh wheels and all. Boys dropped the power core unit, too, I guess."

"Reassemble it at once and bring it here!" Magnan commanded.

Noun nodded. "And the old implants?" he queried. "Get 'em in next week, right, before the big shindig?"

"What 'shindig' is it to which you refer?" Magnan demanded icily. "The GFU banquet was tonight."

"Naw, its duh Old Boys Get-together," Dock corrected impatiently. "Alla boys out on parole'll be there, and we always have rock-goat stew; tougher'n a tump-hide tarp. Kinda a virility symbol, see, if a guy can chew it. Right now," he mourned, "I cun't chew prime blurb-beast." He gnashed his gums to demonstrate his masticatory deficiency.

Magnan jotted. "Flint-steel satisfactory?" he asked the surly fellow.

"Sure," was the reply. "On'y sharp, you know what I mean?" After a moment's pause he added: "Might's well have the old power-chop attachment too, like I seen about inna mag I found inna privy."

As Magnan chatted with the local, a crowd had been gathering in the street ahead. It parted, and the battered husk of the Embassy limousine appeared, advancing slowly, pushed by half a dozen of the blue-hided variant of the local Bloorian type.

"Heavens!" Magnan exclaimed. "They've reassembled it all wrong, Jim! Look, the steering wheel is on the left front, without even a tire! And the jump-seats are on the roof! His Ex will be furious! You know he likes to have Marvin and Herb in the jump seats, directly in front of him, so he has someone handy to flay while stuck in traffic! And there's no glass in the windows. They've put the rear fenders and the deck-lid there instead. I daresay there are other discrepancies as well, under the hood, if the hood wasn't wired to the rear. And why are they pushing it?"

"Duh boys found out it don't run so good wid duh power cell out," Noun supplied.

"Well, put it back!" Magnan suggested tartly, as the battered Monojog was pushed to the curb.

Dock shook his lumpy head. "Nix, chum. We swap it off to duh Reprehensible bunch fer a portable john dey foun' someplace."

"So *that's* what happened to His Ex's Johnny-on-the-Spot!" Magnan crowed. "It's an outrage! I demand you return the facility to Embassy Stores at once!"

"Well, make up yer min', pal," Dock urged. "Dat's six items I'm s'pose to do at oncet! Ain't possible, Bub. Gimme a break!"

"There are moments, Jim," Magnan addressed his junior, "when I doubt Bloor is sincerely desirable of an amicable relationship with Terra."

"Depen's," Dock supplied. "If you'd stick to handing out free stuff to duh citizens and all, which I and my boys can collect and sell back to you—at reasonable prices, too—dat's cool—"

"So that's it!" Magnan exclaimed. "Just the other day Colonel Underknuckle and I were wondering why it is that the shrapnel the rebels and the counter-rebels have been firing into the Embassy compound had Terran foundry-marks."

"Sure," Noun agreed. "We don't waste nothin'. Now, fer ensample, giving perfally good booze and eats to illiterate peasants that woik alla time, and can't even read none, and tractors, too, *that's* wasteful! Keep 'em cold and hungry and you get the hope-vote. Also, they're too miserable to brood and get together and plot insurrection."

"Yours, I see," Magnan said, "is a pragmatic approach to the problems besetting Bloor."

"Ya got it, chum." Dock wagged his head in

agreement. "Like now. I bet you boys got a couple valuable watches and PCs an' duh like a fella could get a nice price fer at Sparky's."

"Are you suggesting," Magnan demanded in tones of outrage, "that you intend to rob us?"

"Naw, nuttin' like that," Noun disavowed the charge. "Yer gonna han' it over, inna in'er'st o Bloor-Terry relations and all, like His is always bloviatin' about."

"Well, in that case . . ." Magnan muttered, unbuckling his brand-new thousand-guck personal communicator *cum* time- and place-piece, with tape library, a gift from his Aunt Haicy on the occasion of his last visit to Terra.

He offered it hesitantly; it was grabbed by Dock's mittlike hand. He bit it and said, "Ouch! Must be somma that new eka-bronze." He looked intently at Magnan. "Oughta melt down fer a hunnert guck, easy."

"'Melt'!" Magnan gasped. "My dear Mr. Noun, or is it Dock? The circuitry is worth—"

"Not to no chop-shop that don't care what time it is," Noun sneered. "And Sparky already knows where he's at, and he don't like Terry music, especially that new shake-and-howl dat's all the go nowadays. Nor no telephone, neither. Sparky wants to talk to somebody, he sends some boys out to fetch 'em." He pocketed the loot sullenly, and looked at Retief. "You don' plan to contribute, pal?" he inquired.

"How about a trifling rupture of the spleen?" Retief suggested, planting a boot at the site of that organ. Dock staggered back, thrust two fingers into his already bruised mouth, and uttered a shrill whistle.

"Oh, dear," Magnan gulped. "Jim, look!" He pointed along the street, where mobs were approaching from both left and right.

"Thanks," Retief said to Noun. "Saves the trouble of looking for them."

"Hey," Noun wailed. "You fergot the goods, pal!"

Retief seized the eight-foot bruiser by his scruffy dark-green hair and slammed his head against the adjacent wall hard enough to raise dust from the mortar joints.

"Jim." Magnan caught at his arm. "Don't you think a trifle of placation at this juncture—" His plea was cut off as two squat, orange-tinted locals hurled themselves at Retief, who kicked one under the chin. The other he threw on top of Dock. At once the two locals grappled and went down in a snarling tangle of muscular limbs.

Retief took Magnan's arm. "Shall we be going, Ben?" he suggested. The two Terrans flattened themselves against the brick wall as a torrent of locals of both green and orange persuasion flowed past, intent on aiding one or the other or, in some cases, both of the local factions.

"Not only the Unspeakables," Magnan gasped out to Retief, "but the Unthinkables as well, and I think I caught a glimpse of some Unimaginables, crouched low and biting at the kneecaps of both groups!"

"I see a bunch of Execrables assembling up ahead," Retief commented.

"We'd best go the other way!" Magnan wailed, digging in his heels.

"You prefer the Abominables?" Retief inquired, urging his chief forward. Just then, the lead squad of the Execrables arrived and dived for their prey, high, low, and at belt-level. Retief stamped on the low man, ducked under the high one, and met the belt-buckle attacker with a knee in the mouth. Magnan shrank back against the warehouse door and kicked the low fellow in the jaw as he skidded past, face-first.

"Jim!" Magnan yelped. "I think that top one is getting ready to—" Just then Retief seized the ankles of the diving Execrable and swung him in a wide arc to impact on the brick wall. Retief dropped him and turned to deal in similar fashion with the next attacker. Down below, Magnan crouched against the wall, and, as a brutish Execrable impacted beside him, jabbed the new arrival sharply in one crossed eye with a sharp stick he had found ready to hand. The unfortunate fellow started to get to his feet, but was felled by his back-up man, just arriving. Retief fended off two more of the aggresive locals and came to Magnan's side.

"Ben, I'm a little mixed up. I understood the Execrables were the traditional allies of the Unthinkables, but now they're attacking each other—and anyone else they can get a hand on."

"To be sure," Magnan replied, raising his voice over the roar of the spreading riot. "The situation here on Bloor, alignment-of-factionwise, can be, to the uninitiated, a trifle confusing, due to the overlapping and interlocking allegiances due to clan, tribe, party, and Tsang-orientation."

"I think I'm getting initiated pretty fast, Ben," Retief told his companion. "But it's still confusing."

"Now, that fellow"—Magnan indicated a burly lout who had come to rest upside-down beside him—"shows the epidermal pigmentation of a classic Unspeakable, but you'll note he also bears the tribal tattoo of the Raunchies, the honorary lobe-perforation of Clan Atrocious, and the *pro tem*. paint-pattern of the Democratic Socialists. Thus, his allegiances require him both to support and to attack all Unimaginables, as well as to pursue a policy of unswerving neutrality anent the Reprehensible moiety and to remain aloof as regards Com-caps and Liberals. What a pity dear old Ambassador Smartfinger didn't realize the complexity of the local social structure when first he offered largess to a starving beggar who just happened to be the Chief Interrogator of the Disgustings, sworn enemies of the Despicables, thus gaining Terra the implacable hostility of all factions, the sole issue on which *de facto* agreement exists."

"The Survey Team wasn't able to do a full assessment, I understand," Retief yelled in Magnan's ear, "because they'd inadvertently violated the Shrine of the Disgustings, which happened also to be the taboo Bad Place of most of the other factions."

"A gaffe which netted Team-Leader Gangplank a nasty entry in the 'Handling of Emergencies' column of his ER," Ben explained. "And I suppose His Ex hardly improved relations when he referred to the starving Despicables as 'kin' of His Ferocity, simply because they're closely related, through hereditary feud partners. An understandable error, but a fatal one. Now, it appears, we're personally about to precipitate the *next* rupture in Terran-Bloorish relations. Jim, get us out of this!"

The narrow metal-clad door which the Terrans had previously broached was half-open beside them. Retief thrust Magnan through into the stygian darkness with its dense aroma of half-cured hides. Magnan struck a permatch and stared in dismay at the bales of furs stacked in rows, almost to the sagging ceiling joists.

"Good Lord!" he gasped. "Retief! Look at all the bales! Someone's been poaching on a grand scale, in direct defiance of the Most Favored Species Agreement! His Ex will be furious. And I, as well, noted pet-lover that I am!"

Retief was fingering a pink-and-green dappled pelt in the nearest bale. "Looks like prime frinkle-furs," he noted. "Not the best pets, Ben. More like a dangerous pest. And over there I see Glavian hell-hound hides; they'll be no loss."

"Jim! How can you be so heartless?" Magnan protested. "Useless and even pestiferous as these animals can be to us, they're still Nature's living creatures, and under our protection!"

"Too late now," Retief pointed out. "Nothing short of a Groatian twaffle-master could help these fellows."

"Good thinking, Retief!" Magnan caroled. "I've a holiday coming up, and I'll just dodge over to Grote and talk dear D'ong into coming along to attend to the chore!"

"Whoever's gone to the trouble of skinning these hides out and partly tanning them might take a dim view of that," Retief pointed out, "to say very little of the confusion that would be occasioned when a few thousand frinkles and hell-hounds suddenly burst out of confinement and start roaming the streets."

"Trifles, Jim!" Magnan enthused. "We'll have the fellows from Wildlife Control on hand to scoop them up, and in an hour they'll be on their way home, as happy as clams, eating each other and fighting with their own kind for mating rights!"

"Sounds halcyon indeed," Retief agreed. "So maybe we'd better figure how to escape from this locked dungeon in time to catch the Two-Planet to Grote."

" 'Locked'?" Magnan yelped. "Whatever do you mean?"

"This is the basement of the bonded warehouse, Ben," Retief reminded his chief. "The exits are locked tight. Supposed to be full of foof blossoms for the Tinkerbell trade!"

"Indeed it is!" Magnan agreed as he looked around carefully for the first time, noting the OFF LIMITS signs on the nearest wall. "The scamps have been smuggling illicit skins under our very noses!" he yelped. "Maybe we'd better leave the same way we came in." He turned to the shattered door where a seven-foot Abominable was wrestling with an eight-foot Reprehensible for possession of a ten-inch Bowie knife. "Or perhaps not," he amended quickly. "But there's no other way out except the triple-locked Security gate!"

Retief shoved the battling pair back out the doorless

doorway and pushed a bale of colorful hides in position to block it.

"I guess it's the gate, then," Retief concluded cheerfully. "Let's go."

Trailed by Magnan, Retief made his way along the crooked aisle into the reeking, lightless depths of the cavernous room to a steel-barred partition half-covered with placards warning, in three local languages plus Terran and Groaci, of the dire consequences of meddling therewith. Retief selected an inch-thick vertical bar and, bracing a foot against the lower horizontal member and pushing up on the upper one, he yanked the bar from the sockets.

"Retief!" Magnan yipped. "One *mustn't*! That's tested to Level Four; it can't be breached without a hydraulic press!"

"Local contractors!" Retief remarked. "Flimsy construction." Magnan peered closely at the forge-mark on the badly bent bar.

"Category One Flint-steel!" he yelped. "Retief! No force less than that of a hundred-ton hydraulic jack would twist *this* into a pretzel!"

"Well, not exactly a pretzel, Ben," Retief protested. "More of a french fry."

"In any case," Magnan went on, "I'd best go through first, being the slimmer." Magnan turned sideways and slipped through the gap left by the removal of the bar. Just as he was smoothing his lapels, a hand the size of a deep-sea grapple clamped on his shoulder, lifted him, and rotated him to face a shiny, blue, huge-fanged Unforgettable, who lowered a jaw like a dragline bucket and said, "Hah! Thought youse could pull a fast one on Blarp Show, eh, which I'm pulling duh duty dis week. I guess you gotta get up earlier'n dis here to do a sneak past *me*!"

"Let me go, Mister Show!" Magnan bleated. "We were only—!"

"Skip all that," Blarp snapped. "I got no time fer no apologies an' all." He jumped as Retief seized the biceps of the arm holding Magnan. Show dropped Magnan, and, rubbing his arm aggrievedly, said, "Say, when I tell Mr. Ambluster about this here atrocity youse boys done on me and duh whole clan, he'll fix yer wagon!"

"It ain't broke, bub," a deep voice spoke up behind Blarp. "Dis here's my pal Retief," the newcomer went on addressing the sullen Blarp. "Which he taken my best buffet widout even blinking. He's OK wit me!"

"Mr. Grand Inquisitor!" Magnan blurted. "What are *you*—? I mean, doubtless you learned of the crime being carried out here—"

"Thanks, Wim," Retief said at the same moment that his left hook impacted on Blarp's solar plexus, causing him to fold like three deuces and sprawl on the floor.

"Retief," Wim growled, "youse Terries shun't of come back here—it's off limits to ever'body but genuine Unforgettable."

"Why, it's our very own bonded warehouse," Magnan sniffed. "Besides, I'm practically Counselor of Embassy for GFU Affairs, so I guess that gives *me* entrée—and Retief is my second-in-command!"

"Youse guessed wrong, Cul," Blarp informed him, still wheezing. "Anyways, what's that 'Gee-eff-you'?"

"That is an acronym for the Goodies For Undesirables program," Magnan informed him. "An organization which was created to bestow largess on Those Less Fortunate Than Ourselves. And I might point out that the charter, embracing as it does all undesirables, undoubtedly includes *all* the inhabitants of Bloor, of whatever persuasion. So you, personally, will get in on the goodies—if you make a favorable impression on the administrator thereof, specifically, myself, Counselor Ben Magnan, CDTO-2!"

"Jeez!" Blarp muttered. "If I woulda knowed, I woulda stepped in sooner, before old Smig Bash lock' the lift an' all! Now I guess it'll be maybe a coupla decades before somebody finds yer mummified remains, yer withered arms still reaching troo duh bars fer duh grub which it's just outa reach. Sad. Sorry about that, Retief."

"Don't waste it, Blarp," Retief said. "We're not staying. Do you happen to know who owns all the furs?"

"Sure," Blarp Show supplied eagerly. "They're His Ferocity's here. Taken 'em in a raid on Repulsive HQ last week. Had alla new handguns he bought and snuck in from Boge wid duh fun's youse Terries give him fer uplifting the deserving rabble and all. Gunned down the Repulsives easy and taken two year's catch. Kinda stinks, at dat." Blarp snorted. "We gotta move the merchandise quick or it'll onney be good for the rag-and-bone trade. But it's OK; we got space booked on duh *Tree Planet* in here today."

"Why, that's the very carrier that's bringing the Semi-Annual Requisition supplies!" Magnan gasped. "Can it be—?"

"Old Cap'n Sloont bitched a little at first," Wim acknowledged, "when we esplain to him he gotta cancel the return cargo o' local chow fer the refugees you Terries set up over on Plunch V, which they're homesick fer Down Home eats. But he come around soon's he thought about how much better a million guck cash was dan gettin' drownded inna municipal cesspool and all," the arrogant fellow explained blandly.

"Imagine!" Magnan mourned. "A cargo of illicit flink hides smuggled out aboard an official CDT—and GFU—mercy ship! The media—Jim, we mustn't let Hy get hold of this one!"

"What'll you give me, Ben?" Wim demanded. "Iffen I don't hold a press conference?"

"You *wouldn't!*" Magnan gasped. "A hundred guck, cash!" he offered in desperation.

Wim grinned, a dreadful display of well-rotted teeth. "Don't kid me, Ben," he urged. "Dis is big-time. Try me wid fifty thou."

"Do you realize, Mr. Grand Inquisitor," Magnan came back, "that fifty thousand guck represents a large multiple of the annual salary of a dedicated public servent such as myself?"

"Naw, youse don't get it, Ben," Wim protested. "I di'n't mean guck; I mean hard currency: Bloorian flugs—fifty guck to a flug, legal rate. Black market's twict dat—a hunnert to one onna street! Youse got to have flug to deal inna market here on Bloor. Dat's duh onney place in Tip Space a fella can buy a coal-black blue-eyed blonde non-mutated-hardly Terry wench, or get his mitts on a planet-wrecker bomb. Fifty t'ousan' flug is letting youse off easy. When His Ex gets the word, Terry diplomat-hide'll drop below flink-skin! Think it over—fer about six milliseconds— I gotta split!"

"Done!" Magnan bleated. "Fifty thousand flug it is, you scoundrel! Heaven knows where I'll get it, but I shall come up with it—somehow!"

As Magnan was negotiating with Wim Dit, Retief, noticing that Smig Bash was creeping up behind Blarp Show, moved along to the end of the steel-bar partition, where the horizontal members were socketed in concrete. He put a foot on the lower bar and pushed up on the upper one, which groaned and popped free of its socket. The heavy grille fell inward, pinning Wim to the concrete floor. Retief stepped up on the confining grating and strolled over to look down at the trapped Unforgettable. Magnan hurried over to gloat.

"Ah, there you are," he greeted the fallen extortionist. "By the way, old chum, I hear Hy Felix is after your hide. That hot poop you sold him last week about the kickbacks on the commissary items kicked back on its own. It appears Undersecretary Longspoon was the financier of the scheme, and he's exiled on Iceberg Twelve now, writing his memoirs. Hy was furious at buying stale news."

"Keep him away from me, Retief!" Wim begged. "I heard when Hy gets out duh skinning knives he means business! Duh guy got no restraint! Whattaya say, chum? Tell Hy I shipped out fer Nauseous territory, over North Continent, OK? Doing a little bull-devil hunding. Out inna swamp fer weeks at a time and nuttin to eat but sperlt meat-hawk. He'd hate it out dere. Just tell him to fergit he ever seen me. Sorry about duh bad dope, Ben, but it was stoled in good faith! I'll get back to dat Abominable sucker dat I got it from!"

"That's neither here nor there, I'm sure, Mister Grand Inquisitor," Magnan contributed. "The point is, after all, Wim, is that you yourself seem to be in charge of the monumental cache of contraband! What have you to say to that? And after His Ex has favored you with admission into his inner circle of trusted confidants, too!"

"Ain't my fault Sam Swinepearl got no judgment," Wim carped. "Anyways, I onney come down here inna vault to do a like recce: feared some slickers from duh Nasty Party was plotting to, like, hijack duh load. Hark!" Wim paused dramatically at a sharp *ping!* from the darkness behind the fallen grating. "Hey!" he stage-whispered. "I heard a sharp *ping!* over duh freight lift! I bet dem sneaky mudders is tryna hot-wire it!" He threshed under the weight of the wrought ironwork. "Hurry up, Ben! Tell Retief to get offa my chest where I can get some air! Let's *get* dem miscreants!"

" 'Miscreants'?" Magnan gasped. "Are *they* involved too?"

"Calmly, Ben," Retief soothed. His Ferocity will no doubt deal with the situation; you may rest easy."

" 'Rest easy,' duh guy says," Wim snarled, "and me wit tree hunnert kilos o' ironwork laying on my lunch, which it wasn't too good at dat! Bean soup! No wonder duh PM brung a lunch!"

"I shall ignore your ill-considered remarks anent Terran cuisine, Mister Grand Inquisitor," Magnan told the unfortunate official, "inasmuch as you are under a certain, shall we say 'pressure,' at the moment, and not fully responsible." He turned to Retief. "*Noblesse oblige*, Jim, in its purest form. No harm in making a few points with the scamp in case we find the footgear on the other pedal extremity at some time."

"Masterful, sir," Retief applauded his chief's ploy. "Should we go all the way and let him up?"

"Not just yet," Magnan counseled. "First I want to see for myself just who else is invading the sancrosanct precincts of the bonded warehouse. Come." He walked across the grille, eliciting groans from the careless fellows lying pinned under it. From the deep shadow ahead, a voice spoke urgently:

"Shake a leg, Foor Pool! I got a hunch—"

Magnan waved Retief back. "We'll wait here and eavesdrop," he decreed. "That sounded to me like that two-faced chap from the ministry, Jum Derk! And he was talking to Foor Pool, the Deputy for Nefarious Affairs, I shouldn't wonder. I shall have a word to say to the Minister, you may be sure. Imagine! Even as I negotiate the final details of the grant, they plot to steal our gifts, and to smuggle the stolen goods out on our very own mercy ship! It's vile, do you hear?"

"Sure, I hear, Ben," a voice came from the darkness. "But it ain't no Vile; it's us Horrids, and a coupla Nasties as hired hands, like Wim said."

"Have you no shame?" Magnan retorted.

"Had a Shameful fella onna staff, but hadda let him

go," Pool's voice came back sadly from the shadows. "Guy was tryna rope us loyal Unbearables into some kinda intraclan rumble! How low can youse get? We get a nice little coalition working here, tryna build it up, say where we can take over and get alla loot fer ourselfs, and dis bum woulda busted it wide open. If we was to jump some o' the Viles, say, in our bunch, alla resta dat moiety would bolted duh coalition. And den trieda set up some kinda bootleg alliance on der own, to do us outa duh goods." The tirade concluded with a hearty *smack!* as of a fist against gristle. "Lay off, Smad Bell!" Foor snapped. "Inna dark, you hit *me*, accidentally!"

"Hey, Mister Depitty!" an aggrieved voice protested. "Whassa idea? *I* got no beef with duh coalition! I'm true Puce! It was old Smelly here making duh cracks!"

"Shut up, youse idiots!" Pool hissed. "If we don' wanna get nabbed inna ack, we better woik fast and quiet!"

"Oh, yeah?" Jum spoke up spiritedly. "Who elected *you* boss?" Scarce had his voice fallen silent when another hearty *smack!* sounded, followed by others, until, in a few seconds, a full-scale riot was in progress in the darkness all around. Retief felt his way to the service panel and switched on the dim glare-strip, revealing half a dozen Bloorians of varied shades, tattoos, and badges flailing at each other indiscriminately. Two were already *hors de combat*; the relatively short, squat Minister of Nefarious Affairs, who was crawling on all fours directly toward Magnan, who halted, arranged an expression of Righteous Outrage (74-a) on his narrow features and exclaimed:

"Why, Mr. Minister! Whatever are you doing, prowling here in an off-limits area, in the company of this riffraff?" Magnan indicated with a wave the four smugglers still on their feet, who had apparently forgotten their differences, and were standing in a ragged line gaping at the Terrans. Wim Dit, slightly the worse for wear, was front and center.

"Hey, Boss," the smallest of the group, only a seven-footer, addressed his chief, who was now pounding his gnarled ear with the heel of his hand. "I hadda idear dis was s'pose to be a confidential caper," the little fellow carped, "which when we snuck in via duh secret tunnel from duh kitchen an all, we had it made: but it looks like a Terry convention, wid, uh, about two of 'em watching us swipe duh stuff!"

"I *tole* Jum to play it cute," Pool protested, "but no, he hadda start settling old scores right inna middle o' duh biggest haul since we made off with Mister Ambluster's personal landing-craft, which duh whole tape liberry was dat wheezy organ stuff!"

"Sorry, Foor," Jum offered. "But when dat Inexcusable weisenheimer tryda crack wise about us Viles being cozy with duh Horrids and all, I guess I los' my head some. Din't mean to clobber yuh inna ear dat way, sir."

Pool came to his feet in a lunge to confront the cowering Jum. "*You* was the one done dat, Derk?" he yelled. "I'm gonna be hearing duh birdies singing in dat ear fer a fortnight, I trow!" With that, he felled the hapless offender. When the next man in line protested, Foor clobbered him, too, then stood glaring at his two remaining conspirators.

"Anybody elst?" he yelled. "Come on, youse slobs are s'pose to be duh toughest hit-guys inna guild! You gonna stan dere and take it?" Then, after a momentary pause, "Nobody got nutting to say, hah?"

"Allow me," Retief suggested, and as Foor turned, surprise writ large on his battered countenance, Retief modified that assemblage of unattractive features with a roundhouse swing which sent the loud-mouthed leader skidding, face-first, back among the baled hides. Wim dithered, complaining faintly.

"Hey! You Terries are s'pose to be pantywaists and all! Who figgered *you* to do anything reasonable inna circumstances, which us downtrod locals are onney expressing our, like, legitimate grievances and all? Just wait'll I tell Sam Swinepearl about dis here atrocity, which you pounded old Foor's favorite nostril flat an bent his jaw right outa line, where he'll be hard put to chew his mummified ulsio at duh big celebration tonight!"

The mourner approached his fallen chief and quickly checked the pockets of his greasy overalls, netting a shabby wallet and a well-bitten gold sprug. The others still on their feet said "Dibs" in unison, then closed in. After the division of spoils, together they assisted the semi-conscious Foor to his large, flat feet. He pushed them away. "Lemme be," he growled. "I never seen dem udder tree guys!" He turned to peer suspiciously into the shadows.

"Where're dey at?" he demanded. "Jess feed 'em to me one at a time, where I can get a good swing!"

Retief tapped him on the shoulder. "Did I hear your fellow genetic deficiency say he'd be chatting with the Terran AE and MP?" he inquired.

"Retief!" Magnan protested. "I'm sure it was a mere figure of speech! You can't imagine that His Excellency is in league with these—" He paused as all mob-members still functioning turned to glare at him.

"Yes, Ben?" Foor prompted. "Youse was about to characterize I and my boys as . . . what?"

"Misguided entrepreneurs," Magnan supplied. "Led astray by bad companions, poor fellows. See here, we're all reasonable beings, so what say we just let bygones be bygones: you leave here now, quietly, and promise not to violate the Embassy stores again soon, and I'll tell His Ex security is as tight as a belly-button tick!"

"Dat ain't what His Ex said, when we made duh deal—I mean arrangements—fer duh like informal distribution of duh loot—I mean duh relief supplies an' all," one of the only slightly cowed thieves complained without enthusiasm. "He tole us—"

"One moment!" Magnan interrupted. "Are you alleging that Career Ambassador Samson Swinepearl entered into some sort of agreement with you fellows to loot the warehouse with impunity?"

"Naw, Old Impunity's out," Foor corrected. "Got likkered up and fell and broke his mooby-bone. An' he never alleged it, he just said it."

"Retief," Magnan said in an aside to his colleague, "something must be done about these bootleg translators that are flooding the market and imparting grossly fallacious concepts of grammar, syntax, and diction to these poor, unenlightened scholars, yearning as they are for higher education. Why, this fellow doesn't even know the meaning of the simple verb 'allege.'"

"Do, too," the lanky illiterate snapped. "Lissen: 'n. l. a horizontal, shelflike projection on a building or a cliff.' Dat's right outa duh Webber Dickanary, Ben."

"I didn't say 'a ledge,' you ninny, I said 'allege'!"

"Sure. Dat's a, like, horizontal, shelflike projection on a cliff or a building, jess like I said, Ben," the stubborn fellow persisted.

"No," Magnan came back stubbornly. "'Al-lege,' not 'a ledge'! Can't you grasp the distinction?"

"Ain't none," the scholar dismissed the matter. "Anyways, last time I was chinning wid old Swiney, he says: 'now, Pool, my boy'—he calls me his 'boy'—"

"I must protest!" Magnan cut him off, "'Old Swiney' is hardly a proper mode of reference to the Terran Ambluster by a mere . . . mere—"

"'Thief,'" Retief suggested.

Magnan recoiled, "Jim! Not where they can *hear* you!" He showed the crestfallen thief an improvised We Must Make Allowances for Gaffes Committed By the Young (1075-w), which the ungrateful fellow dismissed with a shrug—a passable 27-1, Magnan noted *en passant*—at the same time wondering briefly who had tutored the scamp in the subtleties of Nullspeak.

"I insist," Magnan resumed haranguing Foor Pool, "on knowing just what it is you allege His Ex said to you!"

"I'm tryna tell you, Ben," the saucy fellow protested. "Every time I get to duh pernt, youse butt in wit some irrelevant crack about us high-class Nasties or like that!"

"Whom, I?" Magnan squeaked. "I'm quite sure I've made no mention of the Nasty Party—"

" 'Clan'," the argumentative local corrected sharply. "Dat's duh trouble (one of 'em, anyways) wit' you foreign devils: can't keep stuff straight. Like a feller's got his basic racial identity to defen', his clan loyalty, his moiety alignment, an' o' course his union membership. Not to say nuttin about duh various civic clubs, sports organizations an' like dat he collects along duh line. An you got to remember a guy's close clan pals might be in a declared war (or maybe undeclared) wit' his buddies inna union and all. A dumb guy dat don't lissen could get mix up. Then he's gonna make hisself some deadly enemies, get onna wrong side in duh fracas and all."

"As a Terran diplomat," Magnan brayed, "I, and my assistant Mr. Retief as well, am above all such petty allegiances as well as their concomitant hostilities! So just get back to what Old Swiney had to say. Just a second while I activate my corder." He twitched his lapel and said, *"Et, Tvo, Tre, Fyra,"* which boomed out deafeningly through the echoing godown. He made a hasty adjustment, and tried again, then touched the translator button, and the device said, "*Uno, dos, tres, cuatro.*"

"Drat!" Magnan muttered, and adjusted again. This time the device said, "*Yit, blit, yot, zlot,*" before lapsing into a sullen silence. "Go ahead!" Magnan commanded Pool. "Bother the record!"

"Sure, Ben," his surly confidant agreed. "All he said was about upping his cut and all. Greedy fellow, Sam. An' duh mug had duh noive to ask, nay, demand, a slice of duh local action, too!"

"Are you implying, Foor," Magnan put it precisely, "that His Ex himself has condoned, or even participated in, the nefarious activities of the criminal element here on Bloor?"

"Naw, nuttin' fancy," Pool refuted the suggestion. "He onney wants his fair cut o' duh take, in return fer not siccin' no Terry cops on us nor nuttin'. 'Cept fer duh local constabulary, o' courst, which him and dat weasel Bam Slang got togedduh and set up a bunch cops to try to tell us local riffraff how to run our own rackets! Course, along wit duh coppers we got to have duh lawyers, and even some judges. Tough to fin' anybody unprinciple' enough to take on dem jobs, but I guess somebody hadda do it, or we'd be fallin' behind duh Galactic Norm and all, which no self-despising citizen would opt fer dat, so now we got Terry legal eagles come in here to Bloor City setting up in business, to compete wit' our own native-bred shysters! It's bad, Ben. What's dat bunch just rended duh old jail for law offices? Something about 'Tupp, Futter and Swive, P.A.' Dem boys is tryna take duh trade right outa duh hands of duh local ambulance-chasers, which I guess dey got enough on dere plate witout dey gotta watch a bunch Terry bloodsuckers, too!"

"I shall look into the matter at once, Mr. Pool," Magnan reassured the outraged local. "And just a tip:

when you have recourse to Tupp *et al.*, ask to see Old Mr. Roger."

"Tanks, Ben; I guess I'm gonna need some counsel what wid you catchin' I an' my boys red-handed pullin' a heist right here inna Embassy godown."

"Perhaps," Magnan purred. "I could overlook your presence here if a safe conduct back to the Chancery could be arranged."

"To wait just *one* moment!" a breathy voice cut in from a deep alcove between ranked bales. "To be unable to credit my auditory membranes, Ben!" the Groaci voice went on relentlessly. "You, of all people, to be openly attempting to suborn this miscreant from the clear path of duty, to the discredit of all members of the diplomatic community here on Bloor."

"Hardly 'openly,'" Magnan protested. "I'm way down here in the sub-basement, an area, I might point out, not open to intrusion by foreign diplomatic personnel!"

"A low blow, Ben!" Ambassador Shinth of the Groaci Embassy charged. "After the amicable, nay, cordial relations you and I have established over the decades, it's hardly a friendly gesture to consign me now to the category of a mere 'foreign diplomat,' with only the emoluments of that unfavored status. Why, there's plenty here for all! I have contacts in the Cluster which will absorb the greater part of the flink-hide exports, to say nothing of the constant requirement for sturdy terroid breeding-stock for serfs in areas under Groacian hegemony! You may continue to handle procurement; I shall guarantee prompt and profitable— highly profitable—marketing!" The scrawny alien diplomat emerged into the dim greenish light afforded by the glare strip.

Suddenly the light became brighter: the emergency glow patches automatically activated by the presence of too many bodies in the forbidden area.

"The glow patches!" Magnan yelped. "They've activated!"

"And a good thing, too," Shinth hissed. "In total darkness, we'd have little chance of restraining your suspects from slipping away to the emergency escape route via the concealed hatch in the southwest corner."

"You don't understand!" Magnan wailed. "The automatics have doubtless set off the alarm in the Chancery, the Residence, and the Marine barracks. His Ex and Sergeant Muldoon, too, will be upon us in the instant. We'll be caught red-handed! What are we to do?"

"Let's just explain, Ben," Shinth proposed. "That we were alert enough to detect the presence of interlopers, and have laid the rascals by the heels."

"That's OK for Jim and me," Magnan replied. "But what about *you*? What is the Groaci AE and MP doing here at this hour?"

"An appointment, Ben," Shinth replied urbanely, executing a little jig to glance at the timepiece strapped to his left knee. "The rascal is late, as usual."

"What rascal is that, Mr. Ambassador?" Magnan asked eagerly.

Shinth waved the query away. "Ben! I'm surprised at you! Attempting to snoop in Groacian Embassy affairs!"

"Yes, but—" Magnan offered.

Retief took a firm grip on Shinth's skinny neck. "Inasmuch as the Groaci Embassey is conducting its affairs on Terry property," he suggested, "I think the question is a legitimate one. Spill it, Mr. Ambassador."

"It's Miss Meuhl, Sammy's secretary," Shinth squeaked. "The Usually Reliable Source you've doubtless seen cited in my dispatches you've sneaked a look at."

"I thought that was George, the janitor—I mean

custodian," Magnan gobbled. "But Miss Meuhl! Heavens! She has access to—"

"Lucky she's so homely and shrewish," Retief put in, "or there'd be no secrets at all."

"True," Magnan murmured. "One must look on the bright side. But His Ex will be furious when he finds out!"

"Sammy is *always* furious, Ben," Shinth contributed. "So it makes little difference. In fact, if you set it up just right, you could milk this disclosure for points."

" 'Points'?" Magnan echoed. "Do you imagine I'm interested in mere points when my—our lives are in jeopardy?"

"Sure, Ben," the sophisticated Groaci replied. "There's always tomorrow, and we'll be working for points as usual."

"Not if I perish here, miserably, among the scum of Bloorian society!"

"*I* am hardly to be lumped as 'Bloorian society,' " Shinth protested.

"Very well, the scum of Groaci society!"

"Bah!" Shinth snorted. "Ben, you're incorrigible!" He stamped off into the darkness. A moment later his breathy voice was to be heard again from the shadows: "Now, boys," he whispered. "Be patient, I've got Ben so confused he doesn't know who's paying off whom. Did you get the instructions I so subtly passed to you?"

"You mean about duh secret passage inna sout' corner and all?" the surly voice of Smad Bell responded.

"Exactly!" the Groaci confirmed in his accentless Terran. "Now, you scamps get going, before Ben wakes up and realizes—"

"Before I realize what?" Magnan barked as he approached the conspirators out of the darkness.

"Rats!" Shinth hissed. "The jig is up, lads! He's on to us! It's every being for himself!"

"That s'pose to be some kinda crack?" Pool demanded. "I guess us Bloorians are still humern, even if we *are* mutated a little!"

"By no means, my dear Foor!" Shinth disclaimed. "I only meant—"

"Skip it, Shinth," Pool muttered. "I guess duh point is, like, academic."

"I warn you, Bell, and you, too, Pool!" His Groaci Ex snarled. "I'm holding you personally responsible for these outrages against my person as well as against the proud state of Groac! I'm seeing my attorneys in the morning. I've retained a prestigious Terran firm, well equipped to sue under Terry law as well as Bloorian!"

"Never mind, Jim," Magnan said to Retief, who had come up beside him to urge him to withdraw and deal with the matter in daylight.

"I'm a close personal friend of old Mr. Roger, at Shinth's counsel's firm, Tupp, Futter and Swive, P.A.!" Magnan snapped. "He'll soon deal with those Johnny-come-latelies, Skinnerback and Milkerdown, P.A.! Bob Skinnerback and Fred Milkerdown are neophytes! I, for one, don't fear litigation!" He stamped off to take up a position at the locked emergency exit.

"Jeez!" Foor offered in a stage whisper. "Ben's went and tooken up a position by duh secret excape route! Now how do we get outa here?"

"Right through duh odder Terry," a youngish Bloorian barked, and the entire group charged Retief, ignoring Shinth's faint cries of protest. Retief waited for the first volunteer and floored him with a round-house swipe, catching two more with the return backhand. The others split into two groups and advanced from right and left. Retief ducked aside and allowed them to collide, at which point their long-suppressed natural hostilities broke free and they instantly formed a solid mass of combatants, each intent only on tearing his erstwhile ally limb from limb.

"Argumentative fellows," Retief commented, as he helped three unconscious members back to their feet before propelling them back into the free-for-all. Shinth alone had held aloof from the meelée. He hissed in distress and scuttled for the bale-blocked outer door. Magnan took a step after him.

"Let him go, Ben," Retief suggested. "He'll be easy to find tomorrow, hiding in his chancery, making up excuses."

"What possible excuse could exist?" Magnan demanded, "for the presence of a Groaci Chief of Mission, here in the godown and well after business hours, in the commissary stores, in company of these ruffians?"

"None," Retief supplied. "That'll keep him even busier."

They went around the free-for-all and approached Shinth, skulking by the well-known secret exit.

"What about it, Mr. Ambassador?" Magnan demanded. "Do we get the safe-conduct, or do you prefer public exposure?"

"Bah!" His Groacian Ex dismissed the question. "It's scant explaining I'll be doing, vile Terries! In my capacity as Environmental Coordinator for this Sector, I came here to look into allegations that you Terries have been trafficking in contraband under the guise of bestowing largess! This warehouse is my proof! In the morning, far from doing penance, I shall arrive here with a squad of local vigilantes, as well as Committees of Investigation from both my embassy and your own. I've no doubt Sammy Swinepearl will be as outraged as I when I tell him whom I've caught red-handed!" With that, he slipped behind a stack of bales, darted to the exterior door, and was swallowed by the curious throng which had gathered to peer into the darkness and hazard guesses as to what was going on in there.

"—soun's like old Shinth got duh goods on Ben dis time!" one hazarded.

"—annudder example o' skulduggery in high places!" another countered. "Hey! Dere's duh crinimal now! Let's get him, boys! I guess we can fergit duh old race-riot fer a while and pick it up again at dawn, right where we left off at, refreshed by a night o' mayhem and vandalism!" With a yell, he and two others charged the barricade. As he vaulted over the grating, Retief accidentally palmed him off-course, so that he impacted the floor grin-first. His colleagues, closely followed by Shinth, had started forward with hoarse yells, which changed to wails as Retief flipped the iron grille upright directly in their path. As they piled up against it, he pushed it over on top of them, and tumbled a stack of baled hides down on the grating, effectively pinning all three in place, Shinth at the bottom of the struggling heap.

"Dirty pool, Retief!" the Groaci hissed. "This was a classic 'Book 'em, Danno' situation, and it ill-behooves a diplomat of your experience to thus fly in the face of tradition! Let me up at once! At *once*, I say!" He had thrust his small, lumpy head and one feeble arm through between the bars. "Assist me!" he demanded. "Can't you see that in their struggles these ruffians are savaging me, their benefactor? Wim, stop that!" he commanded.

The Terrans were startled to hear the gravelly voice of Wim Dit complain from the middle of the stack, "Now, Mister Ambassador, you promised no publicity! And yet now Ben Magnan's on to me, and Retief is squashing my ribs. You're on your own!"

"Retief!" Shinth gasped. "I lie here, a victim of treachery, undone by his own better nature! Lend me a hand!"

"Too bad, Mr. Ambassador," Retief commiserated without enthusiasm. He grasped one of the Groaci's five gently waving eyestalks and tugged. Shinth squealed.

"Oops!" Retief commented. "I don't think you're going to fit—unless I pull harder."

"Jim, you wouldn't!" Magnan gasped. "That would make a dismal entry in your Promotion of Chumship column! Release His Excellency at once! And as for you, Mr. Ambassador," he shifted his scolding to the unfortunate alien, "I'm sur*prised* at you! Consorting with absolutely the worst element in Bloorish society! And helping them violate Terry sovereignty, too! And you!" he addressed the Grand Inquisitor. "You're in it, too! What do you have to say for yourselves, you scamps?"

"You wrong me, Ben," Shinth wailed. "In me you see the archetypal selfless bureaucrat, risking all to complete his mission of peace-making and the promotion of vigorous economic activity here on Bloor! You're well aware that all of poor, bleeding Bloor's problems arise from the failure of haughty Terra to provide food, clothing, and shelter for the huddled masses of this unfortunate planet! Had you fellows initiated Goodies for Undesirables a few decades sooner, political chaos would never have eventuated here! So, kindly tell Jim to leggo my eye, and let us resume this discussion in my office at seven A.M. tomorrow morning!"

" 'Seven A.M. tomorrow' or 'seven tomorrow morning' would obviate the redundancy, Mr. Ambassador," Magnan pointed out, then, in flawless Groaci, "to receive your counselor in *my* office at nine A.M. tomorrow morning."

"Ben!" Shinth expostulated. "To try to make points at a moment like this, when I'm about to see, pardon the pun, permanent darkness close in on twenty percent of my visual field, is ghastly bad form!"

"Make that forty," Retief corrected, as he gathered in a second twitching eyestalk.

"I hadn't realized, Jim, that you are so unfeeling!" Shinth protested. "Release my optical members at once! Ben, I call upon you to effect the release of my visual organs from the grasp of your barbaric colleague!"

"First, tell your hirelings to cease their cater-waulings," Magnan directed crisply. "Then they're to stop threshing about. Tell Smad to put the bracelets on the others and line them all up for inspection, and I *may*, just possibly, see my way clear to succor you from the situation in which your greed and impudence have placed you."

" 'Greed'?" Shinth echoed in a tone of Shocked Disbelief (16-b). " 'Impudence'? I can scarce credit my auditory members, Ben: that you, a fellow career diplomat, would so characterize my valiant efforts in aid of the unfoldment of Groacian manifest destiny!"

"Don't waste that sixteen on me, Shinth," Magnan advised in a tone from which cynicism was not altogether absent.

"Hey!" Shinth yelled, as loudly as his feeble vocal membranes could manage. "That was a crack from which cynicism was not altogether absent! Ben, must it come to this, after our years of professional association?—years, I might point out, in which I have risen, step by step, to the lofty rank of Career Ambassador, albeit to a trashy world, whilst you remain stranded in the DSO-1 slot! Show a trifle of respect for protocol and tell Jim to help me up, without recourse to my eyestalks as handholds!" The Groacian slumped exhaustedly, uttering one final "Hush!" to Jum Derk, directly below him.

In the momentary silence, Wim Dit spoke up indignantly. "Mr. Ambluster, you tol' us poor unsophisticated patriots about when duh Terry handouts would go up soon's we kidnapped a couple of 'em and robbed duh store, and all!"

"It *is* traditional," Shinth's voice came weakly to Magnan's ear. "Cryptic Terra always rewards most bountifully those nations which prove their contempt by acts of violence directed against her! Look in your history books! Best of all, of course, is to wage open warfare against her, thereby qualifying for gigantic handouts." Shinth was haranguing Magnan now: "The Terry taxpayer is a curious beast: cheerfully electing legislators who tax him to poverty in order to provide luxuries for those at home who prove they will never upset the social order by doing something useful, and, abroad, those who demonstrate their implacable hostility! It doesn't scan, Ben; but then I suppose such perversity bathes your gonads in a warm glow of self-abnegation. Now, let's get back to business and let me and my associates out of this trap; the formal apologies can wait until later, but make them good, Ben! Especially considering the fact that the projected heist came to naught! Act now, Ben, and I may yet be able to put in a word on your behalf at the hearing!"

"You speak of hearings!" Magnan yelled indignantly. "Do you suggest—?"

"Naw, just the one hearing, Ben," Wim corrected. "When duh Inspectors hit duh Mission nex' mont'. I'll hafta have you had up on a atrocities rap, an all. But don't sweat it. Just you and Jim east outa here and let I and my boys and His Ex, too, get on with duh haul, and I'll even forget about duh trick wid duh ironwork an all. How's dat fer fair, old pal?"

"Equitable enough, I suppose," Magnan conceded hesitantly. "Jim, do you suppose we could . . . ?"

"Not a chance, Mr. Magnan," Retief replied. "Local reinforcements have been arriving steadily via the secret passage. While you were negotiating, or giving up, or whatever, I've been listening to them. They've slipped around us and blocked off all the exits. No way out. I'm afraid Wim's trying to con us."

"Yes, but," Magnan offered, "since we're outnumbered, we can hardly be expected to offer further resistance! Imagine!" he mused on. "Wim Dit himself, personally participating in robbery and smuggling and Lordy knows what else!"

Retief picked up the fallen grille, lifted it overhead, turned, and threw it into the darkness of the aisle to his left. A chorus of yells mingled with the clatter of iron on defective concrete.

"—dirty pool! I never—" Bam Slang carped.

"—easy, yuh said!" Wim wailed.

"—leave outa here!" Smig Bash contributed. "I gotta club meeting to go to, or I lose my status as a Intolerable. T'ree misses inna row an' yer out—an' I already got two!"

"Retief," Magnan objected. "I hardly think further violence—"

"What did you have in mind, Ben?" Retief inquired. "I've just about run out of violent ideas."

"Why, if one were to activate the emergency purge system . . ."

"Good thinking, sir," Retief replied, as he went to the service panel and hauled down on the big red knife-switch. Immediately, with a roar like a primitive ramjet engine, the flushing fans started up, flooding the storeroom with fire-damping nitrogen gas.

"Yipes!" a voice Retief recognized as that of Jum Derk exclaimed. "Perzon gas! Duh tricky Terries is tryna expiate us!"

"Dat's 'asphyxiate,' Dum-dum!" Blarp corrected. "You gotta steal a better translator; you'll give us locals a bad name fer illegitimacy!"

"Dat's 'illiteracy,'" Jum corrected in turn. "Skip duh fine points o' Terry syntax, OK? Right now we gotta learn to live widout breadin'!"

"Say, fellows," Foor contributed, with a deep sigh. "I jus' noticed I'm breadin' good! Maybe we ain't dead."

As the conspirators eagerly compared respiratory notes, Retief got their location pinpointed and, with a brief instruction to Ben Magnan, launched himself like a runaway switch-engine, impacting the tight little group and knocking them in various directions. Recovering his footing, Retief delivered one, two, three, four hearty left hooks to as many unshaven jaws. Only Blarp Show, staggering backward, remained erect. Magnan extended a foot and tripped the burly lout, whose skull impacted the floor with a satisfying *bonk!* The other three thieves, now sitting up and rubbing their faces, saw Magnan towering over their fallen leader.

"Jeez!" Wim Dit blurted. "I wudda laid good odds Ben Magnan was no-price! But look at the sneaky rascal! He done floored all four o' us, especially Bam the Boisterous, which he's a Champeen of One Hunnert!"

"Get up, you trash!" Magnan barked, rubbing his unbruised knuckles tenderly on his pants leg. "Before you get me irritated!"

"Let's go fer it!" Wim blurted, rolling a few feet before jumping up. He sprinted for the dark recesses at the back of the cavelike storage room, and his henchmen followed, ignoring Magnan's order to halt.

"I'll bet they've got a private entry back there," Magnan suggested to Retief. "They could have dug one under cover of the supposed addition to their Consular wing!"

Retief nodded. "We'd better get there right behind them, Ben," he pointed out, "or they'll have pulled the dump-line and closed it behind them."

The two Terrans followed the retreating Bloorians closely, and came up just in time to see Blarp Show slipping through a ragged cleft in the crumbly masonry retaining wall.

Arriving first, Magnan peered in. "I see light!" he exclaimed, then turned sideways and leaned backwards, and squeezed in, before Retief could dissuade him. Retief followed, barely able to negotiate the narrow opening, but it widened after the first six feet. In the dim light, Magnan was nowhere to be seen.

Then Retief heard a sharp *yelp!* from ahead. "Retief! They're—I'm—oh, dear, help!" Magnan's voice trailed off.

Retief pressed on as the passage widened further into a roughly excavated rock-walled cave; the light was slightly brighter here. Now he could see Magnan ahead, crouched in a curiously awkward position: he was caught, Retief saw, in a rope net which had lifted him and was swinging him sideways toward a dark aperture from which large, hard-knuckled hands at the ends of arms like tree-roots reached for the net. Magnan *yip!*ped as the ropes were caught, pulling him toward the opening. More hands grabbed and yanked the loaded net inside the side-passage.

Retief eased around the corner and slid along the wall toward Magnan. There was an abrupt dropoff in the floor, he saw, like a well dug in the center of the confining space, leaving him only a three-inch ledge along which to advance. He reached the opening into which Magnan had been yanked and, leaning forward over the dark abyss, caught a glimpse of dark-silhouetted figures retreating rapidly. Magnan's protests mingled with sharp commands to "shut yer yap!" and the sound of a blow. Retief made the tunnel with a lunge and moved quickly up behind the struggling group. He managed to get close to Magnan's agonized face.

"Take it easy, Ben," he whispered. "Relax and keep it quiet."

"Jim! Do something!" Magnan blurted. At once the

party of abductors halted, thrust Magnan aside and started back toward Retief. He flattened himself against the rock wall and waited until Blarp was eighteen inches away, then felled him with a straight right. The others shoved their stricken comrade aside as he stumbled back. Retief decked a second lout; then he found the net entangling him. He fought free of it, but Wim stooped and threw another fold of the webbing at him. He fended it off, and had just secured a grip on Wim's neck when Magnan leaped at him.

"Jim! I must report this outrage at once! Come along, do you hear? Don't bother with Wim just now!" Magnan grabbed at Retief's hand, clamped on Wim's throat. "You mustn't stoop to their level, Jim! That would undermine our position, moral superioritywise! His Ex will deal with this precious Grand Inquisitor!"

"Go past me, Ben," Retief urged. "Get clear; watch out for the pit."

"Pit?" Magnan clung to Retief's arm, inhibiting his effort to avoid the knife with which a local named Smig was making efforts to slash Retief's biceps. The sharp blade made contact, laying Retief's sleeve open in a three-inch gash and causing him to lose his grip. At once Smig slashed again, missing Retief's throat, but cutting his shoulder.

"Ben! Get back!" Retief demanded, and pushed his boss away, toward the mouth of the passage.

"Retief!" Magnan objected. "I'm surprised at you! Laying hands on your very own direct supervisor!"

"There's no time for the civilities just now, Ben," Retief pointed out, pushing Magnan ahead.

By now all three thugs were piled up against Retief. He knocked two of them back and Magnan took their place, scolding Retief, "Jim! You're wounded! How careless! What——?"

Bam thrust Magnan aside and dived past Retief to a wall panel. He grabbed for a switch and Magnan dropped abruptly from view. A trapdoor in the uneven floor snapped shut over him. Retief delivered a hearty kick to Bam's short ribs; the Bloorian boss lunged for the control panel, opening the trap again just as Retief moved to deliver another kick. Retief fell ten feet to a concrete floor. Magnan was not to be seen. Retief called; no reply. He looked up in time to see Bam's lumpy face above, bruised but gloating, in the opening just before the trap slammed shut. A profound silence descended. Suddenly Wim's voice spoke, with a crackle of defective electronics:

"Terran spies! Confess your crimes, and perhaps I will agree to release you!"

"Certainly, Your Ferocity!" Magnan spoke up from somewhere above Retief. "Just get me out of here, and—" Magnan's voice was cut off as if by a blow.

"What about you, Retief?" Wim Dit insisted. "You gonna cooperate, or what? We usely keep ulsios in that cage. They ain't been fed fer a week. It's time to let 'em in so's they can chow down!"

There was a small *clank!*, a ratty rustling sound, and a chorus of squeals.

In the dim light from the partly closed-off shaft above, Retief saw a pack of the three-pound, hairless rodents erupt from an opening near the floor. As they charged him, crawling over each other's backs in their eagerness to reach food, he did a broad jump, landing in their midst with both feet, leaving a dozen of the creatures in their death struggles. At once, the pack turned to devour their wounded members. Retief jumped clear and looked around for another opening, but the one from which the ulsios had come was the only one. He jumped on the ravenous creatures twice more, diverting them long enough to allow him to go into their burrow head-first. It led around a sharp curve and into what appeared to be an abandoned storeroom. A feeble glare-strip on the low ceiling shed enough greenish light to allow him to explore the dusty chamber. Except for some empty crates stacked against one wall, the room was empty. Just as he was about to turn away from the crates, he heard muffled voices, one of which was Magnan's. He paused to listen.

"—I'm quite sure," Magnan was saying, "that as we're both beings of the world, Mr. Dit, we can come to some mutually agreeable accommodation—and I've already forgotten this trifling incident."

"Yivshish!" Wim Dit's gravelly voice came back. "I've caught you red-handed, Ben, snooping in my most highly classified area! You'll answer for this!"

"But, Mr. Dit," Magnan protested. "I was only— that is, Retief only—"

"Bah!" Wim cut him off. "I've heard reports of your assistant's brutal mistreatment of my people! I *seen* duh fellow's undisciplined behavior wit' my own eyeballs! Wondered why you kept such a boisterous fella around a diplomatic mission. Use him to do your dirty work, I suppose. Still, as his supervisor, *you're* responsible, Ben! An' you can depen' on it, you shall feel duh full weight of Tribal justice, to say nuttin' of duh just and passionate revenge dat will be exacted by duh various clans, unions, blood-brotherhoods, sects, civic clubs and political parties you've savaged dis day! Take him away!"

Once again, Retief heard the faint sibilance of Groaci voices nearby. He put an ear to the wall, which as he had discovered was not a mass of solid masonry, but was more like Swiss cheese, riddled with passages.

"To be at ease!" a stern voice snapped in formal Groaci; the hubbub diminished slightly. "Jump-off at oh-fifteen hundred hours," the non-com went on. "To not worry: you'll get all the action you want before the day is done. To have to wait until *Lugubrious* is docked and the Terry big shots are all present or accounted for: then there's the Interplanetary Brigade under General Hish to await. Don't sweat, it's all bought and paid for—some neat tactics, eh, fellows? Good to know High Command is on the ball; OK, our top negotiators euchred the CDT into dispatching a full brigade of seasoned veterans here that *we*'ll use as support troops! Remember, no name-calling. We all know Blovian root-suckers got funny-looking faces, but we just play it cool as a penal colony on Iceberg Five."

Retief listened a little longer to the assault-troop briefing, then eased along to a gaping crack in the under-spec masonry and got a glimpse of at least a battalion of Groaci Planetary Shock Troops in full battle regalia, seated on benches, shuffling their feet while a top sergeant in simulated-jeweled greaves paced up and down before them, waving from time to time at a detailed map of the port facilities, with the Terran receiving-stand outlined in red.

Retief carefully moved crates aside and exposed a small door, adjacent to the barrack-room. Through it, he could hear Magnan's entreaties and Dit's curt dismissal. He checked the edge of the door, found a tiny aperture, and inserted a lock-pick from his lapel kit. There was a faint *click!* and the door slid aside, revealing an only slightly larger chamber, dim-lit, and fitted up with the latest in Bogan torture devices. Magnan was strapped, spread-eagled, into a massive frame, which, as Retief watched, expanded half an inch in two diminsions. Magnan *yip!*ped and tugged uselessly at the tight straps securing his wrists. Wim was not to be seen.

"Easy, Ben," Retief said quietly. "I'll cut you free."

He stepped into the room and with a quick slash of the ceremonial dagger that was part of his semidemiformal early late afternoon regulation uniform, freed him. Magnan slumped and rubbed his wrists. "Heavens,

Retief!" he bleated. "There was no need to damage the device! You could have simply unstrapped me. Dit will be furious! I sensed that he treasures the equipment in this installation: it's of his own design, you know. He ordered part of the Bogan Set Number Four, and added the autotongs from a Groaci catalog. Now you've spoiled his rack!"

"Tough E-pores," Retief remarked. "What was he after? I hope you didn't spill anything of importance, like where His Ex keeps his private stock of Bacchus red."

"Not a word," Magnan vowed. "I was firm with the scamp. I warned him of the response of Enlightened Galactic Opinion when his gross violation of diplomatic privilege is reported. I can hardly wait to give Hy the details!"

"No doubt you gave him a bad scare," Retief admitted. "But—"

"Hark!" Magnan cut him off. "I hear—yes, they're coming back! If Dit finds me free, and his rack vandalized, he'll—"

"Let's get out of here, Ben," Retief suggested, and helped his direct supervisor down from the blood-and-sweat-stained torture device.

Magnan resisted. "Perhaps if we stayed, and offered suitable apologies for the damage," he babbled, but Retief hauled him toward the exit. "Rather than scuttling away like a thief, if I should confront him coolly and offer to pay for the damage . . ." Magnan proposed.

"He had this thing set on 'auto-stretch,'" Retief told Magnan, indicating the control panel. "In half an hour your arms would have been as disjointed as oven-baked turkey-wings."

Magnan braced his feet and struggled against Retief's viselike grip.

"*Mister* Retief!" Magnan grated. "Release me! At

once! This is kidnapping under Section eight of the Code! I refuse to flee!"

"He must have an improved model brain-laundry," Retief offered, "to get you conditioned this fast." Feet could be heard approaching now.

"I was offered no indignity," Magnan purred. "His Ferocity pointed out certain disjunctures in my view of affairs, and of course I leaped at the opportunity to rectify them. Now kindly unhand me and permit me to compose myself in preparation for continuing negotiations!"

"Forget it, sir," Retief grunted. He eased the door aside, picked Magnan up bodily, and started through, but Magnan spread his arms and legs, forcing Retief to pause and tuck those members close to Magnan's centerline.

Magnan yelled, "Help! I'm being savaged! I call on you, Wim, for succor! Hurry!"

Two extra-large Bloorian Unspeakables lunged into the room, crater-guns leveled.

"Don't shoot, pray," Magnan yelped, threshing hard in Retief's grip. One of the bodyguards fired, scoring a gouge in the rocks and spattering Retief's left arm. Released, Magnan scurried past the two gunners and encountered the burly Chief Inquisitor, emerging from the side doorway with two bodyguards.

"Oh, Your Ferocity," Magnan warbled, "there's been a trifling misunderstanding. Mr. Retief was under the impression, that is, he leaped to the conclusion that—" As he chattered on, Magnan was maneuvering to place himself so as to block the view of the cut straps on the rack. Wim brushed him aside and came to an abrupt halt.

"Looky, fellas," he addressed his henchmen. "Vandalism! See what Ben Magnan done to my brand-new Model Y with embellishments! A deluxe job it was, too, Ben!" He turned to look vengefully at Magnan.

"You di'n't hafta savage duh machine dataway, which I was onney tryna show youse duh class equipment I got, to help straighten out some enemies o' duh state which dey got wrong idears! Look at dem straps! Cut clean t'rough! Finest tump-leather, too. I'm putting in fer compensation, Ben! You're gonna wisht youse never come pokin' in here like you done. Boys, take old Retief out inna courtyard and shoot him a few times. As fer you, Ben Magnan, I'm havin' you up before His Terran Ex! It's t'ree inna morning! You oughta be ashame', Ben!"

"Oh, I am, Mr. Dit, I am!" Magnan declared. "Why don't we just have me pay for the damage and forget the whole thing?"

"I guess you forgot," Wim came back heavily. "I done retained Skinnerback and Milkerdown, P.A., the finest shysters this side o' Groac, to handle my claims against you Terries! They'll tear your Tupp, Futter, and Swive apart inna courtroom!"

"Not that, please!" Magnan begged. "A firm of Terran lawyers prosecuting the Embassy of Terra; it just won't do! Though I confess I'm surprised that even those knaves would consent to take such a case in the first place!"

"Dey di'n't take it inna first place," Wim objected. "I hadda appeal to deir better natures and all. Hadda up the ante to ten percent o' duh take! Some crooks, dem legal beagles!"

"To be sure," Magnan murmured. "But why not save exorbitant legal fees all around. Just tell Bobow Skinnerback to drop the case, and I shall inform Tupp, Futter and Swive of the same. We can clear this up right here, man-to-man! What do you say, Wim?"

"I say duh CDT can pay off a bigger settlement dan a lousy CDTO-1! So it's on to duh lists and duh devil take duh hindmost!"

"Do leave me alone, Retief!" Magnan snapped as

the latter urged him toward the escape-hole. "Pray don't interfere in the negotiation, which is at a critical point just now! If I can get Wim to drop his case . . ."

"They'll be around here blocking the exit any second now," Retief told Magnan. "I can hear them already." He turned away from Magnan for a moment to step inside the escape passage and immediately felled an advancing Unthinkable with a straight right.

Magnan heard the _splat!_ and yelped at Retief: "Jim! You'll spoil the rapport I've established with His Ferocity! Now, come back here and observe! You'll get a valuable lesson in chumship techniques!"

After grabbing another advancing local and throwing him at those behind him, Retief went back to Magnan. "Not much time left, Ben," he told his chief. "We can make it out of here before we're sealed up, if we move fast."

"You're _not_ paying attention!" Magnan wailed. "I've no wish to depart before completing my conference with Wim Dit." He turned again to the towering Unspeakable. "Just consider: all the GFU grant funds will be yours, if nothing happens to upset Bloor's Most Favored Planet status, plus, _plus_, I say, whatever else you can think of. You'll be hailed as the savior of Bloor! Enlightened Galactic Opinion will come over to you in a body, and _then_ you can sue in a Court of Inequity and recover damages that will astound even Freddy Milkerdown! What do you say, eh, Wim?"

"Come on, Mr. Magnan," Retief urged in his ear. "It's now or never." He tugged at Magnan's arm.

Magnan let himself go limp and crumpled to the floor. "Dammit, Jim!" he chirped. "I'm _not_ going to abandon my greatest opportunity to make big points with His Ex! What a coup! _Lowly Econ Officer Pulls Ambassador's Chestnuts Out of Fire, Single-handed!_" Magnan quoted ecstatically. "Doubtless, Hy will receive a promo for the scoop I shall give him, a favor he'll remember the next time he's tempted to assume a critical attitude toward me, and I . . . I scarcely know what else to anticipate, Jim! It boggles the mind!"

Magnan broke off the catalog of dreams and resumed his objections as Retief picked him up and headed through the exit, slamming through the vanguard of an advancing platoon of local enforcers. Magnan grabbed the sides of the doorway with both hands, only to lose his grip as Retief forged ahead, knocking down Unthinkables left and right. Then a heavy steel door slammed in his face. He dropped Magnan, who at once turned to resume his conversation with Wim Dit, who was trailing behind.

"Pray overlook this seeming disorder, sir!" Magnan caroled. "I'm sure Mr. Retief didn't realize—"

"Don' matter what Jim don' realize," Wim cut him off. "Grab Ben, fellers," he added in an aside. The Enforcer sergeant standing beside him bleeding from a split lip started to complain, but a blow on the ear from Wim reminded him of his duty. He made a grab for Magnan, who ducked aside.

"Dear me, Mr. Dit," Magnan appealed to Wim. "Pray don't allow any unfortunate breach of diplomatic privilege to mar our nice beginning—"

"Jeez," the cop muttered to his chief. "If dis pansy t'inks getting croaked in a torture chamber in duh middle o' duh night is 'nice,' maybe we oughta tink dis over!"

"You Imbeciles can leave us Dull Normals do duh t'inkin'!" Wim rebuked, with a hearty buffet to emphasize the command.

As the chastised fellow muttered rebelliously, Wim swatted him again. "Smig! You get to duh rear o' duh column!" he ordered. The reorganization produced general confusion, as the hired thugs maneuvered aggressively to secure a position nearer the front rank and thus closer to whatever loot might be forthcoming.

"Aw right!" Wim bawled. "I can see youse got no team spirit, maneuvering to get in on duh goods and all. I'll see to a equitable distribution: half to me, and youse can fight over duh odder half amongst yerselfs!"

During the altercation Magnan had pulled free of Wim's grip and darted back into the side passage. He halted in dismay, staring around at the cul-de-sac.

"Go back, Ben," Retief urged. "I think Wim will come to his senses and escort you to safety. *I'd* better stay out of his sight, or I'll remind him he's declared a private war on Terries."

Abruptly, Ambassador Shinth arrived via yet another entry. "If you insist," Magnan agreed reluctantly, ignoring Shinth. "But what about you, Jim? How will you manage until I can find my way back with a few Marines?"

"That will require some thought, Ben," Retief acknowledged, urging Magnan back through the archway to confront Wim and his yelling cohorts. "Try not to make any really disastrous concessions, if you don't mind."

"I'll show the scamp he can't—" Magnan began, but wilted as Shinth hissed in his face:

"To have you now, Ben! Free at last of the silly restraints of your Terry-imposed diplomatic niceties! Now we shall see who controls the action at this end of the Cluster!"

"Shinth!" Magnan choked. "Am I to understand by your remarks that a Chief of Mission of proud Groac would indeed stoop to connive with the underworld to rob the Terran Mission, for mere financial profit?"

"Nope, Ben," Shinth confided earnestly. "To be the endangered species itself where the bug guck are. There's the flink hides, of course, and the voop horn—aphrodisiac, you know; real big in the Southern Arm. And lots more—all the stuff you Terries are wasting, trying to stop the natural course of nature. Extinction happens, Ben! Us Groacians face it and make a nice income from it. To be reasonable, Ben: I could even see my way to cut you in personal on the take; that's on top of old Swiney's percentage. The glutton! He insisted on ten points! Can you imagine, the nerve!" As he harangued Magnan, Shinth's less-than-flawless Terran deteriorated rapidly.

"What?" Magnan yelled. "Unhand me, sir!" He kicked Shinth in his vulnerable shin, eliciting a hiss of pain, in spite of the sequined greaves symbolically protecting that member. "You dare to attempt to bribe a Counselor of Embassy for GFU Affairs?"

"To be sure, Ben," Shinth soothed, while still hopping on one spindle-shank.

Then Wim Dit spoke up: "To be pertecking yer innerest, OK. By the bye, I heard about the promo, Ben. Congrats! Next thing you know it'll be Mr. Ambassador Magnan!"

"Not if I'm caught discussing His Ex's cut of the bootleg flink-hide trade!" Magnan pointed out, and bolted.

"That's telling him, Ben!" Retief called over the heads of the half-dozen assorted thugs crowding around the entrance to the cul-de-sac. "Run for it, Ben!" Retief cried.

Magnan fled into the darkness, three of the Bloorians baying at his heels. Retief gave chase. He overtook and tripped Gugly Eye, a loafer he'd often seen hanging around the motor pool. Eye was the last in line. Retief moved up to grab Jum Derk by the collar and dump him sideways. Jumping over the still rolling Unspeakable, he overtook the front-runner and knocked him down, Wim's bellow and Shinth's faint voice shouting behind him. Retief called to Magnan, was ignored, and followed his fleeing supervisor along the echoing corridor.

"That did it!" Shinth hissed. "To close the passage,

Wim!" Retief skidded to a halt and charged back toward the Groaci and his hirelings, but the Bloorian strong-arm squad had already rolled an immense, rail-mounted steel slab in place, sealing off the passage.

Magnan, noticing nothing, continued to flee, unpursued. He reached a narrowing in the passage, where a great bool-wood door stood half-open. He grabbed it in passing and slammed it, in Retief's face. The latch *clack!*ed decisively. Retief skidded to a halt and tried the knob. It was fixed as solidly as the wall of living stone beside him. Before he could move, an explosion threw him back against the opposite wall and down into a pit that seemed bottomless.

Chapter 3

When Retief regained consciousness he found that he was lying on a stone floor scattered with meager straw containing fleas. He could see no light; in total darkness he paced off the dimensions of the featureless cell. Twelve one way, nine the other, with an alcove in one corner. It occurred to him this was the approximate size and shape of the Chancery in the Embassy of Groac, which he had seen a few days before on a goodwill tour arranged between Ambassadors Swinepearl and Shinth. On tiptoe, he could just touch the ceiling—of rough planks, he concluded from the unplaned texture. He found a stout wooden bench bolted to the wall and floor at one side of the stuffy room. Insofar as he could determine, there was no door or window. "Still," he mused, "I got in here somehow."

The floor was an unbroken slab, reasonably clean, even. The silence was total. And while he languished here, poor Ben was doubtless getting in deeper with every utterance.

The ceiling seemed to be the only possibility. Retief noticed that in the corner occupied in the Chancery by the big Fortress £3 model safe, the ceiling sagged minutely. He went over to stand under the heavily stressed planks. He returned to the bench, yanked it loose from its bolts and dragged it over. He disassembled his belt-buckle by feel, working carefully; it wouldn't do to drop anything in the pitch darkness. He freed the tongue, a three-inch spike, from its mounting and worked it clear of the deep-blue tump-leather. Standing on the bench, he found a joint between the ceiling planks where the deflection was greatest. He began to gouge at it. The wood was the tough, aromatic local iron-elm, a mutated tree of Terran origin. It yielded reluctantly, splintering away in three-inch by half-inch chips. After half an hour's careful work, he caught a whiff of Groaci dope-stick through the narrow opening he had made, and a faint glimmer of light gave him his first view of the featureless dungeon in which he was confined. He listened, heard faint, breathy Groaci voices not far away.

"—to express astonishment, Flinsh?" a familiar voice was saying: it was that of Shish, the Groaci Counselor, Retief realized. "What's that you say?" Shish went on, "Do you presume to accuse His Excellency of connivance in violation of diplomatic immunity, and to so far transgress the tenets of bureaucratic solidarity as actually to countenance the employment of sacred Groacian soil for purposes of kidnapping and illegal imprisonment? 'Unthinkable!' you say. But only today at their farcical Awards Banquet, I was chatting with that sneaky Ben Magnan; I managed to dissemble my distaste for his loathsome Terran body odor, and to lull the ninny into total acceptance of my wily assurances. To distort Groac's role in this fiasco is a trifle in the service of noble Groac; no breach of honor! Doubtless the feckless Magnan is even now bending His Ex's auditory membranes in the belief he's finessing him into a false position, contraband-kickbackwise. The dupes! What a pleasure it will be, Flinsh, to gloat, whilst wrapped in the cloak of unstained virtue even as the feckless Terries pay the price exacted by Enlightened Galactic Opinion for the traffic from which *we* reap the profits!"

"I say, sir," Flinsh offered hesitantly. "Is it entirely wise to state the case so candidly, especially while so close to the actual environs of the Terran Mission, just beyond the partition there?"

"You, a mere third secretary and vice-consul," Shish retorted contemptuously, "have the effrontery to question the wisdom of your very own counselor?"

"Well, sir," the impudent fellow attempted. "I only meant—"

"To understand very well, Flinsh," Shish said coldly in the Formal dialect: "To make a marginal note in your ER to the effect that you spoke without thinking."

"Gosh, sir," the hapless vice-consul tried again, an example, Shish reflected, of the persistence which had been instrumental in the boy's glacial rate of promotion.

"After all, you're not *totally* infallible, sir," he plunged to his doom.

"Am I to understand, Flinsh," Shish said in an incredulous tone, "that you take it upon yourself not only to dispute the decision of your Big Boss, but place his very wisdom in question?"

While the occupants of the strong-room were thus contentedly engaged in Pecking-order Ritual, Retief wedged off another wide chunk of the tough wood. He could now see part of the room, including two pairs of jeweled greaves above flat, bunioned feet in trump-hide sandals. The Groaci diplomats were at the far end of the room, fully intent on their verbal ping-pong. Retief eased his left hand through the inch-wide gap he had made, and was able to put his fingertips on a silken throw-rug on which rested one leg of a small end-table. He inched the silk toward him; it slid silently, bringing the table along. Retief could see the top of a cheap Groaci copy of a Yalcan glass pot on the table; it tottered as the table swung around minutely.

Retief paused, watching closely, but the breathy Groaci voices went on, poor Flinsh losing ground with each ill-advised utterance. Shish was shifting impatiently, saying: "Yes, yes, no matter, my boy. You're young: to learn in time." Then he turned and walked directly toward Retief's spy-hole, Flinsh trotting at his side, the side nearer to Retief. Timing it carefully, Retief waited until Flinsh was passing directly by the table, then he jerked the rug. The pot rocked, leaned, and fell with a *smash!* Bits of iridiscent glass scattered in every direction.

"Fool!" Shish yelled. "Clumsy idiot! Look where you're blundering! Do you realize that lamp was of museum quality—a gift from the Yalcan Minister of Culture to my departed colleague Ambassador Schluh!"

"Gee, sir, I didn't even *touch* that table!" Flinsh protested.

"Stubborn!" Shish yelled, a dry wheeze. "As we stand here actually *looking at* the shards of a precious vase destroyed by your clumsiness, you attempt to deny the evidence your own senses as well as mine perceive! Folly, Flinsh! No—don't aggravate the offense—"

"But, sir, I carefully avoided any contact whatever with the table whereon the lamp rested!"

"Don't imagine, Flinsh," Shish grated, "that I fail to notice the implied rebuke in your editing my use of the word 'vase' to 'lamp'! As if this petty distinction in any degree lessened the gravity of the offense!"

"Gee, sir," Flinsh offered. "To hate it that the lamp, I mean vase broke and all, but *I* didn't do it!"

"To be quite enough, Flinsh!" his boss declared. "Never mind! To sweep that up—no, I didn't mean that! To be beneath your rank, after all, incompetent though you are! I go to summon a sweeper!" Shish stamped off to his squawk-box and ordered the Groacian

Marine Guard on duty to send in the duty sweeper. All the while, Flinsh was at his heels, whining.

Retief watched Shish go to the big safe, which partially blocked his view. Shish poked buttons, opened the heavy door, and rummaged, while Flinsh hovered nervously. Shish brought out a sheaf of heavy parchment, folded like a road map and secured by a bright red ribbon and a big gob of sealing wax. Without hesitation, the Groaci Number Two broke away the seal and unfolded the document.

" 'The Ambassador of Terra presents his compliments to the Ambassador of Groac,' " he read in flawlessly accented Terran. ". . . and with reference to a certain nominally contraband shipment of office supplies—' Ha!" Shish scoffed. "Get that 'nominally'! Weasel words, Flinsh, and I have to admit Sam is an expert with them. Still, one mustn't be decoyed from the path of duty by such nefarious attempts at subtlety! '—contraband merchandise,' " he went on, " 'I have the honor to request Your Excellency's assistance in exporting the aforesaid items without troubling the Bloorian Office of Customs and Excise.' Hah! wants us to help him smuggle flink-hides, the hypocrite! Listen to this: 'I expect you will, in accordance with our previous mutual agreement, create a disturbance which will distract attention from the godown in question in timely fashion, to permit selected'—meaning 'bribed,' " Shish interjected, " 'local officials to relabel and transport the aforesaid goods to the Sealed Customs Annex before the scheduled departure time of the Three-Planet liner *Lugubrious*, this date. Please accept, Mr. Ambassador, renewed assurances of my highest consideration.' "

"To confess, Mr. Shish, I'm shocked!" young Flinsh gasped.

"To get over it, lad," the Counselor said kindly. "To have had to discover the truth eventually: ours is a devious calling. 'The end justifies the means,' as the revered Foreign Minister Fishfilth said at the time of his capture. I *had* to delude poor Sammy; it was the only way!"

"But I thought you and that wretched Terry were bosom buddies!" Flinsh wailed. "All the times he's saved your mummified blurb-jowl by honestly lying on your behalf! Actually, I'd conceived a sort of secret admiration for Ambassador Swinepearl, Terry though he is. I'm devastated!" Poor young Flinsh flicked a drop of lachrymal exudant from his middle eye-stalk. Shish patted his carapace comfortingly. "I know, my boy; I, too was shocked in the beginning. On my very first tour, in the Goober Cluster, I had the unhappy duty to 'accidentally' lose a certain document which would have suggested less than total lack of culpability on the part of my revered Chief of Mission in regard to the premature release of certain Terran detainees being held on behalf of Incompetent Fumbler Swive, a poor fool who had been so naïve as to trust us. He paid for his folly when his Mission was incontinently ejected from the Western Arm, where he had secured a toehold unknown to the CDT. A band of bucolic dacoits set upon him in his very chancery and evicted him into the low street. For a while, I felt shamed, but in the end, well, we shall yet see who prevails in Tip Space!"

"Sure, sir," Flinsh replied brokenly, "but this isn't just playing His Terran Ex for a fool, it's condemning all those cute little flinks to extermination! I can't bear it! Something must be done!"

"Something to keep my name out of it, you mean," Shish supplied. "Good thinking, lad. Suppose you just take this potentially compromising document, which I signed tongue-in-cheek and with both outer pairs of coulars crossed, solely to give poor Sam a sense of security. He feared that if the trade agreement became generally known, GFU shipments would cease at once, endangering the success of his Mission, as well as casting himself into disrepute. Poor Sammy. He was only an amateur scoundrel; no chance against the real thing in the person of myself!"

"Right, sir," Flinsh gobbled, taking the incriminating Agreement form. "I think I'm beginning to get the hang of it!" he exclaimed as he eyed the heavy parchment which Shish had given him. "Guess I'll burn it, eh, Chief?"

"By no means, Flinsh," Shish countered. "It constitutes hard evidence of my unexampled virtuosity! I shall yet find a use for it, with a few discreet modifications made by an expert in amending such evidence."

"Gosh, sir, I wasn't thinking, I guess," Flinsh confessed. "Hide it?" he offered.

"Precisely," Shish confirmed. "There—behind that crack in the paneling. Shoddy construction, but it has its uses."

Flinsh went to the designated gap in the imitation berpwood partition, swung open the secret door and thrust the document inside. It landed with a heavy *thump!* beside Retief. He tucked it away.

"Hark! I heard a heavy *thump!*" Flinsh exclaimed.

"Nonsense, lad," Shish soothed. "There's nothing below but the refuse pits. They'd make more of a *splash!*"

"Sure, I guess so, sir," Flinsh retreated. "But if anybody finds that, it would—"

"Forget it!" Shish ordered. "Do you suggest that your very own supervisor would be so careless as—" He broke off at a distinct *creak!* from the floor underfoot. "Here!" he hissed. "What's—?"

"Just this old floor creaking, sir," Flinsh supplied. "You know how careless these local contractors are."

"But this building is the former Grand Imperial Doghouse," Shish protested, "once Headquarters of the Local Order of the Schnauzer! It was built fifty years before the first visit of Ambassador-at-Large Thush! So . . ."

As the two Groaci bureaucrats wrangled, Retief studied the deflected planks under the weighty safe, and noticed newly-exposed fibers of the tough iron-elm, weakened by his gouging, where a new longitudinal split had opened spontaneously. Working silently, he widened the aperture further, while the two Groaci diplomats nattered on above, unnoticing. When the crack was a quarter of an inch wide, Retief carefully tore a narrow strip of parchment from the Memorandum, folded it lengthwise for stiffening and, when the Groaci were at the far end of the room, poked the strip through the opening and gave it a tap which propelled it through, and a few inches away. He waited. After a full minute, Flinsh exclaimed: "Sir! You must have dropped—I mean, clearly *somebody* dropped a scrap of paper, and—" He came up to the safe. Retief noticed the slight further deflection of the floor under the junior officer's added weight.

"Fool!" Shish hissed. "Would you impute your own slovenliness to *me*?"

"But, sir," Flinsh attempted, "I only deposited the secret document just like you said!"

"I said nothing about towing classified papers on the floor!" Shish barked. Speechless with rage, he came stamping over to confront his underling, crowding him back against the safe. Beside Retief's ear, the floor *creak!*ed again, under the added load, and uttered a distinct *pop!*ping as more fibers failed as the straw of Shish's weight broke the figurative camel's back.

"Look out, sir!" Flinsh yelped. "The safe! It's—"

"Quickly, pull it back!" Shish ordered. Both Groaci climbed on the tilting strongbox, as the planks sagged under it; Retief stroked his improvised chisel across the highly-stressed fibers on the underside of the deflecting plank: it gave minutely, then collapsed. Retief ducked aside as the half-ton safe dropped a corner into the gap now yawning in the floor; it slid farther, doing aside the adjacent floor-plank, which parted with an angry *crunch!*; then the safe fell through, in a hail of splinters, to impact on the concrete a yard from Retief's foot. Above, the Groaci diplomats leaped aside, and fled, with sharp cries. When all was silent, Retief stepped up on the great red-painted safe and examined the hole in the floor. He glanced into the empty office above. The outer door of the richly appointed office stood open. In the distance faint Groaci cries were audible. Retief climbed up into the room.

Using the code he had watched Shish employ, he opened the steel wall-depository, and glanced quickly over its contents, mostly well-thumbed Groaci soft porn portraying Groacian ladies emerging from hot-sand tubs, and tight little bundles of local currency. There was one sealed document, which Retief tucked away with the other in an inside pocket.

At a sound outside, he flattened himself against the wall beside the hall door and waited until a five-eyed Groaci head wearing the plumed helmet of a Groacian peace-keeper had poked inside and withdrawn with the over-the-shoulder comment:

"Naw, Mr. Counselor, nothing like that. To be able to smell Verbot Nine at one part in a trillion. Looks like maybe the floor give way, is all. The safe's intact, OK."

"To thank you, Corporal! Now to enter the room and conduct a proper investigation, at once!" Shish hissed. The rebuked NCO threw the door wide and stepped inside, just in time to receive Retief's straight left to his underslung jaw. In falling backward he slammed the door in Shish's face. Retief stood over the dazed cop, who scuttled backward away from him, fumbling at the same time for the big brass whistle at his belt. Retief shook his head and the hapless Groaci went limp and lay looking up at the tall Terran.

"To watch it, Terry—" he started, but fell silent when Retief dug a booted toe into his narrow thorax.

"I'll tell you when to start talking, Sish," Retief told him. "Keep it quiet for now, and you may yet get out of this intact."

"To be very cooperative, honored sir," Sish assured his captor. "I was only—"

"What's it all about, Sish?" Retief persisted. "What's going on?"

"Why ask *me?*" Sish objected. "I'm a mere under-ling, as you well know, Mr. Retief! Nobody tells *me* anything!"

"Very well," Retief replied. "It seems we'd better get Shish back in here. Put on your helmet and give him the high-sign."

"B-but I *couldn't!*" Sish gasped. "To decoy my per-sonal boss into a trap? Reprehensible!"

"Sure," Retief agreed. "Just pretend it's some poor, trusting Terry bent on Doing Good, like Ben Magnan, you're luring to his doom."

Sish straightened his flaring helm and went briskly to the door, yanked it open, thrust his head out, and said, "To step in just a moment, Mr. Shish." He stepped back, holding the door wide as Shish came through in a rush.

"Yes, yes, to show me—" he started impatiently, but recoiled at sight of Retief. "You! The infamous wrecker Jame Retief!" He spat, backing away. Two of his eyes swung to transfix Sish. "Corporal!" he hissed. "Just why is it this interloper on sacred Groacian soil is not in irons?"

"Oh, I guess I forgot my irons, Mr. Shish," Sish explained. "To be just going to . . ."

"Skip that," Retief cut in, confronting Shish. "That's

enough horsing around. Now: What's all this about you imprisoning Terries, and how far up does the involvement in the flink-hide trade go?"

Shish's eye-stalks drooped, miming total incomprehension.

"Don't bother with the twitches, Shish," Retief snapped. "You know we Terries don't understand when you mime 'incomprehension' in your eye-stalk language. Speak up!"

"To know nothing of Ben Magnan being held in the code room under interrogation by Colonel Thilth," Shish gobbled.

"What is it he expects to find out?" Retief insisted.

"Oh, nothing of consequence," Shish replied airily. "Just sort of exploring Ben's psyche, I guess. Asked him how long he had known about the system of secret passages and all, and if Sammy Swinepearl had OKed the hidden entry into the Terry Chancery from our VIP mess, stuff like that. Counter-counterintelligence you could call it. But Ben's hanging tough: says he's not privy to no nefarious stuff and all. He's lying! Ben's in this up to his paltry eyeballs!"

"'In' what?" Retief demanded.

"Why, the scheme initiated by Sam Swinepearl, of course!" Shish hissed. "What else?"

"I thought perhaps you were referring to the trade in contraband flink-hides," Retief explained patiently. "Was that your own idea, or is somebody coercing you?"

"'Coercing'? *Me?* A Groacian Deputy Chief of Mission!" Shish squalled. "Flink-hides, indeed! That was merely a cover, Retief, for Sammy's actual crimes!"

"I'm fascinated, Counselor," Retief prompted. "Pray continue."

"It's unthinkable!" Shish hissed.

"Think about it anyway," Retief directed. "Let's get to the heart of the matter."

"A shipment—nay, ten shipments, a hundred, of Bogan small-arms!" Shish blabbed. "In transit at this moment! With means of slaughter in the hands of the locals, no one will be safe, Retief! We have to abort this tragedy, somehow!"

"'We'?" Retief queried. "Now we're all pals, eh?"

"Are we not? Surely any civilized nation—a category in which one can hardly include Bloor—would intercede to prevent this monumental atrocity. To arm these fratricidal barbarians, who, even bare-handed but for rude implements improvised from the so-called relief shipments supplied by your Terries, have succeeded in decimating their subject populations! Certain interested powers from the Western Arm have succeeded in suborning poor Sam Swinepearl from the path of duty to cooperate in a scheme to depopulate Bloor, thereby making it, as an unoccupied planet, fair game for colonization! The 'relief' shipments are subtly tampered with, and fifty thousand stand of Bogan 2mm repeaters arrived at the port but yesterday, disguised as agricultural equipment. The turncoat Wim Dit has acquiesced to this diabolical plan, in hope of gaining advantages for his Disreputable clique! The heavy stuff is to follow in a few days. It will be Unspeakable against Unthinkable, Unbearable versus Intolerable; Reprehensible will confront Contemptible at the barricades! Instead of the traditional buffets and insults, these naïve dupes will exchange hard shots! Vascular fluids will flow in the gutters! I have it on good authority that Hellbores will be included in the next shipment; even infinite repeaters will be placed in the hands of warring clans, clashing tribes, unions locked in jurisdictional dispute! Bands of irregulars will mow down dacoit hordes; each and every traditional rival on the planet will assault its ancient enemy with massed gunfire, cannisters of Verbot Ten will be as common as hurled rocks are now! The slaughter of valuable consumers will be beyond calculation or the possibility of properly conducted funeral rites, at Groacian bargain prices! There's not an hour to lose, Retief! Let's go talk to Ben, and see what can yet be done, if it's not altogether too late to stop the bloodbath!"

"Lead on," Retief said. "Sish," he ordered the corporal. "You stick around and discourage any meddlers."

"Do as he says, cretinous litter-mate of drones!" Shish snapped. "Nothing, I repeat, 'not anything,' is to be allowed to interfere with our high mission! Come, Retief!" Shish concluded grandly. "The Forces of Right will yet prevail!" Just as Retief and the Groaci Counselor of Embassy opened the door to depart the room, gunfire rattled in the corridor. Shish leaped back. A window smashed inward and a smoking cannister *thump!*ed on the carpet beside Sish.

"Deal with that, Corporal!" Shish yelled.

"Verbot Two!" Sish squealed. "It's every being for himself!" He dived through the broken pane into the darkness.

"Pity," Shish commented, glancing back. "That light-well is six stories deep. But poor Sish had no future in the Cadre in any case. Never did learn so much as the Manual of Arms! Fell down every time he attempted the foot salute!"

They went along the corridor, from which the gunfire had moved on, though the armed local employees crouched at the intersection gave evidence that the disturbance was not yet over; but the scene of action seemed to have shifted to an upper floor. Sounds of carnage came from the stairwell. Abruptly, Ben Magnan appeared, scrambling down out of a cloud of smoke and dust.

"Ah, there you are, Mr. Shish!" he chirped. "And you, too, Jim. I'm *so* relieved you've placed yourself under the protection of the Counselor! I'm sorry I was detained, but it seemed Colonel Thilth *would* have his little chat. One has to admire his élan, nattering of commercial matters whilst crater-guns are booming just outside the door!"

"Ben Magnan!" Shish hissed. "What—how—where is the Colonel now?" The Groaci peered up into the obscurity of the stairwell, where recurrent flashes of gunfire lit the murk fitfully.

"Oh, ah, I fear I quite inadvertently slammed the door on poor Thilth!" Magnan twittered. "After our chat, I had preceded him out of the chamber when a pair of your Marines entered the passage, firing as they came; I fear I shied a trifle and accidentally slammed the door on poor Thilth! I was just coming to let you know, in case you were wondering what was keeping him."

"Thoughtful of you, Ben," Shish purred. "As to your chat, did you cover the, ah, irregularities I fancy I've detected in certain shipments of emergency aid supplies?"

"Oh, dear me, yes," Magnan burbled. "You mean about the jellied blurb-jowls going astray, I shouldn't wonder. But," Magnan wagged a finger playfully in Shish's inscrutable face. "I've not forgotten they're your favorite! It was a mere administrative mix-up; no doubt we'll find them mixed in with the semi-annual requisition. If you'd just buck my two missing bales of Report of Redundant Reports forms back to my office, I'd be most appreciative!"

"Bother the R of RR forms!" Shish spat ungraciously. "And the infernal blurb-jowl as well! I'm a bit off my feed since the local ruffians invaded my office yesterday," he explained. "Actually, Retief has a question or two to ask you, I believe."

"Yes, Jim?" Magnan looked expectantly at his six-three junior. "What was it? You're curious about the new hemi-semi-demi early late mid-afternoon dress codes specified for the banquet, I suppose? By the way, about those flink-hides—"

"What " Shish snarled. "You have the effrontery to bring up *that* matter, right here in a monitored stretch of corridor? Have you *no* discretion, Ben?"

"It's not the flink-hides, Shish," Retief corrected. "Those bales are dummies; the cartons are full of handguns and ammo to fit them, with a layer of moldy hides on the outside. I suppose Wim Dit has taken delivery by now."

Magnan recoiled. " 'Handguns,' you say, Jim! Whatever are they for? If anyone should be so foolish as to place weapons in the hands of any faction here on Bloor, the resultant massacre would make Fort Dade seem like a picnic!"

"Perhaps not so foolish, eh, Ben?" Shish spoke up in a wheedling tone. "Remember that twenty thousand guck has been deposited in your account in the Bank of Groac."

"*Mister* Counselor!" Magnan rebuked. "I thought that contribution to charity in my name was to be *our* little secret!" He stepped to Retief's side.

"A nonexistent charity, by the way," Shish amplified.

"You see, Jim," Magnan continued, "I happened to notice something a little odd when I visited the Consular Office the other day—you'll recall I was a trifle late to Staff Meeting on Tuesday last—and when I referred the matter to Old Swiney—I mean His Excellency the Terran AE and MP—he scoffed at me! Imagine! Me, a Counselor of Embassy for GFU Affairs, dismissed like a nervous recruit! But to return to my thesis: Marv Lacklustre, the Consular Officer, was inundated with Reports of Discrepancy pouring in from every quarter! The Minister of Eats and Drinks was quite furious; he'd diverted a few cases of the jellied blurb-jowl to his hill station, you see, and when his chef opened them—he found, not succulent tidbits, but rather scads of Browning 2mm needlers in cosmoleum! Hardly fitting provender to set before the chiefs of the Reprehensible and the Objectionable clans, under truce, gathered in a spirit of good fellowship to divide the spoils—distribute the relief shipments, that is—anyway, that was only the beginning! The Commissioner of Planetary Pigs, as the locals so colorfully call their cops, was *most* incensed to find that cartons labeled 'school lunches' contained zipguns and crack Tylenol spiked with cyanide, all ready to be insinuated into rival apothecary shelves! Disgraceful! And you'd hardly credit the abuse I've suffered from the Motor Pool Chief, carping about his spare parts shipment! Useless components for energy weapons, he says, though the scamp admitted he'd been able to cannibalize the stuff for energy slugs to keep his rickety fleet in service for a few more weeks! Incompetence on a giant scale, Shish!"

The incensed Groaci turned to Flinsh. "The rot runs deep, my boy," he muttered. "Imagine Ben Magnan pulling a fasty of this magnitude on his old kikistone fingering buddy and fellow veteran of the diplomatic wars! It's not to be borne!"

"So . . ." Third Secretary Flinsh queried breathlessly, "what are you going to do, sir? How will you bring proud Terra to heel and punish this perfidy?"

"I don't have the details worked out yet," Shish confided, "but getting Ben in my hands was my first priority. Now for phase two."

"Could I go along, sir?" Flinsh begged. "Just to observe the master at work, you know. But Ben Magnan's standing right here, sir."

"I so decree," Shish replied, nodding importantly. "Pull yourself together, lad," he commanded. "We mustn't let Ben or Retief see you looking flustered, implying a chink in the armor of Groaci infallibility,"

"Sure not, sir," Flinsh agreed and, aligning his eye-shields, executed an almost flawless foot-salute.

"See, I didn't fall down that time, sir!" he chortled. "Like Sish does," he added.

"Commendable, I'm sure," Shish grunted. "Now, clear the passage ahead of me and put some snap in it!"

"Ah His Excellency desires," Flinsh mumbled and forged out along the debris-littered passage. Retief and Magnan followed. It was a leisurely five-minute canter to the Chancery wing, where Flinsh halted before the strong-room door, which stood open.

"Gosh!" the youthful Groaci exclaimed. "Somebody left the door wide open! I bet it was Ben!"

"Ha!" Magnan exclaimed. "It's just like the scamp to blame me!"

"A less benign Chief of Security than myself," Shish addressed the nearby corporal gravely, "would see you staked out at the sulfur pits for this disregard of primary duty, Sish. Kindly recite the General Orders for me."

"Uh, why, 'I will walk my post in a million different manners,'" the NCO crowed glibly. "'Under no circumstances, that's not any circumstances at all, will I fail to take prompt and effective action upon detecting any apparent breach of security.'" Sish looked pleased with himself, an effect achieved by aligning his eye-stalks front-rear, front-rear, front. On impulse he slammed the heavy door.

"Fool!" Shish spluttered. "Now how am I to gain ingress? Eh? Did you consider that, Sish, when you so rudely slammed the door, practically in my face? Did you, eh?"

"It says 'not under any circumstances,'" Sish pointed out futilely. "Wait a sec, sir, I'll find Sarge!" He darted off.

"Ah, Ben," Shish purred. "I was just about to nip over to your Embassy and invite you to accompany me for the ceremonies."

"What ceremonies?" Magnan demanded bluntly. "His Ex has postponed the award of the Grand Star and Bladder of the Legion, Second Class, to His Excellency the Foreign Minister, as you well know."

"No, no, not that hollow ritual!" Shish objected. "I refer to the touching welcoming ceremony at the port, as noble Groac displays her solidarity with haughty Terra in receiving the GFU shipment! I've laid on a nose-flute troop, and a squad or two of honor guards. I was just about to inspect the guard. Do come along, Ben!"

"Oh, so you're trying to horn in on Terra's hour of glory, eh, Shish?" Magnan replied coldly. "The press will assume you Groaci are the donors rather than Terra's Goodies for Undesirables program. Insidious in the extreme, I'd call that. And what's this about an honor guard? By solemn interplanetary accord, Groac's armed forces, even token detachments, are rigidly excluded from pretechnical worlds! Now, lead me to where you've hidden these troops!"

"Never!" Shish hissed. "Do you imagine that proud Groac would allow envious Terra thus to thwart her realization of Manifest Destiny? My troops are *my* little secret, Ben. They shall remain so until unleashed in the moment of dire need!"

"It isn't fair," Magnan moaned. "What's a Counselor for GFU Affairs to do . . . ?"

"Never mind, Ben," Retief consoled his stricken supervisor. "I'll show you their hidey hole."

"*You!*" Shish hissed. "What could a mere third secretary and vice-consul know of great affairs? The entire matter has been handled under Cosmic Discreet Security! The documentation is secreted in a safe depository where no mere Terran would even think of looking! It's bluff, Retief! Pure bluff! I defy you!"

"Here are the details, sir," Retief said, as he took out the folded parchment he had removed from the Ambassador's safe and displayed it so that Magnan could read the lines he indicated.

Magnan looked, read, gasped, " '. . . a final Solution to the pernicious nuisance of Terran *de facto* assumption of domination over Groac, an invidious claim, the truth of which they have had the audacity to demonstrate publicly on more than one occasion . . .' " Magnan stared at Retief.

"This, it appears, is it, Jim," he gulped. "At last the scoundrels have given themselves away! When I expose this clandestine troop buildup for all the Galaxy to see, the Groaci will be forced to abandon their far-flung empire and slink back to their native sandhills, there to ponder the unwisdom of incurring the rebuke of Terra. Doubtless, Shish"—he shifted targets to the enraged Groaci—"you'll have the elementary discretion to withdraw from your untenable position here on Bloor *before* it becomes necessary for me to advise Freddy Underknuckle to call out the Peace Enforcers . . . now cruising on fleet exercise off Yoon!"

"Never!" Shish spat. "Have a care, Ben Magnan, soon-to-be *ex*-Counselor when it becomes generally known that you Terries have violated the sacrosanct soil of the Groacian Mission, and offered insult to myself, the Beloved of Bloor—had you heard I'd received the honorary title by acclamation, Ben?"

"Congratulations, Shish," Magnan purred. "Now, if you'd just be a good scout and revise your plans for grabbing credit for GFU's distribution of free eats and stuff, I'm sure we can clear up all these petty irregularities without recourse to Draconian measures!"

"Turning it over to the yellow press, you mean, Ben,

in the person of Hy Felix. The scamp would spill the legumes via SWIFT to every city desk in the Arm in a matter of minutes!"

"Milliseconds," Magnan corrected the Groaci's faulty conception of the efficiency of the Shaped Wave Interference Front Transmitter. "And Hy won't bother with petty local presses. He'll dump the entire matter before ACHE, and ITCH as well, for adjudication at the next open hearing!"

"Why involve the Tribunal, or even the feckless Assembly?" Shish demanded. "Their efforts to correct historical events are doomed to Failure. That business about deleting all mention of Native American rape and murder of pioneer women and children under cover of reporting in for free blankets and beads, for example! Irresponsible, Ben! The crime was too well recorded in the contemporaneous record to be expunged now, even by the most diligent efforts of well-intentioned amateurs! Claiming that the practice of scalping was introduced by Europeans is another example: scalping-knife marks on Neolithic Amerind skulls indicate otherwise! As for the silly Assembly's efforts to Curtail Hostilities, why the thing is preposterous, Ben! A bunch of Do-Gooders can't fly in the face of the primary force of Organic Evolution itself. 'The Survival of the Fittest' hardly implies feckless tolerance of the objectionable! Thus, it is inevitable that great Groac and ambitious Terra shall forever grapple in the darkness, seeking advantage—and this time, Ben, it's we Groaci who have seized the initiative and left you Terries with egg on your faces! Do your worst, Ben! My plans are long and well-laid. Even now . . ." The irate Groacian bigwig paused and appeared to be listening, as if for distant sounds. "Even now," he resumed, after a glance at Magnan's lapel chronometer, "my lads, under General Hish, are readying themselves for the grand coup! You're too late, Ben! The wheels of Fate are in motion, and he who would obstruct them is doomed to destruction! Have done! Give it over! You've done all a Terry bureaucrat could have, and I shall personally indict an epistle to Sam, attesting to your efforts. How's that for professional élan?"

"Gosh, Shish," Magnan whispered. "It's magnanimous to the point of self-imolation—!"

"'Immolation'?" Shish gasped. "Just how do you mean? I have no thought of being myself consumed in the holocaust set by an aroused Bloorian populace!"

"It's just that when they see all those guns slipping from their grasp and falling into the hands of their sworn enemies," Magnan clarified, "they're likely to be a trifle upset."

"But I didn't—you *wouldn't* thus abort my lovely plan!" Shish screeched. "In my wildest xenophobic imaginings, I never considered that an old associate would actually commit an act of such bestiality! Picture the atrocities: Incorrigibles grabbing off wire-guns slated for Clan Execrable, the Teamstresses' Union glomming onto brass knuckles clearly addressed to the Seamsters, otherwise known as the Bitches and the Beasts! It's not to be countenanced, Ben! Call off your fell design and I'll tell you where the last shipment disappeared to—and you'd best be quick because I have it from a Usually Reliable Source—"

"You mean George, the janitor," Magnan snarled. "Yes, yes, go on."

"No, no," Shish objected, "George is a 'Classified Source'! Anyways, I'm tryna tell you!" he whimpered. "To have discovered that even now the cache has been discovered to the Reprehensibles, who are attempting to buy of the Deplorables with a promise of a posthumous allotment of firearms, and—"

"Enough!" Magnan decreed. "There's no time to waste! When word gets out that the flink-hide trade is actually a gun-running scheme, the fat will be in the fire for fair!"

"Please, Ben!" Shish objected. "You know how I hate alliterations, especially fricative ones!"

"Sorry about that," Magnan muttered. "But what do you say, Shish? Should we join grasping members just this once, to avert carnage on a vast scale? Groac and Terra, shoulder to shoulder, fighting the good fight!"

Shish extended a tentacle. "Done and done, Ben Magnan," he cried in as ringing a tone as his feeble voice could manage.

A few minutes later, Magnan spoke quietly to Retief: "I'm amazed at the effrontery of the scamp," he said. "He virtually admitted that he had planned to muscle in on our distribution ceremonies, elbow His Ex aside, and claim credit for the Goodies! Thereby becoming the Power Behind the Throne here on Bloor!"

"Nice work, Ben," Retief congratulated his immediate supervisor. "If we can keep the rap pinned firmly on Shish, the Terran Embassy may very well survive unburnt."

"Oh, my, yes," Magnan murmured, then, "What? What do you mean, Jim? Are you implying—?"

"Nope, I'm proclaiming," Retief corrected. "If we can get His Ex to lie low while Shish gets his skinny neck all the way in, we're home safe, and you'll probably come out of the discreditation and collapse of GFU with a promotion to Career Minister."

"'Collapse'?" Magnan gasped. "Tell me, Jim, just what did I do, or am I about to do that's so clever? Actually, I don't know what to do about Shish's little surprise in the form of a battalion or more of seasoned troops about to descend on the port and grab all the credit."

"Never mind, Ben, I mentioned the matter to Buck Muldoon, and I imagine he has the matter in hand."

"But how could you have known?" Magnan gasped. "I hadn't even explained it to you yet!"

"Just a hunch," Retief told him. "A hunch that developed when I saw the Bill of Lading for today's GFU shipment—it had been crudely altered."

"Why, the nerve!" Magnan gasped. "Tampering with the virtually holy mission of my proud bureau!"

"We'd better get out to the port, pronto," Retief suggested. "When those crates clear Customs—"

"Look here, Shish . . ." Magnan turned to the spot where the Groaci had been crouched against the wall.

"Why!" Magnan blurted. "Where's the scamp gotten to? He's gone, Jim!"

"Right," Retief confirmed. "He did a sneak down the service passage while you were being indignant about the Bills of Lading."

"Why didn't you stop him?"

"I thought it would be a good idea to follow him," Retief explained.

"Heavens, Jim!" Magnan nagged. "I don't imagine Shish will stop with waylaying our cargo; he'll be up to further mischief, I don't doubt!"

"Not if we catch him," Retief offered.

"He might even start a rumor that we Terries are at fault!" Magnan grieved, as Retief led the way along the dark passage to a side exit.

"Wait, Jim!" Magnan yelped. "I've heard that once lost in the tortuous maze of secret passages which riddle the Groaci Embassy, one is never seen again!"

"Then let's not get lost," Retief proposed as he forged ahead.

After ten minutes' groping progress along the dark, rubbish-littered passage, during which Magnan lost count of the splits and side-turns, they emerged in the garage of the Terran Embassy.

"Jim!" Magnan yipped. "We're—we're in the garage!
Our garage! I mean, this is the bay His Ex leased to
his Old Car Club! See, there's Herb Lunchwell's
restored 1936 Hupmobile! Shish must have come here
to steal a car! Where—?"

"Over there," Retief suggested, as the groan of an
early self-starter sounded from the shadowy corner
where Hy Felix's 1913 Stutz three-passenger coupe
was parked. With a creak of ancient springs, it moved.

"That Bendix is an aftermarket item some owner
installed," Magnan muttered. "Pity. If he'd had to
hand-crank it, we'd have laid the thief by the heels."

The voice of Bob, the motor pool chief, rang out
abruptly. "Hey, you, in the Stutz! Hy never said—!"

"That's right, Bob," Retief told the excited guard.
"Better lock the main doors."

This Bob hastened to do, and the Stutz fetched up
impotently before the closed portal. Shish was honking
the Klaxon frantically, but the audioelectric cell failed
to respond by swinging the steel portal wide. The frustrated Groaci hopped down and scuttled around to
search in the gloom for the manual override, muttering, "Drat!" and casting murderous glances from
entwined oculars.

"Don't give *me* that G-142-c If Looks Could Kill,
Shish!" Magnan yelled, forging ahead; and Shish,
abandoning the effort, fumbled with his hip-pouch and
brought out a Model F all-band tuner, which he used
to open the adjacent door. Even as Magnan rushed
the final yards, Shish hopped into the stately Stutz
and gunned away into the crowded avenue, the crowd
parting so reluctantly that more than one luckless
Bloorian was forcibly propelled from its path, yelling.

As Magnan turned to notify Retief that Shish had
made his escape, he was forced to leap back as the
Mercer Raceabout which was the apple of Ambassador

Swinepearl's eye squealed to a halt beside him and Retief motioned him in.

"Quick!" Magnan squalled. "I mean 'quickly'!"

"I won't count that one, Ben," Retief told him. "Anyway, 'quick' is correct."

"Bother grammar!" Magnan snapped. "I'm surprised, Jim, that you'd even mention so esoteric a matter in this moment of crisis!"

The Stutz was almost lost among the crowd of towering locals, all, it appeared, eager to lay hands on the driver thereof to express doubtless legitimate grievances.

"The little wretch will be lucky if he's not torn apart by the mob!" Magnan bleated, then winced as a hardshot rang out and the most aggressive of the Bloorians assaulting the Stutz fell back, still yelling.

"He wouldn't!" Magnan moaned. "Jim, he *shot* that fellow! Now—"

Retief, following the relatively open trail Shish had cleared through the riot, gunned ahead in time to see the wounded Bloorian jump up and point an accusing finger directly at the oncoming Mercer. The mob at once coalesced, blocking the way.

"Hang on, Ben," Retief advised. The elderly fourbanger roaring, he steered directly toward the biggest loudmouth, who shut down that organ and leaped for safety, starting a general stampede which opened the way effectively. The little topheavy Stutz three-seater was just rounding a corner into a side alley known as Civvy Street. At it leaned perilously, Shish almost lost control, veering up onto the sidewalk, where he scattered a cluster of fruit-and-veggie stands. As the squashes and eggplants showered down, the sturdy peasants who had trundled the produce into town shook their fists, some clutching pitchforks, after the departing Groaci.

"Heavens, lucky Herb's aunt didn't leave him a

Bearcat," Magnan observed. "We'd never have caught him."

"We still haven't," Retief pointed out—but, on the straightaway, he was rapidly closing on the fleeing car.

"He's headed for the port," Magnan observed, as they thundered past the last retail establishments and scattered houses and entered the open countryside.

"Nice country," Magnan commented, hanging on desperately as the ancient sports car leaped over the potholed and rutted road. "Pity there aren't enough industrious Bloorians to keep it all under cultivation."

"If they did that," Retief pointed out, "there'd be no need for GFU."

"True," Magnan mused. "I suppose one shouldn't question the established order."

"Except when it's shooting at us," Retief demurred, ducking as a sharp report rang out. Magnan pointed. "Over there, Jim! Behind the shed! It's a fellow with a blast rifle!"

Retief nodded and concentrated on his driving. Ahead, Shish veered off down a side road, shaking a puny fist from his side window toward the rifleman.

"Seems he was aiming at the Counselor," Retief noted, and followed into the farm road, which was even worse maintained than the highway. Shish had halted and was out of his stolen car, hastily setting up a tripod-mounted apparatus through which he sighted toward the barn, like a student surveyor. The Groaci jittered as more hardshots kicked up dirt nearby, but persisted in his twiddling with a cable-linked box.

"Good Lord!" Magnan yipped. "It's a Glavian implosion-gun! He's gone insane! If he fires that thing—!"

The shed where the gunman had been hiding erupted in a white actinic blast, accompanied by a *clap!* like thunder near at hand. A column of dust rose over a wide crater. The Bloorian, having jumped clear,

was running at a brisk pace across the unplowed
pasture.

"Help! Stop!" Magnan was yelling, treading the
floorboards in an instinctive effort to apply the brakes.
Retief slowed and pulled up by a sagging fence. The
erstwhile shooter veered away and made for a clutch
of buildings across the field, from which a crowd was
emerging to intercept the Bloorian.

"Let's let him go," Magnan offered.

"We don't have much choice," Retief pointed out.
"Unless you feel like climbing that fence and chasing
him on foot right into the midst of a lynchmob."

Shish had folded his potent weapon and tossed the
compact pack into the backseat of the Stutz. Now he
was back in the driver's seat, gunning his engine. The
ungainly coupe lurched, freed itself from the ruts, and
rolled briskly off along the bumpy road.

"Look!" Magnan yelped. "It's not the Bloorian
they're after, it's Shish! They'll cut him off!"

The unpaved track curved to the left, and half the
strung-out mob had split off and was streaming toward
an intercept point a quarter of a mile ahead where
the path squeezed between two parallel fences. Shish
was rolling along briskly but not frantically, apparently
unaware of the mob closing on his right flank.

"Hurry, Jim!" Magnan pled. "After all, he *is* a fellow
diplomat. We can't let them tear him to pieces before
our very eyes!" he moaned.

Retief gunned the Mercer, while Magnan frantically
worked the outboard bulb-horn. When they had
closed to within fifty feet of the Stutz, Shish looked
back indignantly, making "go away" motions, but the
movement on the right caught one of his outer eyes
and he gunned ahead, ignoring the Mercer closing in
on him; he seemed intent on beating the mob to the
ambush point. The first of the locals was already over
the fence when Shish slammed through the narrow

point, sending eager attackers back over the barbed wire. The Mercer blasted through the shaking fists of the thinning crowd in the road. Looking ahead, Magnan saw the unruly mob that had forged ahead of the Mercer was pouring over, through, and under the fence to block them off.

"They don't seem picky as to *whom* they menace," Magnan commented. "They ought to be *help*ing us! After all, we're pursuing their exploiter! Can't they see it was Shish who committed the atrocities, while we're merely benign bystanders?"

"Maybe they thought it was rude of us not to stop and inquire after their health," Retief suggested, clinging grimly to the Stutz as it executed a sharp right slalom and vaulted the embankment of the modern Terran-built approach-road to the port. Once on the hardtop, the little Stutz showed its horsepower, the same as that of its close relation, the race-winning Bearcat, and quickly receded into the cloud of dust raised by the main body of the mob as they swarmed over the guardrails into the right-of-way. Shish ignored them, sending a number back over the rail in headlong dives. Retief followed him closely, skidding the big Mercer around the sharp turn.

"Keep going, Jim!" Magnan cried. "We can't stop now!"

The would-be living barricade melted away as they realized the oncoming Mercer had no intention of halting to be assaulted. Magnan got a glimpse of bared teeth, flaring eyes, and shaken fists as the Raceabout flashed past them. Ahead, Shish, in his Stutz, was just doing a turn on two wheels into the parking area.

"We've got him now!" Magnan exulted. "When he stops to get his ticket—"

Shish sheared off the ticket dispenser at ground level and went careening, not toward the flag-decked reviewing stand, where a crowd of Bloorians was already gathered, but around it, making for the service area. Retief stopped and allowed Magnan to debark beside the Terran ambassador's stretch Turbocad.

Magnan released a sigh of relief. "Safe at last!" he breathed, and ducked as a shot rang out. "Jim! A shot rang out!"

Retief nodded. "It came from the cargo pick-up area," he commented. "Save me a place, Mr. Magnan; I'll be back." He drove off, leaving Magnan staring after him.

As he rounded the end of the long, low Operations Building, a spindle-legged Groaci peacekeeper in tarnished greaves and plain GI eyeshields stepped from between stacked crates and unlimbered a Bogan-supplied blast-rifle.

"To halt your conveyance and descend instanter!" he hissed. "To display proper ID, and to go to Perdition, Soft One!"

Retief halted the Mercer, stepped down, and brushing the rifle aside, seized the sentry by the neck and upended him in a rubbish barrel. He then extricated the weapon and bent the barrel into a U, while the non-com screeched in fury.

"Quiet, Tish," Retief ordered the irate peacekeeper. "Just hang loose while I put the lid on. Looks like a nice airtight fit, too," he commented as he settled the heavy steel slab in place.

"To be destroying issue property of the Groacian Autonomy!" the Groaci's weak voice echoed inside his can.

"Not yet," Retief countered. "I've only laid you aside for destroying later, if necessary. Don't worry, it won't be long, if the information you're going to give me is accurate, that is."

"To tell you nothing, vile Terry!" the muffled voice yelled. "OK, a deal: I tell you at what moment we plan to spring the Big Surprise, and you make it back here before I asphyxiate!"

"Get it right, Tish," Retief admonished.

The corporal bleated out the timetable.

"I'll see you later, Corporal," Retief said. "Unless you got something wrong, that is."

"Perhaps," Tish hissed, "I may have erred in the timing of the sharpshooters. Actually, it will be just as the Terran Ex extends the meretricious hand of amity to Counselor Shish! Sorry about that."

"Still wrong," Retief replied. "Shish can't make it."

"To outrage!" the canned alien hissed. "To have gone too far this time, Retief! Yes, to know you, infamous wrecker that you are!"

"Gosh, I'm famous," Retief replied in mock astonishment.

"To stay your hand, rash Terry!" Tish squeaked. "To rue this fell deed in a matter of seconds now!"

"The ceremony doesn't start for half an hour, Corporal. What's going to happen in a couple of seconds?" Retief inquired.

A faint sound came from overhead.

"A major realignment of influence here on this vile world, that's what!" Tish hissed. "Hark!"

Retief had noted the near-supersonic whistling, which had been growing in volume, heralding the approach of a covey of VIP landing craft. Now the sound had risen to a clearly audible screech. He pounded down the lid on the trash receptacle, muffling Tish's outraged yells, and drove the Mercer around to the FREIGHT-INCOMING area, where he saw Shish's Stutz parked behind a row of crates, and the Groaci Counselor in a huddle with a group of locals in soiled line-whites.

Retief pulled the Mercer into the lee of yet another sizable stack of heavy beelwood crates awaiting processing. He had just noted the code BG-X stenciled on

the sides, when Shish, trailed by two Bloorians twice
his height, came scuttling toward his position. When
the Groaci appeared to be about to hurry past, Retief
spoke:

"'Seized contraband held in bond, awaiting CDT
disposition,'" he interpreted the code. "What's it
doing here, stacked in the 'duty-free' area on a non-
pact world, Shish?"

The Groaci shied, losing a jeweled eye-shield as his
oculars snapped erect in reflexive readiness for fight-
or-flight.

"You!" he hissed, deftly retrieving the bauble.

"You got that one right, Shish," Retief confirmed.
"What's going on here? What's your hurry? You didn't
set a track record getting here just to show Sam
Swinepearl how zealous you are to display Groac's solidarity with Terra in sponsoring the Goodies For
Undesirables program." He glanced upward where the
incoming covey of shuttlecraft was now naked-eye visible, coming in in a tight Omar formation.

"Expecting guests?" Retief asked the sputtering
Groaci official.

Shish attempted a leg-sweep, netting himself a dent
in his greave.

"Doing your own legwork now, Shish?" Retief queried. "No pun intended. That was Wim Dit and his
top aides you were huddling with. What big plan have
you sold the poor suckers?"

"It is you who create a pocket of depleted molecular
density into which atmospheric pressure forces ambi-
ent gases!" Shish objected. "Your Terry figures of
speech don't translate all that well," the confused
Groaci commented *en passant*. "In spite of that, in a
few moments now, to stand in awed admiration of my
finesse! Sammy Swinepearl will rue the day he excluded
proud Groac from the published list of honorary

sponsors of GFU!" Shish paused, jut as Ben Magnan came up, puffing.

"That's preposterous, Shish!" Magnan snapped. "Groac did all she could to force a measure through EGO to prohibit the very program you now claim to co-sponsor!"

"But we relented, Ben, and cast our vote *for* GFU!"

"That was, I presume, immediately after you'd hatched the fell scheme you're hoping to implement here today!" Ben snapped.

"Cynicism ill-befits you, Ben!" Shish snorted. "And as for 'hope,' no need for it, Ben!" he went on triumphantly.

"Look there!" he pointed to the descending assault-craft. "One thousand of hand-picked Groacian Rangers! And the Interplanetary Brigade as well! What gambit can you offer, haughty Terrans, in riposte to my deft ploy?"

"Only a thousand?" Retief queried disparagingly. "Heck, I called out a whole squad of Terry Marines."

"You *did*n't!" Shish gasped. "What miscreant leaked the top GUTS plan to you? I shall personally see him staked out!"

"Those sulfur pits are going to be pretty crowded, Shish," Retief interrupted. "You, and young Flinsh, and Corporal Sish, and a lot of others all provided pieces of the puzzle."

"*I*?" Shish screeched. "You suggest that a Groacian Counselor of Embassy would thus sabotage his own precious plan? Ridiculous!"

"You led us through your Embassy," Magnan pointed out, "when we could scarce fail to note the numerous evidences of preparation for war and revolution; you fled when you could, and then led us to this precise spot, just as——" His voice was drowned in the bellow of braking-rockets as the arriving boats settled in amid whirling gales of stinging dust particles a hundred yards from the spectators.

"Drat!" Shish spat as he stamped off to collar the pilot of the last vessel, which had landed almost atop the stolen Stutz, covering it with dust. "Hy will be furious!" Shish hissed through the dying roar of jets.

"Retief!" Magnan squealed, batting futilely at the dust obscuring the view of the debarking troops, no two of the same species, who hustled down the gangways to form up smartly on the ramp.

"When the Department agreed to sponsor new uniforms for the Interplanetary Brigade," he blurted, "it was with the clear understanding their participation would be solely in the role of honor guard! What treachery is this, bursting in on the ceremony prematurely?"

A lone Groaci wearing a particularly ornate helmet with a great flaring rim reminiscent of the headgear worn by Roman gladiators scurried around to face the first rank.

"General Hish!" Magnan muttered. "I thought the scamp was confined at hard paperwork for life on one of the penal planetoids, after the fiasco at Slunch!"

"Hah!" Shish jeered, returning to trot alongside Magnan as he approached the heavily armed detachment of ill-assorted troops. "A squad of these savvy Interplanetary Brigade irregulars trepanned the General from durance vile—"

"Please," Magnan objected. "You know how I hate clichés, Shish. *Do* speak more creatively!"

"Bother creativity!" Shish rejoined. "To have expended the fruits of my genius on the present coup, one which will yet ring resoundingly in the annals of interplanetary one-upmanship! Grind your teeth, Ben, in frustration, as you see your own puny efforts negated by a superior diplomatic intellect!"

"I don't see anything very diplomatic about a bunch of assault troops!'" Magnan dismissed the taunt.

"*Au contraire*, Ben!" Shish hissed. "The select body you so callously refer to as 'assault troops' are, as you well know, an honor guard, fully authorized by solemn interplanetary accord. They have been drawn from the armed forces of one hundred worlds, carefully selected for the honor by a committee of noble Groacian bureaucrats, qualifying on the basis of virture alone to so participate in this gesture of multiplanetary solidarity! Observe! Even now these paragons are falling in to pass in review before Sam Swinepearl and Ambassador Shinth, and, but for your pernicious interference, myself!"

"You people conned Secretary Headfeather!" Magnan charged in a tone of Deep Shock (738-m).

"Don't waste that rather inept 738 on *me*, Ben Magnan!" Shish snapped. "About an *n*, wasn't it? You were as aware as anyone of the deliberation of Headfeather's Interplanetary Tribunal for the Curtailment of Hostilities!" He offered an elaborately ribboned and sealed document.

"Don't try to bring ITCH into this!" Magnan demanded. "That ineffectual panel of failed Cultural Attachés! You can't escape responsibility for this atrocity by attempting to implicate retired Terry bureaucrats motivated only by the highest principles! I'm sure they had no idea they were giving sanction to armed invasion when they generously agreed to sponsor a purely symbolic multinational force to participate in the proceedings!" All present looked up as a line-cart braked to a halt beside them, and Ambassador Shinth stepped down.

"The dotards had done well to read the fine print before they appended their signatures," Shish riposted, before turning to greet his chief; then he turned back to Magnan. "Listen to this roll call of distinguished signatories, Ben!" Shish unfolded the impressive charter and read aloud:

" 'AE and MP Herky Thunderstruck, CDT-CM (ret).

" 'Deputy Undersecretary Ajax Spraddle.

" 'Former Special Envoy Samson P. Longspoon,' et cetera, et cetera."

"All superannuated retirees in advanced senility!" Magnan dismissed the cheeky Groaci's pitch, as he nodded with his chin. "All trotted out by you Groaci for a last brief moment in the limelight! A moment which will live in infamy alongside that in which FDR committed Terran youth to war and death in order to save Communism from Hitler's tender mercies!"

As the diplomats chatted, the honor guard had formed up in a column of ducks, left-faced, and presented a bewildering array of arms, ranging from a compound bow in the hands of a squat dirt-miner from Goblinrock to a triple-lens Daser-gun gripped by a professional wrestler type dragooned from Goldblatt's World. Their uniforms were as varied as their armaments and faces, which included a number of nearly pure-strain Terran types, a whole range of sub-human Goods, and a lone barely-humanoid Geek with a greenish hide, his inconspicuous yellow antlers barely projecting above his unkempt olive-green Afro.

General Hish whispered a command to his wrist, and a burly Furthuronian master sergeant stepped forward and bawled what sounded like "Smeer!" to the roughly-aligned soldiers. They hung their heads and, eyes-righted, shuffled their feet and dress-right-dressed into a precise rank.

" 'Kay," the sergeant barked. "Now lessee some snap here!" He proceeded to put the troop through a highly-modified Queen Anne drill. As each man tossed his weapon, spinning high, caught it, and snapped to present arms, the NCO turned to Hish and came to the salute.

"Two!" Hish rasped. The saluting arms came down with a *crack!* of hand against pants-seam.

"At ease! Smoke if you got 'em!" the non-com ordered, and the ill-assorted but well-drilled troops went into a relaxed crouch, each with one hand near his slung arm.

"Now what?" Magnan yipped. "It's clear these picked thugs of yours are ready to commit any bestiality you may choose to order. But—Mr. Ambassador, you wouldn't . . . ?"

"So now it's 'Mr. Ambassador,' eh, Ben?" Shish whispered. "What happened to 'Mr. Ambluster,' and 'miscreant,' and so on? Lost some of your arrogance, have you? Face it, Ben, you've been outfoxed by your superior at the game! My troops, duly authorized—" he slapped the charter against one of his palms—"perfectly legally, ready, as you suggest, to implement Groaci policy in any fashion I may select—so just what are you going to do about it?" He broke off to speak to the general, who barked at the sergeant, after which the lead squad went directly to the nearest stack of crates, unlimbered crowbars, and began ripping slats from the containers, exposing a layer of heavily cosmolened brown paper which the sergeant promptly tore aside to reveal closely packed power rifles, dully glinting in the late sun. A moment later, each of the honor guardsmen had two or more of the potent small arms in hand briskly, on command, fell in, about-faced, and rejoined their platoon, handing out the guns to one and all. After the third case was emptied, every man had at least two weapons, including one or more of the rifles, at right-shoulder-arms.

"They're only awaiting the order for the massacre to begin!" Magnan wailed. "What can be done, Jim?"

"Let's find out," Retief suggested. He strolled over to General Hish.

"Highly disciplined fellows," he complimented the

officer. "Tell them to present arms." Hish relayed the command to the sergeant.

Faced with the problem of presenting multiple arms, the troop broke up into a chaotic mob, haranguing each other and casting resentful glances toward Hish.

Hish recoiled, miming incomprehension by allowing all five oculars to collapse limply across his narrow, cartilaginous skull.

"Are you quite mad, Retief?" the general demanded.

"Just a little," Retief conceded. "After all, you spoiled our show."

"Regrettable, but necessary!" Hish hissed. "But what has that to do with a simple soldier like myself, simply carrying out his orders?"

"The orders are changed," Retief told him bluntly. "Call the sergeant over here."

"A Groacian general officer hardly takes orders from a Terry *Civilian!*" Hish announced.

"But I'm bigger than you are, Hish," Retief reminded the officer, and simultaneously took a careful grip on three of his limp eye-stalks.

"Retief! You wouldn't!" Hish complained. "Remember, eye-stalk-twist was covered in Article Two, paragraph nine, line five, of the New Geneva Convention!" Retief gave the oculars a tentative tug.

"They seem firmly anchored," Retief commented. "I wonder just *how* firmly." He applied a steady pressure to the now frantically twitching organs. Hish went limp, but regained his footing as he found himself supported by the members in Retief's grip. "To let go!" the Groaci wailed. "Oh, Sergeant! To come over a moment!" He folded a handy pair of tentacles and mimed impatience by erecting his center eye-stalk and drumming the other free one on his cranium like a man might drum his fingers to display boredom. The sergeant ordered his company to parade rest and hurried over to stand uncertainly before the two big shots.

"Sergeant," Retief spoke up before Hish could speak. "Come to the Position of a Soldier, but first hand me that sidearm."

The non-com looked dubiously at Hish, taking due note of the drumming oculars. He did the top-formal Six Rank or Higher salute, employing both primary manipulatory members, three eyes, and both skinny legs; then he unholstered his Borovian wire-gun and handed it, butt first, to Retief.

"To snap out of it, Whish," Hish snapped, "before you dislocate something, Corporal!" The general returned the honorific with a casual flip of an ocular.

"But I'm—" Whish started, then snapped-to, his eyes on Retief.

"You mean you *were* a sergeant," Hish corrected his underling, who began an objection, but was sharply silenced. "I shall do the talking," Hish snapped. "You know Retief, here, a Terry civilian with a reputation—"

"Thanks, General," Retief cut him off. "I'll take it from here. Sergeant," he went on, "things have come unstuck, it appears. Certain usually reliable local elements have changed sides and are even now approaching the port, intent on tearing limb-from-limb all foreigners not blessed with Terryhood. I may be able to save you boys, if you'll be nice."

"Sure, sir," Whish gasped. "I always said not to trust that Wim Dit sell-out! Sure, to be nice is my specialty. Ain't that right, General?" He paused, awaiting approval that was not forthcoming. Instead, Hish hissed:

"Avoid the particle 'ain't' when speaking Terry! It's *declassé*, and we don't want Retief to get the idea we're like these unsophisticated locals!"

"But everybody says it, General, sir!" Whish protested.

"Ignorant rabble, possessed of cheap, no-name-brand translators," Hish dismissed the impertinence.

" 'Ain't' is actually the Scandinavian negative particle 'inte,' introduced in the days of Old English by the Viking invaders—"

"But to have thought Terra to never have been invaded!" Whish carped.

"Certainly not!" Hish confirmed. "To have meant not Terra itself, but an outlying world called Britain which suffered the depredations of the Swedes!"

"Guess I was inna brig or the pest-house the week they covered that part at the NCO Academy, sir," Whish mourned. "But now to have gotten that stuff out of the way, what about this Terry here?"

"General," Retief interjected gently, "you know just how to answer the sergeant's legitimate query."

"To be well aware of that!" Hish sniffed. "Sergeant, to regret to disillusion you, but for compelling reasons made known to me, I have just turned over command to Mr. Jame Retief. You will carry out his orders with an alacrity which will reflect credit on Groaci military training. Do it!"

"Huh, sir?" Whish gasped. "But he's a Terry, pure stock, and it was the Terries we were s'pose' to sucker!"

"Change in plan, Sergeant," Hish explained tersely. "Rot in high places, it appears. Counselor Shish, whom you see deep in conversation with the infamous Ben Magnan just over there, is deeply involved. Notice the snappy late-model coupé he's driving, received, doubtless, as a part of his payoff."

"To be *his* pay-off," Whish grunted, "but where's mine?"

"Right here," Retief said, and showed him the butt of a 2mm at his hip. When the Groaci noncom recoiled in horror, Retief commented, "That's the way it is, Sarge. Now tell your lead squad to load and lock one round of ball ammunition."

Whish scuttled back to his ranked troops and hissed

orders. The troops snapped-to, did "inspection arms," loaded and locked their pieces. Whish turned, offering Retief a casual tentacle-salute. Retief returned it with a snappy one-two.

"Deploy the first squad in line of assault to envelop the rest of the platoon, and report to me," he ordered. Whish complied. General Hish made clucking sounds in his throat-sac.

"What in the world to intend—?" he started, but Retief cut him off.

"Watch," he ordered curtly. When Whish again presented himself, Retief ordered him to form the entire platoon into an open phalanx, and box in the rest of the company. That accomplished, with much muttering and dragging of feet on the part of the multinational troops, Retief told Whish to form up the entire debarked battalion flanking the landing area where the second of the troop shuttles was now making planetfall.

"To look here, Retief!" Hish started blusteringly, but Retief told him to remember that he was strictly bound by the policy of AE and MP Shinth, who was nattering casually with Magnan and Shish near the port detention building, a small but fortresslike structure where arriving suspects were detained awaiting the cursory Bloorian naturalization process.

"Barbarians!" Hish snorted. "This confounded world is well-known to be the refuge of every scoundrel unhanged in this end of the Arm!"

"General," Retief said quietly. "That's a slight exaggeration: there are still a number of petty bureaucrats and cops on the loose in Settled Space. It will take years to round them all up. Luckily, only moral lepers would consider accepting such posts, making it quite a simple matter to identify them."

"But . . . you diplomats are yourselves bureaucrats, in the loose sense!" Hish objected. "Do you include yourself, personally, in your blatant dismissal of governmental flunkeys as rascals?"

"Watch how neatly I'm going to ace you out of a battle group," Retief suggested, "And *you* answer your question."

Hish gnashed his mandibular plates and fell silent. Sergeant Zoob was back, hesitating briefly between the general and Retief as recipient of his report, but at a nod from Hish, addressing Retief:

"Sir, to have the battalion, including Brevet Lieutenant Grunge, all fell in and awaiting orders yonder."

"So you have," Retief concurred. "The second vessel is about to land. Now get your troops in line of ambush behind those crates—all except you, Sergeant. You take up your post at the foot of the gangplank when the shuttle runs it out, present arms with a full magazine loaded, and when the Colonel comes down the ramp, disarm him and fall his battalion in behind yours."

Zoob scurried back, and deployed his force to take the new arrivals in hand; there was a brief conference with the debarking colonel, a hulking Clunchan Black Beret, with five rows of campaign ribbons *and* the Groac Star of the Legion. After much arm-waving, the sergeant pointed at General Hish, who erected all five oculars in a commanding gesture. Then the colonel intercepted his company officers as they came down the landing ramp. They hurried off to dispose their respective commands as Retief had specified. General Hish was controlling himself with an effort evinced by the slow change in the hue of his carapace from a deep olive to a pale chartreuse.

"To suppose you'll order the complements of the first two craft to capture each of their fellow contingents as they arrive!" Hish fumed, then stepped up to confront Retief. "You, sir, to be a rascal!"

"Thanks very much," the Terran replied graciously.

"Coming from an expert in the field, that's high praise, indeed."

"You are crafty, Retief," Hish acknowledged, "but no craftier than my own confounding of Simon Proudflesh and his silly ITCH committee. An 'Interplanetary Tribunal for the Curtailment of Hostilities,' indeed! Why, it's an open attack on dedicated career military personnel! You've doubtless heard how I finessed the entire delegation of busybodies into an ice cave on Goblinrock, and let them languish there for three weeks before making *big* points with Enlightened Galactic Opinion by accidentally discovering and rescuing them! Simple Simon almost fell on his face in the effusion of his gratitude!" Hish paused to point to one of the many spectacular jeweled starburst decorations on his mud-colored tunic. "I got this for that one," he purred.

"Far more sophisticated than the mere capture of an armed task force, General," Retief admitted. "Would you mind taking over at this point and gathering in the rest of the boys, personally? Just form up a battle line defending the port. When the Terran Marines arrive, turn your boys over to Sergeant Muldoon."

"What? A mere non-com—no offense, Sergeant Whish—to command a full brigade of Indestructibles?"

"Unless you'd rather fight it out with O'Rourke," Retief offered.

Hish considered briefly. "And an entire squad of Terry Marines?" he queried as if incredulous. "No way! It's 'Field Marshal O'Rourke,' if you say so!"

"I do," Retief assured the Groaci veteran. "Your legislature can handle the paper work later, so let's get going. Call the colonel over."

Hish uttered a near-supersonic *whist!* and, when the busy colonel paused and looked his way, Hish pumped a tentacle up and down, then waved it in a circular path over his head. The colonel, whose face resembled a gutted carp, pointed to himself, miming interrogation, and Hish flapped his eye-stalks in vigorous affirmation. The colonel beckoned to a captain standing nearby, exchanged a few words, then returned the junior officer's salute and came loping toward Hish. He swung in a wide curve so as to come up on the side opposite Retief, and threw a snappy salute.

"To kindly hold the hand salute until I return it, Colonel Smank," Hish said coldly, and waited while the chastened field-grader reassumed his salute and held it until Hish's leisurely return was completed.

"Yessir, General, sir," Smank puffed.

"Out of shape, eh, Colonel?" Hish commented. "Now get this: in a moment a Terran official will arrive here, and you're to turn over command to him at once. You can take off those eagles and fall in at the tail end of the last squad."

"B-busted, General?" Smank gulped. "But all I done—did—was fall out the boys like always, and all of a sudden Major Thuck is showing me his Mark Ten and telling me about some kind of a foul-up—"

"No foul-up, Smank," Hish rebuked. "The Indestructibles have been sold out," he snarled. "Betrayed, decoyed into an untenable position. Rather than lose crack troops in a frontal defense, I have tendered my surrender to overwhelming Terry force, treacherously insinuated here on this peaceful world with the express intention of spoiling my career—and yours as well, Space'n."

"Cripes!" Smank muttered, saluting again just for good measure. "I spend thirty years working my way up from deck-ape to bird colonel—and now I lose it all, just because some lousy Terry . . ." He turned and swung a roundhouse at Retief, who deflected it casually and returned a straight right to the woundlike countenance of the Slunchan, knocking him back into the arms of Randy O'Rourke, who had come up quietly, with his squad at "at ease." The sergeant avoided the colonel's desperate kicks and elbows and tied his arms up in a break-it-if you're-not-nice hold.

"Par' me, sir," the lad addressed Retief. "Can't do no salute whilst I got this here feller. What should I do with him?"

"First," Retief decreed, "let him go, then salute him, and offer your apology for not observing the military courtesies."

"Jeez," O'Rourke grunted, noticing the not-yet-removed colonel's eagles. "A full bird, huh? Well, par' me, Colonel, sir; I thought you were just drunk."

Smank twisted free of O'Rourke's relaxed grip and snarled. Muldoon grabbed him by the lapel and snarled back: "Let's watch yer language, Mister. Colonel or no colonel, yer my prisoner! Right, Mr. Retief?" He glanced up hopefully.

"Exactly right," Retief confirmed. "Colonel Smank is a smart fellow; he won't give you any more trouble. Anyway, he's a private now."

"Now, Private," Retief addressed the crestfallen captive. "The horsing around is over. It's up to you— by the way, Randy, it's 'Sergeant Field-Marshal O'Rourke' now. An appointment in the Groaci Military Auxilary, right, Hish?"

"To handle the paperwork ASAP," Hish gulped. "I'll see to it the marshal's baton is delivered via my next packet-boat."

"I don't get it, Mr. Retief," Randy told the Third Secretary of Embassy of Terra. "How's come all these here militia types are deployed in a Barnum around the port? And what about the armed mob headed this way from town? We hadda persuade a few of them boys we had the right-of-way." He rubbed his knuckles reflectively.

"Just a little off-letting of steam," Retief assured the youthful field-marshal. "You lucked into a big promo,

Randy. It's legit: the Corps will have to recognize the rank and will probably bump you to Senior Master."

"Nice pay increase," O'Rourke commented.

"That's not all," Retief told him. "A Groaci F-M gets a hundred thousand guck per annum, in your case retroactive to your date of rank in the Corps. That's about half a million—cash. Don't spend it all in one place."

"To make payment in full so soon as the Embassy Budget and Fiscal Officer can be apprised," Hish stated as one dealing with trifles.

"What do I have to do for it?" O'Rourke wanted to know.

"Just take the ex-colonel in hand and tell him what to do," Retief advised. "Better snap to it; I see the eager beavers of the mob are breaking down the perimeter fence now."

"All right, Corporal, or whatever you are," Hish said roughly to O'Rourke. "You can walk on my left and slightly to the rear, and I'll let you know when to speak."

"You were very big on the military courtesies a few seconds ago, Hish," Retief put in. "Better remember them now."

"Ah, to be sure," Hish waffled. "If the Field Marshal pleases, my, that is, your company-graders are even now assembling for further orders." Hish did an elaborate seven-grade knee-salute and stepped aside while Randy inspected his new command, and appointed his Marines as Company officers. O'Rourke returned a Groaci major's casual hand-salute and went over to the cluster of uncouth-looking non-coms of the Interplanetary Brigade, which he had ordered to fall in off-side.

"Hold your fire, gents," he commanded after returning their ragged salutes with a snappy Corps one-two. An exceptionally tall, green-furred Hondu staff sergeant pushed past his fellows and planted himself before Randy.

"I never heard about no Terry taking command of the Indestructibles," he mumbled. "Lessee some ID, OK?"

Twenty feet away, Retief cleared his throat. The Hondu looked at him. "Oh, I didn't see you, Retief," he mumbled. "Now, maybe we better get down to cases, eh, sir?" he said to O'Rourke.

"At ease, Captain," the Field Marshal ordered easily. "I don't want any unnecessary bloodshed. So keep your troops on a tight leash. I'm going over to talk to these civilians." He walked off toward the leaders of the oncoming mob.

"Oh, dear," Magnan whimpered. "I fear the lad will come to grief. Wim Dit is in no mood to parley."

"He's subject to mood swings," Retief said. "I think Randy will do OK."

Retief watched from a distance as O'Rourke confronted Wim Dit at the head of his mob, and promptly sent the rabble packing. The Marine returned to report to Retief.

"Now, Randy," Retief said. "Get the Indestructibles sorted out, and see to it they understand your gyrenes are their new company-grade officers. You'd better keep the field-graders on the job for the present. Colonel Smank here wants to help out."

"Right, sir!" the Clunchan officer agreed eagerly.

"Vessel number three is on final approach," Retief continued. "Flag her in, and have your double-battalion ready to reorient the ship's complement one by one, as they debark. Then use the recruits to take the next, and so on, until the whole squadron is on the ramp, and the whole brigade is formed up to Pass in Review. Post a three-man guard on each ship: the Groaci task force is still standing by off-planet, waiting for landing orders. We'll think of some. Right, General Hish?"

The Groaci, who had sidled close so as to eaves-drop, leaped as if goosed by a Glavian unicorn and agreed volubly. "Better to get those boys down right away," he hissed. "They've been in orbit for three weeks now. By the way, they're a penal battalion, and don't take kindly to discipline."

"Just be careful to explain to them," Retief cautioned the general, "that we're all one big happy family here; no hostilities."

"To be sure," Hish agreed, eyeing the rank on rank of Interplanetary Irregulars eagerly awaiting the command to attack.

Chapter 4

Three hours later, back at the Terran Embassy, Magnan was completing his explanation to Ambassador Swinepearl.

"... so you see, sir, the whole flink-hide scam was just a cover-up for the arms smuggling scheme, and now that the arms—plus the mercenaries—are safely tucked away aboard the prison hulks, with the hatches welded shut, you've not only neutralized the threat to Galactic peace, you've acquired a handy strike-force ready for whatever use your Excellency may choose." Magnan sat back, glowing inwardly with rosy visions of massive promotion and an ER which would serve as an exemplar toward which lesser diplomats would aspire in vain.

"What the devil are you smirking at, Ben?" the Ambassador snapped as he discarded his scribble-pad and unwrapped a new one. "You propose to burden me with the administration of a prison fleet, and simultaneously, you expect me to assume command of the most boisterous gang of misfits in the Arm! What am I to do? Abandon my post to launch an attack on that secret Groaci installation on Doldrum II? Sit idle, entoiled in administrative detail, while the situation here on Bloor goes from bad to worse? What?"

As his Ex's never soothing voice rose to a bellow, Magnan shifted nervously in his chair and cleared his throat tentatively. "Well, sir, Mr. Ambassador, I mean—"

"Speak up, dammit!" Swinepearl roared, turning on Magnan, thus effectively paralyzing his subordinate's vocal apparatus. Then His Ex resumed his hip-u-matic chair and stubbed the talk key on his direct-line to Sector.

"Ambassador Extraordinary and Minister Plenipotentiary Samuel X. Swinepearl here, on the job at Bloor!" he yelled. "Get me Admiral-General Promo at once!"

"OK, Sammy, I'm here," a drawling voice came back. "What's up?"

"You may well ask!" His Ex snarled. "I've some sixteen hundred dacoits on my hands, duly disarmed and locked up aboard their own vessels. I suppose that in deep-space mode, the ship's systems will sustain them for some months, but thereafter, I shall be obliged to open up and see to their needs! Otherwise, they'd starve to death, and that wouldn't look at all well in the Empathy with Inferiors column on my next ER! I'll need a battle group at minimum to control the riffraff! Meanwhile, I have a heavy squadron of armed warships piling up demurrage at an alarming rate! I disclaim further responsibility, Rex! *Do* something!"

"What do you have in mind, Sammy?" Promo inquired, sounding wily. "I hope you're using a tight beam. This stuff could be misinterpreted."

"Certainly, it's tight!" Swinepearl confirmed angrily. "Do you take me for a neophyte?"

"A being's sexual preferences are no concern of mine as long as it gets the job done," Rex stated flatly. "OK, what's the plan? A sneak strike on that Glavian mining property out your way sound OK? We could sell to GenMines through a dummy corporation for enough to balance the planetary budget, and cover it as a legal preempt under Paragraph IX."

"Damn the planetary deficit!" Swinepearl yelled. "It's Mrs. Swinepearl's boy Sam I'm concerned about! As for Paragraph IX, it's well known that's a weasel-worded statute inserted in the Law by reactionary elements intent on selfishly sequestering rights to their own property. I rather favor Sub-Section 103—paragraphs V-XII, you know, where it says about '. . . preemptive action and right of emninent domain' and all, and some gobbledygook about protecting the moral purity of miners and that—my legal boys can interpret that until we get a full Hail the Conquering Hero reception, when we dock at Aldo with the loot all legally registered in our own names—"

"Easy, Sam," Promo cautioned. "Let's not be *too* candid. Don't get me wrong: I'll go along," Promo reassured the AE and MP. "I've got to hand it to you, Sam: you can make Regs sit up and talk—and say just what we want 'em to. That's a useful skill, Sam, and I'm just the boy to help you cash in on it. Sixteen hundred crack troops, you say? I heard about the Indestructibles being shipped out your way—figured it was another foul-up, but I underestimated you, Sam! How in the name of Good Government and Better Business did you manage to sew 'em up inside their own destroyers?"

"Oh, a trifling matter I handed to my Political man, Ben Magnan. I commended him on his efficient handling of the affair, of course."

"You didn't cut *him* in on the action, I hope," Promo yelped. "We can't pay off every Tom, Dick, and Meyer in the Corps! This Magnan's a mere underling, just following orders! He's got no claim—!"

"Quiet!" Swinepearl snapped. "He's standing right here! Don't give him any ideas!"

" 'Ideas'?" Magnan echoed in a tone of Shock, Deep, at Implications (97-C). "Why, I wouldn't dream of employing a captive battle group to pressure recalcitrant elements of the Galactic community to pay a fleet-maintainence surtax, or anything like that!" he protested, his voice flagging as the full scope of the concept became apparent.

"Rex, are you still there?" Swinepearl quavered.

"Hell, no," the general came back heartily. "I'm halfway to Budget and Fiscal to turn in an old satchel I found in the closet, full of used currency. Want to hand it over to a few key legislators, you understand, to restore it to its rightful owners. Ta!"

"Look here, Benny," the Ambassador wheedled, gazing at Magnan appealingly, an expression not unlike that of a lovesick elk on spying its intended. "I do hope you won't misinterpret the general's light-hearted jesting as serious proposals! He's bored, poor man: sitting there at Sector with all the responsibilities of the CinC Strike Command—the most powerful attack force ever assembled—and, due to envious reactionaries on the Strategy Committee, powerless to hurl his seasoned troops into action in defense of hallowed principles! You'd go a little bonkers, too."

"I *heard* that, Sam!" Promo's amplified voice burst out. "You've got a bad ON/OFF switch on your talker— or else you forgot to shut it down. I got that, and so did anybody else within two lights, I expect. What about that Magnan fellow? Is he still hanging around? Hold everything, Sam: Problem. You remember the Council's bagman, that sneaky little bird from Lumbaga? That Colonel Bob Switchback? He dropped by just now and told me he just got orders to put half my Strike Force on standby for Maneuvers in the Goober Cluster. Threatened to throw 'em at HQ, and put me under arrest unless I make him my adjutant in charge of collecting the loot after the strike! Lucky I happened to have some dirt on him. But he's still complaining, the treacher! Oh, hi, Bob, you still here? Hold on, Bob!"

Swinepearl rolled a bleary eye at Magnan. "Sit down, Ben," he suggested, almost gently. "You've heard too much—you've doubtless gained an erroneous impression you're yearning to communicate to Hy Felix, who'll relay the false impression to the Agency, who'll spill the beans to the yellow press. We have to stop this miscarriage of, ah, justice before it goes any further! What would you say to, er, five points, eh?"

"*Mister* Ambluster!" Magnan blurted. "You *aren't* actually offering me a percentage of the villainy in return for my silence!"

"Sorry, Ben, I spoke without thinking," His Excellency alibied. "Pooh! Five points is for leg-men, mere accessories. A career diplomat of your reputation deserves at least ten! I'm sure General Promo will go along; he has problems of his own. I know that conniving, favor-currying Switchback; *he'll* demand at *least* ten! So what do you say, Ben? Is it to be cooperation all around, and everybody happy, or selfish conscience-indulgence for one and bitter deprival for the rest?"

"Why, sir, I wouldn't think of depriving anyone," Magnan hazarded. "But—"

"But me no 'buts,' Ben," Swinepearl boomed, rising to extend a set of well-groomed fingernails. "Deal!" he stated. "I knew we could count on you! But what about that assistant of yours, Jim Retief? Can you bring him into the fold? Of course you can," he answered his own question contentedly, and resumed his chair. Magnan backed from the Presence and made his way back to his office, muttering to himself.

"Oh, dear," he wailed. "What's a career bureaucrat to do with his bureau collapsing around him?" He moaned as Retief came in.

"Oh, Jim," he spoke up brightly. "I fear I've bad

news: I was just on to General Promo, of Sector, and he seems to have gotten wind of the presence here on Bloor of a mislaid battle group. Has some wild idea about adding it to his Strike Command forces and taking some sort of preemptive action or other. I'm quite confused by it all. He's already set wheels in motion, I fear! He could precipitate a general collapse of the Truce! All because he misinterpreted some idle remark of mine! Jim—what can we do?"

"The first thing is to reorient the Indestructibles, I think," Retief suggested. "They have a tendency to act on their own, you know. Right now, I imagine they're about ready to mutiny and train their guns on the capital and start issuing demands."

"But I distinctly told General Hish," Magnan protested, "to disable the battle-board on each and every vessel, so as to preclude just such an eventuality!"

"I know," Retief acknowledged, "but judging from the salvo they just fired at the Port Authority blockhouse, I suspect the general failed to follow orders. I was just coming to get authorization to get Field-Marshal Sergeant Muldoon on the job."

"Of course! He'll soon deal with Hish! The scamp! And after I _trusted_ him, too!" Magnan mourned. "You get Randy and his Marines in position, plus those local levies under Wim Dit and that other fellow—Colonel Ack Jass, I think it was—commanding the household troops. As you said, we have to reorient the Indestructibles before it becomes generally known—"

"If you don't mind, Ben," Retief suggested, "I'll handle that part."

"Jim!" Magnan gasped. "If only you _could_ make some sort of deal with them! But don't promise full immunity! After the prisoners are pacified, Randy's Marines would take over and all would be well!"

"Maybe the Marines have done better than you

think," Retief suggested. "Randy wouldn't take kindly to Sarge Thrash interfering with his command."

"Poor Randy," Magnan mourned. "Very well, Jim. See what can be done. If we should unseal the ships and allow those caged killers to swarm forth, unchecked—" He left the rest to the imagination of the readers of the yellow press, even as he called Hy Felix.

"Information Agency," the veteran pressman's voice came back wearily. "That you, Ben? What's up? Another big awards dinner coming up, so we can publicly praise another local hoodlum to the skies—and not even get any points for it? These locals think we're nutty, handing out ribbons and orders like free lottery tickets. What lousy little jerk's hind-end do we need to kiss now, in full view of the cameras?"

"It's not that at all, Hy!" Magnan protested. "You know I disapprove all this favor-currying with petty dictators and mob-leaders! This is far more important! This can earn you that bump in grade and that cozy desk back at Sector, Hy! *If* it's handled discreetly, of course."

"Oh, some sneaky business of dubious legality, eh?" Hy gloated. "Shoot."

"There can be no doubt regarding the legal status of what I have discovered!" Magnan stated flatly. "It is *il*legal in the highest degree! I'm only filling you in on the current status, just to ensure there's no confusion or misinterpretation of this affair."

"Par' me while I fan myself, Ben," the cynical former poultry editor for the *Caney* (Kansas) *Gazette* said jeeringly. "Illegal, eh? What else is new?"

"War," Magnan intoned solemnly. "Rapine. Insurrection. Mutiny. Piracy. Bloodshed on a vast scale. Do you want to go for stretching of Regulations *beyond* the breaking point?"

"Slow down," Hy mumbled. "I love it, but I've got

my tapes snarled here. Sounded like you said 'breaking Regs'!"

"Precisely!" Magnan confirmed. "The Manual, and Basic Regs as well, are founded on the principle of noninterference in local politics, of course. But in this case, if we don't interfere, chaos will ensue! We *have* to appear to interfere! But subtly, mind you! Nothing obvious; a matter of interpretation, you see. When is dacoitry 'intervention by a peace-keeping force'?"

"An all-out raid?" Hy almost choked on the words. "Ben, you call that subtle?"

"It's not what I call it that's important!" Magnan corrected the impulsive newshawk. "Be calm, Hy! It appears the impounded battle group we have at the port is lobbing shells into the Customs and Excise shed. I shall be forced to take vigorous action. At the same time, Ambassador Swinepearl is under the impression I'm about to use the same fleet to launch a preemptive strike against certain potentially hostile elements in the Arm." Magnan paused for breath.

"Wow!" Hy said, his usual monotone almost modulated to express a trace of excitement.

"Don't go ape on me, Hy!" Magnan shouted. "I'm counting on your cool cynicism to help defuse the situation!"

"Easy, Ben," Felix responded flatly. "I guess I can handle it. Who's His Ex planning to raid? Figures to hand Sector a *fait accompli*, eh, and hold 'em up for looting rights, or 'collection of war reparations,' I usually call it, under Section XXI? No censorship, you understand, Ben, just a matter of optional diction. See? Nobody muzzles Hy Felix when he's Revealing All to the Trusting Galactic Public!"

"Sure not, Hy," Magnan agreed soothingly. "Just please, as a personal favor to me, don't breathe a word to the TAP about a quick takeover of Goblinrock and maybe a quiet little police action with reference to some outlying Glavian miners—and—"

"Oh, Sector is finally getting around to confiscating those fat core-fragments, eh? Good move: it'll fund the planetary debt. Glad those stuffed shirts back at the Department are doing something constructive!"

As Hy finished, Magnan burst out: "Hy, No! You mustn't spread any unfounded rumors! It could scuttle the whole operation. Listen here, Hy, I called just as a professional gesture to let you in on which way the wind is blowing! I assumed I could count on your discretion!"

"'Rumors'?" Hy echoed sarcastically. "Nope, Ben, I got this right from the Political Officer hisself! How's about some details: When does the strike launch? What will you do with those two thousand or so captured Indestructibles you've got locked up aboard ship? I'm assuming it's their ships you plan to use to hit Glave and Goblinrock and all . . ."

"Assume nothing, Hy!" Magnan directed the irresponsible fellow. "A strike in force is precisely the disaster I am struggling to defuse!"

"Nuts and fruits," Hy scoffed. "You're going to order the Indestructibles to stand down when they smell blood? That Sarge Trash or whatever won't stand still for that, and neither will his boys!"

"You may leave Supersergeant Thrash to me to deal with," Magnan sniffed.

"*You*, Ben, up against Sarge Thrash?" Hy laughed. "I get it, Ben: nothing going on, so you're pulling my leg, right?"

"Hardly," Magnan contradicted. "I only wish . . ."

"It's OK, Ben, I get a little bored myself, filing all these honors lists full of nothing but known thieves and swindlers. I'll go along. Thanks for lightening up my day, Ben: I'll see to it you get full press coverage, weasel-worded, of course, so if anything goes wrong, it'll come back on Sam Swinepearl, not you. Hej Så länge!"

"Oh, dear," Magnan sighed. "I fear I've muddled the waters further," he told himself aloud. "I merely wanted Hy to align Enlightened Galactic Opinion in a way that would forestall cries of 'Battleship Diplomacy!' Instead, the scamp intends to announce—and thereby launch—all-out war on a grand scale!"

"Take it easy, Ben," Retief soothed his distraught supervisor. "I'll go have that chat with Thrash and get the reorientation under way."

"Splendid notion, Retief," Magnan commended.

Chapter 5

At the port, Retief drove across the dusty tarmac, deserted now, like the empty streets of the city. Wim Dit's impromptu army of mutually hostile malcontents glowered from behind the hastily erected barbed-wire enclosure of the newly designated detention area. Retief parked beside Herb's Stutz, slightly battered by its wild drive, but still ready for service. He sat for a few minutes studying the roughly aligned row of battle-scarred warhulls standing like desert rock-spires across the ancient, blast-burned concrete. All seemed quiet, with the exception of a lone space'n rappelling down from the fore service-hatch of *Malodorous*, the flag-ship of the battle group. Retief reported to Major Raunch, the cop chief, that he was about to talk to a smaller but highly potent vessel, a destroyer still in Borundian colors, *Expedient*, and went over to the thousand-tonner, skirting the still hot stern tubes, checked for a cool spot in the residual radiation aura, and approached the service ladder. He attached his induction-talker to a metal rung and spoke:

"Use your X channel; put your captain on. This is

Retief of the Terran Embassy. Would you boys like some fresh air?"

After a noisy interval when at least ten coarse voices yelled at once, mostly curses, some of which Retief hadn't heard before, the racket subsided and a deep growl cut through intelligibly:

"Super Sarnt Thrash talking, *Mister* Retief."

"Was that name 'Trash'?" Retief inquired as if guilelessly. " 'Sarnt Trash,' eh? Are you empowered to guarantee there'll be no disorderly conduct if I allow you and your crew to emerge in groups of ten, for exercise, pending resolution of the problems that stand in the way of your regular incarceration in a permanent facility?"

"I lost you, Nance, after 'empowered,' " Thrash came back indifferently. "You gonna undog the hatches or what?"

"First, Mr. Thrash," Retief replied in as prissy a voice as he could manage, "I want your personal assurances you'll behave yourselves. I can't abide boisterousness."

" 'Boysters will be boysters,' " Thrash replied. "You know my name now, huh? That 'Trash' business was a mistake, Nance. You fancy-britches fellers don't know much, do you?" he inquired lispingly.

"Oh, I imagine I'm conversant with a few facts," Retief/Nance responded. "For example: what is the 'Mororovicik Discontinuity'?"

"That's where Steve—we call him 'Chick'—ducked a little slow and got this gap where his front tooth useta be," the Sergeant/Captain replied smartly.

"Excellent, Sarnt," Retief congratulated his pupil. "Now, what's the 'Schwarzschild Singularity'?"

"Everybody knows old Swartzy only got one—you know—insteada two," Sarge told him bluntly. "Borned that way. Never got kicked in the crouch nor nothing." Thrash's voice cut off and a moment later his head, unclipped, -washed, and -combed, popped out from a clean-cut scuttle near the keel stern-tube. He tossed down a cable, then got his shoulders through the tight opening, and swarmed down the line. On the ground, he spat on his rope-burned palms, rubbed them on his pants leg, and swaggered over to Retief.

"You're doing splendidly!" Nance crowed. "Let's move right on to the more difficult portion of the quiz; to wit: is clam-digging to be considered as fishing, or, alternatively, as agriculture?"

Thrash looked sullen. "Yer too fulla questions, Nance," he growled. "How's come? Why you so nosey, hah?" He reached for Nance's neck just as Retief stooped to examine a curiously-shaped object on the ground. He picked it up and rose just behind the abortive grab, which had closed on the empty space occupied a moment before by Nance.

"Stan' still, Nance!" Thrash barked, and lunged for his putative victim. Nance, preoccupied with his find, took a step to the right just then, and Thrash's toe accidentally got hooked over Nance's still extended ankle, causing the attacker to impact, snarl-first, on the rough tarmac. He spat a yellow tooth and got to his feet, cursing, and charged again.

"Gracious," Nance said. "Such *dread*ful language! I always hate to hear anyone using *language*! It reflects its vileness back on the user, you know." As he chided, Nance was peering wonderingly down the barrel of the 6mm needler he had picked up. Apparently finding nothing of interest there, he reversed the artifact, so that the heedlessly aimed weapon was bearing on Thrash's leg, while Nance fingered the trigger. Thrash halted his advance and put out both spread hands as if pushing on a barrier. "Pernt that six em-em some other place!" he yelled. "I still got a use for that knee-cap! Lookee, Nance," he continued in a wheedling tone. "So, OK, I got my signals mix up a little. Deal, OK? See, I got this 'arrangement,' he calls it, with

Boss Nandy over Ward Nineteen, where he gets a exclusive on the hot small-arms, and I glom onto the dope traffic, plus a cut o' the pearl smuggling. OK. Fat deal: them rackets alone would retire the planetary debt on any six worlds in Tip Space. But what the heck, is old Sarge Thrash knowed as the greedy kin'? Not me, pal. Say I git you in for a full five points, and you go con some other poor sucker—"

Thrash broke off to make a grab for the carelessly held needler, and found his wrist locked in Retief's grip as if clamped in a scrap-crusher. He lunged in vain and stopped, red-faced. "Leggo my arm, pal," he growled. "If anybody sees this, it's mutiny and a cheap space-funeral! I got a reputation to uphold! I'm the toughest mother in space, that's why I'm Commodore o' this here battle group!"

" 'Battle group'?" Nance echoed wonderingly. "I was told, by a *very* reliable source—"

"Oh, you mean Ferd, the ramp-sweeper," Thrash put in. "Well, see, Ferd had this little accident, fergot to get outa the way when I wanneda walk where he was standing, and—"

"That's *hard*ly germaine to the issue!" Nance scolded. "What I was *try*ing to say was—"

"Yeah, about my battle group and all," Thrash prompted. "Impressive, hah? Sixteen spaceworthy fleet boats parked right here, and another one hunrit attack units standing by off-planet, not counding them fifty Groaci cruisers, which I figger I'll hafta capture them and put prize crews aboard. Hafta deep-six them Groaci crews, I guess."

"To hardly find that acceptable, Commodore!" the breathy voice of Shinth, the Groaci Information Agency chief, spoke up, as its owner emerged from behind an adjacent rubbish bin.

"Just to be back here checking for carelessly disposed-of incriminating material," he explained offhandedly, brushing flecks of garbage from his plain GI greaves and the hem of his rib-sprung hip-cloak.

"Yes," Retief nodded. "I trust you got Trash's confession on your taper."

"To be sure," Shinth agreed, nodding his lumpy, cartilaginous skull, all five eye-stalks erected in an expression reflecting On the Ball This Time, You Betcha (21-c).

"Hold it right there!" Thrash barked. "I ain't gave no confession! I was onney bragging a little; maybe I won't even be able to con Admiral Thilth into the deal; I figgered to offer him a cut o' the pearl traffic, see, but maybe the guy don't *like* pearls, so where does that leave me? Just another dreamer with busted dreams, eh?" Thrash paused to assume the tragic expression of a dreamer of busted dreams; he stifled a sob. "Sad, ain't it, when a boyhood dream o' martial glory goes *pftt!* in the face of growed-up disillusionment and all? Who'd of figgered Nance here to throw down on me, eh? I ast you, Shinth, does it figger?"

"The person you refer to as 'Nance,'" the Groaci intoned impressively, "is none other than Jim Retief, the notorious wrecker, spoilsport and sworn enemy of the Groacian people! Had you laid him by the heels, proud Groac would have shown herself to be not ungrateful. Instead, you allow him to reduce you to lachrymose impotence! Bah! The deal is off, Sergeant! I mean all the way off!"

"You mean, no brevet Admiralty inna Groach Reserves?" Thrash mourned. "No personal pleasure-planetoid? No fully restored genuine Deusenberg Model J, with body by Hibbard and Darrin, which there's only the one in the known Universe? No bevy o' unmutated Terry hookers, no villa onna Shallow Sea? No purty suit wid like Austrian knots and them gold epaulettes an' a fake jool sword? No play-purties atall?" His voice turned accusatory: "You led me downa garden path, you five-eyed sapsucker! Wait'll I get my han's on you—" Thrash took a step toward the cowering Groaci newshawk, and was jerked up short by Retief's grip on his arm. He turned to expostulate, but threw himself flat as a resounding *Ka-boom!* threw dirt and rubble up in a boiling column while the pressure-wave knocked the baggage shed flat. Shinth and Retief, also flat on the pavement as the dust went whipping over them, looked at each other. Rubble rained down all around. Among the debris pattering down Retief noticed pink pearls.

"Treachers!" Shinth spat. "I could have been killed!" He scrambled up, brushing ramp-dust from his ruined hip cloak, and grabbing for the few unshattered pearls gleaming amid the debris.

"You planned it this way!" he charged, aiming all five eyes at the protesting Thrash. "Have you forgotten it was *I*," Shinth yelled as loudly as his inadequate vocal apparatus allowed, "who endowed you with the sacred trust of leadership of this superb fleet, along with the glorious title of Temporary Acting Assistant Deputy Cadet Grand Admiral of Reserves? And this is how you repay my largess! You detonate my personal cache of blood-pearls, cleverly secreted yonder in the dummy firefighting apparatus—and you very nearly destroyed myself as well! Fool! Renegade! I wash my hands of you!" The irate Groaci turned and started toward the perimeter fence, where a crowd of irate locals had gathered behind Wim Dit's army, pressed against the fence shaking their fists.

Retief grabbed the Groaci. "Not so fast, Shinth!" he cautioned. "I think that's Gad Bye's bunch over there backing up Dit. They have a grudge against you Groaci, remember, ever since Filsh ran one of them down on the highway yesterday, when the poor fellow was only trying to hijack him."

"To be sure," Shinth muttered, attempting to

reassemble his dignity. "To be going to forget the matter for now, and instead of prosecuting the devious Thrash, to instead make further use of his brute abilities! Release me, Jim. To be acting in the best interest of all civilized entities, a category which does not include the inhabitants of this vile planet!"

Retief thrust him back toward Thrash. "Go ahead," he urged. "Use him."

"Sergeant!" the Groaci diplomat hissed with as much menace as his breathy voice could muster. "I call upon you now to expiate your high crimes against the Groacian state in the person of myself by bringing under your de facto control the treacherously surrendered vessels under your nominal command, and deploying them in battle array off-planet, ready to strike at my command! Do it!"

"How'm I s'pose to do *that*?" Thrash inquired guilelessly. "That feller name of Magnan had the hatches welded!"

"I notice Captain Rooch of *Unreliable* descending to the ramp only now," Shinth pointed out, referring to the lone figure just disentangling himself from the rappel-lines at the stern of the tarnished hull of the condemned armed freighter a hundred yards distant.

"To explain to the captain," Shinth went on, "that he is to ready his vessel for immediate liftoff. You may then proceed to the second vessel in line, yourself climb to the welded hatches, and free them up, using the line equipment just there." He pointed to an abandoned red-painted line-cart, fully stocked with emergency gear. "Remember to be diplomatic," he enjoined, "since much depends on your former officers' willing, nay, eager cooperation! You'll find both hull-cleats and a cutting torch aboard," the officious Groaci reminded the protesting Sarge, who trotted off obediently, and after rummaging, began to fit the hull-climbing cleats to his well-worn boots. Captain Rooch gave him a

wide berth, but Thrash yelled, and his subordinate
approached hesitantly. As soon as the latter reached
him, Thrash felled him with a haymaker amplified by
the heavy wrist-cleat strapped to his left forearm.

"Drat!" Shinth spat. "An inauspicious beginning, eh,
Jim?"

"Just about right, I'd say," Retief replied. "Sarge is
savvy enough to communicate with his boys in a language they can understand. Let's see what his next
diplomatic maneuver is."

" 'Diplomatic,' indeed!" Shinth whispered contemptuously. "The lout knows no more of the high art of
diplomacy than does a mud-crab from Krako Eight!"

" 'The art of the possible,' someone has called our
profession," Retief reminded his Groaci colleague.
"Now, shall we get back to the down-and-dirty?"

" 'The possible'?" Shinth hissed. "What is possible,
sir, is that the miscreant you have so casually dispatched as your emissary to the captive crews will turn
his coat yet again, and make off with the fleet to commit further nuisances on *our* persons, to say nothing
of the innocent bystanders!"

"He's passing over number two in line," Retief
pointed out. "Smart move. That's Jack Raskall's tub.
Number three looks more promising." By then Sergeant Thrash was halfway up the keel and just aft of
the coil compartment.

"To kill himself, the cretin!" Shinth objected. "Doesn't
he realize we need him alive, to deal with these pirati-
cal crews?"

"It probably slipped his mind," Retief suggested,
"when he saw the antipersonnel orifices tracking him."

"But Ben Magnan distinctly told me the vessel's
offensive capabilities were neutralized!" the Groaci
carped.

"Not the close-in defensive circuits," Retief explained.
"Let's see how Sarge handles this."

Thrash paused momentarily, clinging to his dizzying perch, while he awkwardly unclamped and reclamped in a new orientation the heavy magnetic climbing cleats, so as to approach the stern emergency hatch.

"Surely the hatch to be sealed!" Shinth offered.

"Should have been," Retief agreed as Thrash reached and opened the inconspicuous entryway.

"I trust you will invoke dire yet equitable administrative action upon the slacker who failed in his duty," Shinth announced. "As a caution to others tempted to slack their responsibilities!" the Groaci added, remembering the Groaci Image.

"Lucky he was lazy," Retief commented. "Otherwise our apostle to the barbarians would be peeking down from ten stories up, with no place to go."

"To be sure," Shinth conceded grumpily. "Look, he's gained ingress."

A moment later, the unguarded hatch snapped open again, and a man was thrust violently out: he fell, arms and legs windmilling, to impact on a heap of builder's sand left carelessly, and luckily, in the parking area, by a paving crew.

"Was that the good sergeant?" Shinth gasped. "Or . . . ?"

"'Or,'" Retief told him. "It's Skunky, one of the Indestructibles' less civilized fellows."

"Less than what?" Shinth breathed. "The etiquette of the most polished of their senior officers would rival the table-manners of a mud-pig!"

"Skunky's OK, I think," Retief commented, as the fallen gang-leader got to his feet, unholstered his sidearm, and took aim at the aft insulator box. Retief yelled, "Hold it, Skunk!"

The burly evictee spun to cover the two diplomats.

"You guys come over here," he ordered.

"To assure you, vile miscreant," Shinth hissed. "To

have had no other intention! You are to remain where you are and aim that piece at your own foot!"

"Wiseguy, hah?" Skunky came back breezily. "I heard about you little five-eyed sharpies. Getting a little too big fer yer britches, ain't you? Now, you, Mister," he changed targets to Retief. "Don't be ascairt, I won't hurt you none, less it works out thataway. Just you grab aholt o' that there Groaci's neck, OK, so's to remind him to mind his manners and all. Hurry up! I got Sarge Thrash to deal with yet!" He fired a bolt into the pavement at their feet, sending hot vinyl spattering.

"You'd better unload that piece," Retief told him mildly. "We don't want to make you sign any statement of charges for damage to public property."

"I was *going* to," Skunky muttered and dropped the power cell from the butt of the pistol.

"Now holster it," Retief ordered. The Indestructible did so, looking resentful.

"You ain't scairt of an empty gun, are you, fella?" he inquired artlessly.

"No. Empty heads are more dangerous," Retief corrected.

"That sounded like some kinda crack," Skunky complained.

By then Retief had reached him. "I'll tell you what. You go climb that squat-strut, like Trash did," he suggested casually.

Skunky dutifully went to the base of the massive landing jack. "Time I get to the top, old Thrash'll kick me inna face again," he predicted mournfully, not grabbing the handholds.

"A kick in the gut wouldn't be much better," Retief pointed out, moving into position.

"Now, now," Skunky protested, putting a foot on the first rung. "You ain't got to do nothing unfriendly!"

He scrambled upward, out of reach. "I'm going, ain't I?"

"We'll be watching you," Retief told the ascending ruffian.

"*He'll* be watching me, too, ever foot o' the way!" the latter complained. "He's watching me right now. Time I get to the hatch, he'll open it, and I'll get the boot!"

"Just ease up and get flat against the hull, off to the left of the hatch," Retief ordered. "When his foot sticks out, grab it and give him a free ride down to your sand-pile."

"Could, I guess," Skunky conceded. "Unless he gets careful and takes a look first."

"In that case, you can kick *him* in the head," Retief explained. Skunky reached the top of the jack and maneuvered over by the hatch. It popped open and Sarge's arm poked out, gun-first. Skunky struck down at it with a free hand, knocking the weapon from Thrash's grip; then he grabbed the pirate captain's wrist and jerked him clear of the opening, holding him suspended over the seventy-foot drop.

"Be nice and I'll drop you onna sandpile," Skunk offered. Thrash replied with a violent lunge that dislodged Skunky's grip on his wrist; he fell with a wild yell, kicking madly, to impact at the thin edge of the cushioning heap. Half-dazed, he stumbled to his feet. Retief came over and told him it was time to move on.

Skunky was peering down cockily from his perch inside the open emergency hatch. Retief called up to him:

"Debark ships' company and fall them in on the ramp!"

"And what if I don't?" Skunky returned.

"In that case," Shinth cut in, "to have no choice but to order my command to destroy you on the ground!"

"Oh, yer sticking *yer* oar in," Skunky objected. "That's no fair, Retief, using the Groaci to jump a feller Terry!"

"So now it's all good fellowship, eh, Shinth?" Retief remarked cynically to the furious GIA agent.

"Never!" the Groac hissed. "To attack the rogues in defense of the prerogatives of proud Groac, alone!" he told Retief; then, craning upward at Skunky's retreating face:

"To declare this planet and its resident fleet a protectorate of the Groacian Autonomy, to be defended against the threat of a band of landless dacoits! Now to do as Retief ordered, Skunky!"

"Easy, Shinth," Retief soothed. "Siding with me this once won't lose you your charter membership in the Terry Hater Underground Directorate."

"To fear not, Jim Retief!" Shinth spat. "To be in no danger of expulsion from THUD! To know all the names and addresses and to have access to secret files which would put paid on the careers of all the behind-the-scenes powers in THUD, a group which, I learned to my horror but a few days since, is in the employ of Terran Intelligence! Patriotism alone would demand I denounce the treachers! I have restrained myself thus far only out of reluctance to expose so many of Groac's most honored bureaucrats to public disgrace, to the detriment of the Groacian public's confidence in those few of us who weren't in their conspiracy!"

"That's an item Hy Felix would love to get hold of," Retief commented casually.

"Retief! You wouldn't! Or, yes, I suppose you would," Shinth dithered. "Hy would spread it all over the Arm! Perhaps we could reach an accommodation: as soon as Skunky has his thieves and murderers nicely lined up to pass in review, I'll sneak around behind them and pretend to be inspecting the rear rank. You put Skunky and his chief lieutenants in irons, and I'll shoot a few tail end Charlies just as an example to the rest. General Hish will be along soon with his Special Detachment to disarm the rabble."

Magnan arrived on a line-cart in time to overhear the Groaci's words.

"Special Detachment?" he cried. "I don't think our Division of Spheres of Influence Agreement included provisions for a secret Groaci swat team inside Bloor City!" Magnan dismounted to await the Groaci's excuses.

Shinth ignored him.

"As for your precious General Hish," Magnan resumed hotly, "he's the incompetent fumbler who failed to disable these captive vessels in the first place! Where's he gotten to? I have a word or two to say to that gentlebeing!"

"Right here, Ben," Hish supplied, emerging somewhat untidily, from the adjacent refuse bin. "To be sorry about the foul-up," he apologized casually. "To have been so busy suppressing sixteen mutinies, I may have overlooked . . ."

"Never mind," Magnan cut him off. "That's past history. What's important *now* is to get this gang back under control. Shinth, what do you have in mind?"

" 'In mind,' you say, Ben?" the Groaci responded in a disparaging tone. "I took the opportunity, Ben, whilst you were busybodying yonder, to call Admiral Foof aboard his flagship *Devious* and call in a space-strike on this gaggle of decrepit ex-warships! He'll be along momentarily, I imagine, so we'd do well to vacate the area pronto! Let's get out of here!" So saying, Shinth jostled Magnan aside to take his seat at the controls of the cart. Retief upended him and deposited him in the cargo bin, already half-full of sharp-cornered line equipment. Sarge Thrash scrambled aboard as the cart dug off toward the operations building.

"Slow down, Ben," Retief urged. "Listen!" he offered his direct supervisor a lapel talker.

Magnan listened intently, while braking to a stop. "Ye gods!" he yelled and thrust the offending communication device back into Retief's hand.

"It's Rex!" he yelled. "He's—it will—I expect there's going to be trouble!"

"What to be *that*?" Shinth wailed, pointing skyward at a ring of bright points visible at extreme range.

"Oh, that's just General Rex (Buck) Promo taking exception to a Groaci task force forming up over Terry-mandated territory," Magnan told him jauntily. "He'll clear your Admiral Foof out of the way in a moment or two, so there's no real need for hasty evacuation." Magnan retrieved the ground-to-space talker and after listening for a moment, cut in:

"No, Rex! Don't do it! After all, the idea *isn't* to precipitate an interplanetary incident! Just group your command in a Barnum to encircle the captive units you see on the ramp here!"

"Sold me out, eh, Ben?" Promo's yell came through clearly to all present. "Made a deal with those five-eyed scoundrels, have you? Thought you'd get Buck Promo into a compromising position, did you, and then milk the situation. Forget it, Ben, the scheme flops hard! See, I already pulled a little switch on *you*! Remember Colonel Switchback? The chiseler tried to undercut me by spilling the whole plan to Intermediate Command—Admiral Hardbutt's outfit. Ha! The trick backfired! Hardbutt offered me a reserve squadron that was in for depot maintainence at Ringsta II and just signed off yesterday, for a full half-cut! The robber! I gave him twenty points is all. But Bob Switchback's prolly got more treachery up his sleeves. And I don't trust the admiral any farther than I could spit in a whirlwind!"

"A parlous situation!" Magnan declared. "One hardly knows *whom* to trust! I—"

"This is no time for Old English datives, Ben," Promo objected. " 'Trust'? Ha! Trust nobody, that's who! Now let's quit bellyaching; we've got work to do!" He paused for breath.

"You got these paroled convicts quieted down some, Mister? As soon's your bunch is ready to lift, I'll give you the numbers for a rendezvous off-planet that'll have the five-eyes up all night writing out explanations to be discovered on their remains!"

"Bother the paperwork!" Shinth contributed. "Retief, I call upon you to halt this betrayal before further damage is done to the prospects for Groacian-Terry détente! What we do here today could well determine the future of Galactic politics for a millennium!"

"I'm afraid Shinth is right this time, Rex," Retief told the indignant general. "At the moment, the Groaci units are participating, unwittingly, it's true, in the rather delicate job of neutralizing the only combat-ready armed battle group on the planet, before they realize they're in a position to dictate terms."

"Oh," Promo replied, as one Only Now Being Informed of the True Situation (1904–x).

"Dear me," Magnan muttered to any Unseen Chronicler who might be monitoring the situation from on high. "One *does* wish that amateurs untrained in the subtleties of nullspeak would refrain from essaying the millennial series, at least. That nineteen-oh-four could well be mistaken for a discreditable twelve-two (I Guess You Got Me, Pal) with who knows what harm to the negotiation!"

"Luckily," Retief pointed out, "no one was paying any attention, they're all watching Sarge Thrash trying to sneak up on Skunky. Twenty guck he gets decked for his trouble."

"Done!" Magnan replied, slapping his palm to

Retief's extended hand. "Skunky's an uncouth fellow, but well versed in Shugo-II!"

"Right," Retief agreed, "but Thrash is a pink belt in Shugo-III."

Just then, Thrash took three quick steps to close the gap with Skunky, who ducked a high leg-sweep and grabbed the proffered limb, giving it a good two-hundred-seventy-degree twist before dumping the sergeant on his rear. Thrash howled and raised his haunch so as to comfort his bruised tail-bone.

"Fots dirty, is what the skunk does!" he grieved.

"Sure do, Sluggy," Skunky acknowledged proudly. "How you think I got the name 'Skunky'?"

"Name ain't 'Sluggy,' " the fallen non-com grumped.

"Is *now*!" his conqueror declared. "Fer 'Sluggish,' see? 'Sluggy' it is, right, Mr. Retief?" As he turned to his sponsor for confirmation, his expression changed from triumphant to shrewd. His eyes narrowed, and he made a grab for Retief's arm, but somehow instead met a sword-arm that impacted his neck with sufficient force to put a glaze on his squint. He staggered and tripped over Sluggy, who at once took a one-handed grip on his throat. Skunky made curious squawking sounds and threshed violently.

"I was fleet champ until this sneaky feller dumped me," Sluggy told a breathlessly waiting world. "So that made him a super-champ. So now I'm croaking him with one hand; that makes me a distinguished super-champ, right, Retief?"

"Something like that," Retief concurred. "By the way, I'm a double-distinguished hyper-champ," he went on. "So you'd better let old Skunky have a little air. I'll need him in breathing condition to testify at your trial."

"*My* trial?" Sluggy yelped indignantly. "After I done like you said and taken this here super-champ down a peg or two and all?"

"Alas," Retief told the burly fellow as he scrambled to his feet, dumping the gasping Skunky carelessly aside. "Such is life. 'The evil that men do,' and all that."

"I don't know nothing about Shakespeare!" Sluggy declared vehemently. "Anyway, it says about how the good is oft interred with their bones. That guy was dead, see? And I'm not!"

"That could be rectified quite easily," Retief reminded the sergeant, at the same moment extending a foot to trip Skunky as he made a lunge for freedom. Sluggy took advantage of the distraction to throw a left-handed haymaker, which Retief ducked. In an almost leisurely way he took an elbow-breaker on Sarge's extended arm, evoking a howl of pain and rage, the big man crumpled to his knees, lunging in vain against the restraint. Skunky, observing the byplay, reached out from his prone position at Slug's feet and seized the booted foot kicking at his face. He rotated it half a turn and netted a kick in the teeth. He fell back, cursing.

"Looky what you let him do to me, when I was tryna help!" he invited Retief, removing his hands from his goblinlike face long enough for Retief to get a glimpse of red ruin.

"I woulda done worser'n that, if old Retief wouldn't of had aholt of my arm," Slug declared.

"Ha! If he wouldn't of trip' me first, you never woulda got the chanct!" Skunky came back with the tone of One Who Knows Dirty Pool When He Sees It (2031-a).

"Heavens," Ben Magnan contributed, approaching cautiously from the position he had selected well out of the area of disorderly conduct. "Imagine a lowlife of this Skunky's stripe attempting the double-mil series!" he appealed to Cosmic Justice. "It's grotesque!" He stood over the malefactor, looking down sternly. "That could well have been mistaken for a two-thousand thirty-one-d (I'll Get You) by one with a less perfectly trained eye than mine! Think what a vendetta could have resulted, my man! One doesn't lightly tamper with subtleties honed over a millennium of intensive harsh experience in the great arena of Galactic diplomacy! A two-oh-three-one, indeed! Get up, you rogue! You're going straight to the local lockup, a place I know well, due to the gross inefficiency of native officials, abetted by the venality of yet others! Get up, I say! Retief, make him get up!"

Retief went over to Skunky, who scuttled backward, then got to his feet. "I was *going* to!" he told his biographers in an indignant tone. "What's the big hurry, anyways?"

"Mr. Magnan just thought you might prefer to go to jail with your long bones intact," Retief explained gently. "Now go over there to Sergeant Thrash and apologize."

"Me?" Skunky cried in a tone of Moral Outrage (a feeble 901-b). "What do I got to apologize to old Sluggy for?"

"Existing, for a start," Ben Magnan supplied. "In fact, you owe us all an apology for that. Start now."

"Well, par' me," the chastened brigand started uncertainly. "Par' me for living! I guess a pore boy that never got no Christmas prezzies ain't got a right to breathe the air. Prolly 'cuse me o' smothering somebody which I used up *his* air! Ha! I guess a blue bicycle under the Christmas tree when I was twelve, if we woulda had a Christmas tree, and I wouldn't of never took to a life o' crime and all!" Skunky leaped toward Sluggy in response to a gentle kick in the seat of the pants from Retief.

"Now, Jim, we mustn't be guilty of brutality!" Magnan objected. "Please, Mr. Skunky, if you don't mind," he went on, "if you could just express to Mr. Thrash

your sincere regret at past misunderstandings, I'm sure
. . . well, I'm not quite sure what I'm sure of, but—"

"OK, I get the sketch," Skunky grunted. "And I
ain't 'Mr. Skunky.' Skunky is my given name; the sur-
name is Obtulucz!"

"Oh, I sorry about that, Mr. Obtulucz!" Magnan
exclaimed. "A person's name is his most precious possession! I didn't know—"

"Skip it," Skunky suggested curtly. "Now . . ." His
tone became more brisk. "Before I apologize to this
Sluggy person, he gotta apologize to me first!" Skunky
halted and folded his arms, assuming an obstinate
expression. Retief prodded him again.

"I'm going, ain't I?" Mr. Obtulucz yelled indignantly, and collided with Sergeant Thrash, who had
been standing by sullenly, fingering a swollen lip. He
repelled Skunky with a hearty shove.

"Keep that degenerate away from me, and we'll get
along OK," he growled.

"*Mister* Thrash!" Magnan objected. "He was only
trying to express his sincere regret for past differences,
and to offer his hand in comradeship! Isn't that right,
Mr. Obtulucz?" He solicited confirmation from Skunky,
who, having regained his balance after the shove, was
approaching Sluggy from behind in an elaborately
casual saunter.

"*Mister* Obtulucz!" Magnan yelped. "Don't—don't
even *think* about assaulting Mr. Thrash from behind!"

"That's *Serg*eant Thrash!" Sluggy protested. "I guess
I still got the rank. This here *Mister* Objectionable or
whatever, he's onney a tube-scraper-third! He better
show a little respeck!"

"Of *course* he will," Magnan cooed. "Won't you,
Skunky?"

The felon thus addressed stooped as if to fasten a
bootstrap and came up with the switchblade dropped
earlier by Shinth. "I'll show the lousy slacker some

respeck!" he stated, in a tone suggesting that this was precisely what unseen forces had tried in vain to prevent. He skirted the sergeant and when abreast of him, said in a gravelly tone: "I think my lef' boot is a little bit dusty, Bo. You better buff both of 'em up a little."

Thrash turned slowly, like a bull elephant looking back to see what's biting his behind. "You talkina *me*, worm?" he demanded.

"Now, now," Magnan interjected soothingly. "There's no occasion for any misunderstanding, gentlemen! I'll see to the trifling chore myself!" He took the monogrammed hanky from the breast pocket of his pearl-gray late midafternoon blazer and, stooping, whipped it across the tips of Skunky's scuffed and grease-caked ship-boots. "There," he caroled. "That's ever so much better, isn't it?"

Skunky gave him a flat glare and snorted. "I don't see no difference. Them boots is *s'pose* to be *blue*, dum-dum!" Dum-dum at once knelt at the insolent fellow's feet, the better to inspect the battered footgear.

"Oh, look!" he bleated. "I see a little bit of blue, right there!" As he pointed to an ungreased patch which had been concealed under the latch-flap, Skunky attempted to stamp on his fingers, but instead fell heavily as Retief knocked him back.

"Jim!" Magnan protested. "I wasn't *fin*ished yet!" He rose and scrambled after the retreating object of his scrutiny. "Say, Skunky," he addressed Mr. Obtulucz brightly. "I've an idea: why not just slip off your boots, and I'll be able to do a *much* better job!"

"You figger to get me out here barefooted!" Skunky accused. "Not me, chum! Mrs. Obtulucz's boy Vergil—that's my real name, see?—ain't gonna fall fer *that* one! Nope!" He stared defiantly at Magnan, who had finished dusting his knees and was gazing sorrowfully at Retief.

"What's a Deputy Chief of Mission to do, Jim?" he

wailed. "Goodness knows I've *tried* to reason with this savage! He's incorrigible! I may as well take him directly to jail!"

"Yeah?" Skunky jeered. "You and what army? What's that 'Incurably'?"

"This one right here," Magnan returned, pointing at Sergeant Thrash. "Sergeant," he continued without pause. "I deputize you as a Peacekeeper Second, and I direct you to take this fellow in charge and escort him to the local civic lockup!"

"Me, a cop?" Thrash scoffed. "That's a hot one! I *never* had no ambition to get into the big-time crooked stuff!"

"Sergeant!" Magnan said coldly. "That was a direct order! Do it!"

Thrash, as if reluctantly, feinted at his prisoner's arm, then grabbed him by the neck, and rammed a stiff right to the gut when Skunk expostulated.

"Don't get the idea," he told the gasping detainee, "you got any cherce inna matter, just 'cause I never ast fer the job." He thrust Skunky ahead of him, and started off toward the terminal building.

"To hold everything!" Shinth rasped. "What assurance do you have, Ben, that these two miscreants won't join forces and abscond, once out of sight? I say to shoot them now," he offered eagerly, "and offer pious mottoes over their remains later!"

Thrash and Skunky turned back and rushed to Magnan, seeking shelter behind him. "Don't let him do this thing, Master Magnan!" they gabbled in unison. "We wun't try nothin'! Honest! Would we?" They looked to each other for confirmation.

"All we want—" Thrash started.

"—is a nice safe cell inna lockup!" Skunk finished for him.

"As you were!" Retief ordered, and the two fell silent, eyeing Shinth uneasily.

"Retief!" Magnan blurted. "Where's Hish gotten to?" He stared around wildly, miming Astonishment at a Totally Unprincipled Breach of Tacit Understanding (3120-c).

"Ben," Shinth put in, "stick to the double-m series for now, OK? I admit I have trouble distinguishing between the suffixes above three thousand."

"Sorry, Shinth," Magnan apologized. "Actually, I usually reserve the triple-m for hearings before Boards of Inquiry. About the only way to protest some scamp's tendency to try one by implication, without being charged with contempt!"

"Stand fast," Retief suggested. "I think Hish is playing a little game." He went to the rubbish bin from which the general had emerged a few minutes before, and setting his blaster on low-beam, irradiated the contents for a full ten seconds. With a hiss like an aroused alligator, General Hish emerged from among the fruit rinds and ramp-sweepings, uttering Category Inth oaths in Low Groaci.

"*General* Hish!" Magnan objected. "*Do* you mind your vocabulary! I'm astonished that an officer of your exalted rank would be so conversant with the jargon of the scraping-chamber!"

"To be sorry about that, Ben," Hish said contritely. "To have risen from the ranks, you know—and I'd like to see *you* concerning yourself with niceties of speech when *your* copper athletic supporter has just been heated to one hundred degrees Crumblnski by induction! That fellow Retief is a menace! He knew full well . . . !"

"Sure did," Retief acknowledged as he reset the blaster at SERVICE LEVEL 2 and holstered it. "That'll smart enough to remind you who's in charge here."

"General," Magnan addressed the diminutive Groaci reproachfully. "Just why, if I may ask, were you concealed in the dustbin?"

"To fulfill the requirements of policy, for reasons of high state, not to be divulged to lesser life-forms," Hish snorted. "Stand aside, Ben; I fear I've lost an eye-shield." The wily alien stooped and began to sort through the spilled rubbish, seemingly intent on his task. Retief went around him and picked up the general's two-way talker: it was somewhat sticky, but its telltale still glowed pink.

"To be all set at this end, Hish," it said in a breathy whisper, in the High Groaci dialect. "To have diverted the noddies' attention?" the talker went on. "To be ready to launch at your signal."

"Swell," Retief commented. "That sounded like Admiral Foof. I thought he was staked out on the sulfur pits for malfeasance and conduct unbecoming and a few other things."

"A trifling breach of pettifogging regs!" Hish spat. "Foof is a valuable officer with extensive field experience, not to be lightly set aside! I myself trepanned him Yan and reinstated him on my personal staff."

"I remember his last trial," Retief commented. "He saturation-bombed his own observation station on Yoon with Verbot Ten, as I recall. Maybe he didn't know there was a delegation of twelve Groaci inspectors in the complement, or maybe he didn't care. That was a little too rich for the vascular fluids of the High Command, even. They took away his play-toys and exiled him to Yan."

"Ah, but the good admiral had thoughtfully detached a full squadron and sent it in to Blinsh for depot maintenance," Hish gloated. "And now these same superb fighting units, fully refurbished, are standing by, ready to do battle with the forces of tyranny!"

"You mean he's going to attack Groac City?" Retief inquired in a guileless tone.

"Yes!" Hish agreed hastily. "The scoundrels will rue— No— (Dammit, Jim! You're deliberately trying to confuse me). It's another pack of scoundrels entirely which I've targeted! You'll know soon enough!" He paused as a high-frequency whistle sounded, followed by a *crump!* across the ramp. "Into the bonded warehouse, on the instant! The admiral is here!" he yelled, then, "Stop it, you damned fool!" Hish snarled into his talker. "It's Yoon all over again! Only this time there'll be no kindly General Hish to succor you, the same having been blown up in your precipitate attack! I *told* you to await my signal!"

"Sorry about that, Hish," Foof apologized tonelessly. "But it seems like I got a little mutiny on my hands here. Super Chief Hooth and some o' the boys lock me up inna head. To have gotten the idea there's loot for the taking, there on Bloor."

"Hooth!" Hish hissed. "But Super Hooth is the very non-com on whom I myself conferred the Grand Bladder *with* dangle berries, of the Legion of Apathy! Surely—!"

"Yeah, and to remember the scandal when the bladder showed up in the Thieves' Market on Drood, six months later!" Foof countered. "Seems like Hooth hocked it to feed his jazreel habit. Hadda bust him back to tube-scraper-third, remember? Got to be a malcontent after that."

"Bah!" Hish dismissed the matter. "To clap the scamp in irons at once!"

"They won't let me outa the john," Foof mourned. "And I keep my irons lock up inna armory. Can't get *in*, even if I get out!"

"Um, pity and all that," Hish commented perfunctorily. "Can't you buy off one of your sub-chiefs? Get him to lay Hooth out with a spanner, perhaps?"

"Tried that," Foof carped. "Sumbich took my money and then played me false; tipped old Hooth, and got him pissed, so he ordered the compost bin

dumped into my can here. Phew! Them decaying
snarf-bugs is potent! Hold on sec! I got a idea!"

"Foof," Hish yelled in vain. He gave Magnan a five-
eyed glare, his eye-stalks rigid in indignation. "The
incompetent fool!" he hissed. "I suspect this talk of
mutiny is but a ruse to cover his betrayal of the
Cause!"

"What cause is that, General Hish?" Magnan inquired
as if naïvely.

"The cause of Galactic Justice, of course!" Hish dismissed the frivolous query. "As embodied in the doc-
trine of Unquestioned Groacian Supremacy!" Hish did
a complex double-m, involving all five eyes plus both
bope-nodes, which Magnan was unable to interpret.

"Excuse me, General," he stammered. "I fear I've
not mastered the subtleties of Groacspeak above the
single-m series."

"Naturally not, Ben!" Hish snapped. "Few even of our
own most seasoned diplomats can handle the double-m!
Not one in ten, I trow, would have correctly interpreted that as a 2091-a (Astonishment at the Presumption
of Inferiors)! Don't trouble yourself: I shall endeavor
to limit my eloquence to the simplistic, hereafter."

"That's thoughtful of you, General," Magnan purred.
"But how is it that you, a career military type, are
conversant with Total Security Groacspeak, access to
which is, as you suggest, denied to all but the top
echelon of Groacian bureaucrats?"

"It's amazing what a few truckfuls of guck will do
to smooth away obstacles to one's meteoric rise in the
service," Hish pointed out blandly.

"When I ran through a virtuoso series of ritual gri-
maces in front of the Board of Examiners, the poor
boobs didn't know whether to faint or go blind. 'Here,'
they said, 'to be some mistake: this fellow is clearly
privy to great affairs; doubtless he's the protégé of the
Prince himself! We'd do well to bump him three

grades over the heads of lesser colonels who don't have his connections!' Ergo, my first star, at the tender age of third carapace! That's about ninety years in your terminology, Ben."

"Yes, I know," Magnan gobbled. "Amazing! I congratulate you, sir!"

"To forget it, Ben," Hish dismissed the tribute. "Ancient history. It's close to the time, actually, when I should be preparing a coup of similar proportions for performance before the Assembly, to get that third star. First, of course, I need to sweeten the pot a trifle with something like, for example, a Patent of Annexation of the habitable world Bloor."

"Hish! You wouldn't!" Magnan gasped, miming Horror at a Jape in Very Bad Taste (195–j). "Not after you were invited here to participate in the Liberation festivities! That would be unthinkable!"

"Think about it anyway, Ben," Hish suggested callously. "Unless, of course, you could see your way clear to come to a reasonable accommodation in this matter—one which frankly acknowledges Groac's legitimate vested interest in the development of Bloor along lines conducive to the—"

"Yes, I know!" Magnan burst out impatiently: " '—to the orderly unfoldment of manifest Groacian destiny'! Nonsense! Terra has clear priority here, as you well know! Now, what do you propose to do to get your figurative chestnuts out of the allegorical fire, eh?"

"As to that," Hish snarled as if he were stating the obvious, "it is to you, Ben Magnan, that I look for constructive disengagement at this point in the collapse of civilization!"

"Well, now just let me see . . ." Magnan mused. "I have in mind that Rex Promo needs a trifle of discipline, and as for Admiral Foof—well, perhaps we have the basis of a trade-off after all."

"I kind of lost my place, Mister," Sergeant/Captain Thrash interjected. "But if you're thinking about selling out, I . . ."

"More of a rent-out, actually," Magnan corrected coolly. "You see, Jim"—Magnan turned to Retief— "after the honeymoon is over (it will take the foolish Groaci a couple of years to discover they've been had) they'll commit some trifling technical breach of the small print, and we'll kick 'em out and have the entire haul for the Forces of Good!"

"Ha!" Hish butted in triumphantly. "I heard that, Ben! I'm surprised at you, after all your mealy-mouthed utterances over the years, your repeated declarations of impractical principles; now you openly propose tricky dealing and overt malfeasance! Congratulations, Ben!" His tone changed from caustic to saccharine. "I thought you'd never wise up, and that Groaci wiliness would forever lay your plans at naught! Now I need to revise my thinking a trifle to take into consideration this unexpected new factor!" Hish subsided, muttering.

"Pity and all that," Magnan commiserated perfunctorily. "But don't imagine that my devotion to exalted principle extends so far as to permit your sneak force to have its way here on Bloor!"

"Does it not, Ben?" Hish agreed. "In point of fact, even now . . ." His voice trailed off as he gave his attention to the voice emanating from the talker set in his lapel.

"Impossible!" he cried in reply. "You must be mistaken, Foof! I myself—"

" '—screwed up,' " Retief supplied. "I don't suppose you paid much attention when Shinth reported that a derelict scow had been sighted adrift off the squadron's port quarter."

"Hardly!" Hish confirmed. "I don't clutter my intellect

with trifles! I've matters of moment with which to deal!"

"Sure do," Retief agreed. "At this moment it's the failure of Admiral Foof to execute his orders in a military manner."

"Sir, your jest is in poor taste!" Hish chided. "Would you imply that a flag officer of the Groacian Navy would be in flagrant derelection of duty in the face of the enemy?"

"What enemy?" Magnan put in worriedly. "There's no one here but the native Bloorians, you, and us Terrans, all united in the effort to bring enlightenment to this poor, bleeding, backward—"

"Skip the alliterations, Ben," Hish snapped. "I suppose you were about to further characterize Bloor as 'benighted.' Bah! The place is a hotbed of every form of criminal activity yet discovered or invented! Anyway, that 'allies' jazz is all very well for press handouts, but the inherent divergence of interest between Groac and Terra will continue to govern their relations for so long as honest Groacian bureaucrats draw breath!"

"You're avoiding the issue, General," Retief pointed out. "Check your CR scanner and you'll find that Foof's command is still firmly in skew orbit, in direct defiance of your orders."

"Why, that's ridiculous!" Hish whispered, uncasing his continuous readout terminal for a quick glance. "But—that's impossible!" he gobbled, then, to his talker:

"Admiral Foof! *What* are you doing? By now you should have eased into position for the preemptive strike, at the very least! In fact, the strike itself is three minutes overdue!"

"General!" came the frantic reply, "I can't—my command panel! Even the idiot lights—my gunnery chief reports no charge to his plates! It's—"

"It's mutiny, Foof!" Hish hissed. "I order you: get

into battle array at once. At *once*, do you hear?" He glanced at the CR, which showed no indication of any change in the formation of Foof's powerful battle group. Hish threw the unit on the pavement and jumped on it, netting a painful pad-bruise.

"It's not Foof's fault," Retief told the frustrated commander. "His equipment is knocked out. That 'garbage scow' was *Irresolute*, the flagship of the PDF, Capt. Pete commanding. It made a pass by your entire force and beamed a saturation EMS surge at every unit. They're dead in space."

"*Mister* Retief!" Hish spat out the name, turning on its possessor. "Am I to understand that even as you Terrans babbled so eagerly of 'peace' and 'spheres of influence,' you were treacherously preparing this dastardly blow directed at poor, trusting Groac? Ben—" he shifted targets. "*You* must have authorized this! It's not to be borne!"

"Well, actually," Magnan started, but Retief cautioned him: "You wouldn't want the general to get the idea you're not in control of your own subordinates, would you, sir?"

"Now, how silly," Magnan rejected the idea. "I'm sure we must have conferred about the scheme, but it had slipped my mind, it seems. It's just a silly misunderstanding, Hish," he told the Groaci. "I'm sure— that is, I hope—anyway I'll try to arrange for a Class V apology, alluding favorably to your own restraint under apparent provocation, General!"

"I trust the Class V carries an adequate honorarium!" Hish snapped.

Magnan made no reply but turned to Retief. "Now that Powerful Pete's neutralized Foof's battle-wagons," he whispered, "What next?"

"I guess I got a word to say about that," Sarge Thrash spoke up, having recovered a good measure of his unfounded arrogance. "I and my boys are still full of spit-and-vinegar! We're raring to go! I got to get back aboard my command and tell my captains to rig for deep space!"

"Not so fast, Sluggy," Magnan put in quietly. "The reorientation is not yet complete."

Retief had just turned his talker to the CDF band. He caught Pete's voice in mid-report: "—little problem area here, Retief. Just before we finished the EMS sweep, one of the tricky devils lobbed a torpedo into my aft lazaret. Blowed my reserve chow and funny books all to hell! Got a good mind to—"

"Don't do it, Pete!" Retief countered. "There's more at stake here than *Ultraguy and the Red Menace*. Stand fast and keep an eye on the Groaci. I'll get back to you. Over and out."

"Gracious!" Magnan contributed. "Jim! Does this mean you're in collusion with that dreadful Pete person in some sort of scheme to frustrate Groaci strategy?"

"I sincerely hope so," Retief replied.

"Mr. Retief!" Hish groaned. "Did you pause to give due consideration to the damage such an outrage would do to the career prospects of a number of high-paced Groacian dignitaries, not least myself?"

"I sure did," Retief answered unequivocally. "It added to my satisfaction considerably."

"Jim!" Magnan gasped in a shocked tone (not quite a 72-w [Aghast at a Social Blunder of Unprecedented Proportions]).

"Ben!" Hish snarled. "This is no occasion for that rather unsophisticated Seventy-two of yours. It demands the rigor of a full Seventy-nine-a!"

"'A Person Whom It's Not Possible For One to Know'?" Magnan gasped. "But, General, under the circumstances that would mean that I'd be forced to order Retief's eviction from the scene!"

"Precisely!" Hish gloated. "We'll soon set things to

right then!" He turned to Sarge Thrash. "You, fellow!" he grated. "Will report yourself under arrest in quarters, at once!"

Sluggy scratched his lumpy skull with a rutching sound like a banjo pick plied on concrete. "I heard about that, General, sir," he offered. "But I never doped out how a feller would do it."

"Don't whine and grovel!" Hish snorted. "Execute! Now!"

" 'Execute'? you said," Thrash echoed in a Tone of Puzzlement (4-g), and unholstered his sidearm. "Who'm I s'pose to shoot?" he inquired, looking to Magnan for guidance. "Who do *you* think I'm s'pose to shoot, sir?" he pled.

"A round between the feet of that rascal, Skunky, wouldn't be amiss (excuse the pun)," Magnan offered. "He's right behind you, getting set to try a Hai-itchy-guy on you."

"Why the sneaky little sneak!" Thrash bellowed, turning to face the object of his indignation. He put a wild round into his own left boot, fortunately into the space between his opposable big toe and the next digit. He dropped the weapon and hopped on his right foot, howling.

"That smarts some," he remarked, at the same moment felling Skunk with a backhanded swipe. "Not much, though," he continued contemplatively, "considering it blown my toes off."

He paused to pull off the perforated boot and wiggle the surprisingly intact digits. "Hey, that's sumpin!" he exclaimed. "Put a round o' hardshot through the duron toe of my number twelve EE withouten hardly bruising the skin much!" He held up the miraculously intact pedal extremity for Magnan's inspection. "See?" he moaned. "Still got six toes! Coulda been cripple fer life. All because old Skunk was trying a fast one."

"Just a moment, Sergeant," Magnan put in. "It

would be quite unfortunate to make, and act upon, a hasty judgment at this critical point."

"What's critical about it?" Thrash bellowed. "I'm shot, ain't I, even if it nigh missed me!"

"But it was you, yourself," Magnan pointed out, "who fired the shot."

"Shooting at *him*, wasn't I?" Thrash demanded. "Same difference: if he wouldn't of deserved to be shot, I wouldn't of ruint a hunderd-guck duron-reinforced boondocker!" He casually dumped Skunky, who had just gotten his feet back under him. The dumpee sprawled with a plaintive cry and kicked Thrash in the back of the knee.

Thrash collapsed, clutching his leg. "He done broke my laig!" he whimpered, and cast a shrewd glance at Magnan, as he scrambled to his feet. "Just when I was goin' to offer to fergit and forgive! You going to jest stand there, Mr. dipple-matic bigshot, and let that little space-rat maim me? Huh?" He advanced on the cowering Magnan, scowling and hefting a cabbage-sized fist. "Huh? Are you?" he yelled, and dropped abruptly as Skunky kicked his other knee.

Magnan backed away, looking around for Retief. "Jim!" he croaked. "You'd best deal with this brute before he assaults me—and that Skunky person, too!"

"Who, *me*?" Skunky screeched. "After I gone and dumped this here mutineer fer ya? Save you from getting yer mush caved in, too. Some gratitude!"

He got to his feet, fingering various bruises. "Oughta make *me* Admiral o' the fleet, stead o' this here loser," he stated importantly. "Then maybe we'd get some action to clear these Groaci five-eyes outa here!"

"Splendid notion!" Magnan bleated. "Captain Obtu-luck—"

"I'm kinda sensitive about my name," Skunky cut in. "That's 'Cap Obtulucz'! See, 'luch,' not 'luck'! So, OK, now you gotta appoint me out loud where I can get it on my CR taper here. Sealed and official. Go ahead."

"By the authority which should have been vested in me," Magnan intoned obediently, "I appoint you, Skunk Obululusk, to be commanding admiral of the task force heretofore known as 'the Indestructibles,' to assume all authority and responsibilities appertaining thereto. Say, 'I accept the appointment.'"

"Wait a sec," Skunky protested, "what was that part about 'responsibilities'?"

"An inevitable concomitant of authority," Magnan scolded. "A pity some of you would-be 'bosses' don't realize that! It's not all fancy uniforms and yessirs.' It's up to you to get your force in fighting trim, rig for space, and advance to confront the enemy! Now be about it! But first you have to say, 'I accept the appointment tendered to me, to be Grand Admiral of Fleets in the Terran Reserve on EAD—.'"

"That's wid full pay and allowances, right?" Skunky amended. "Right," he answered his own query. "I except the perntmen' tender' to me to be Grand Admiral of Leets inna Terry Reserves. OK; let's have the fancy suit—wit' medals—and I can get going. Stay down, you!" he ordered Thrash, enforcing the order with a kick in the grimace as the battered ex-captain was coming uncertainly to his feet.

"Now, none of that," Magnan interceded. "We have a war to conduct. We can't be fighting."

"I'm getting tireda you civilians tryna tell a Grand Admiral what to do," Skunky snarled and strode off toward *Execrable*, the nearest unit of his new command.

"Oh, Grand Admiral," Magnan called after him, netting no response. Skunky forged on, ignoring the group of crewmen, debarked from various vessels, who had gathered to block his way.

"Oh, dear," Magnan whimpered. "I see that uncouth ex-Captain Chornt, late skipper of *Indistinguishable*, who was stripped of his command and reduced to the ranks by ACHE. An unwise move, I fear, however richly deserved the rebuke was. He's the ringleader of this delegation, I don't doubt!"

Retief nodded and forged ahead. As he passed Skunky, he spoke to him, then angled off toward the welcoming committee, now waiting uneasily, slapping spanners against their palms and spitting. After a moment's hesitation, Skunky walked boldly up to Chornt, halted, and gave him a six-grades hand salute. Chornt returned it perfunctorily and motioned to those beside him, who moved to encircle Skunky.

As the latter turned to gaze back at Retief, now coming up behind Chornt, one of the larger crewmen, a shaggy green Hondu master gunner, pushed aside the spindly Yarch wiper blocking his view and stepped into Retief's path. "Who're you, Bo?" he demanded, showing a fine set of pointed teeth.

"I'm your new instructor in good manners," Retief told him. "For openers, you may inform Space'n Last-class Chornt that he's to lie facedown with his arms extended above his head."

"Oh, a cute one." The Hondu glared and snapped his interlocking fangs. "Better get lost, Professor, before some o' the boys, which we're playing hookey today, take a dislike to you."

"Goodness!" Retief squeaked. "That would be just dreadful! I'm here to reaffirm our mutual chumship! If the fellows would just—"

" 'The fellows,' " the Hondu replied, "are going into town to tear it up a little. We heard about how there was some kinda rumble going on, with fat pickings for anybody wised-up enough to grab 'em. Stand aside!"

Retief happened to stoop just then, even as the Hondu's haymaker whistled over his back. He came up with an empty gribble-grub bag.

"Littering!" he said with disdain. "Now," he went

on briskly, "we must lay by the heels the miscreant guilty of this environmental rape!" Retief shifted his gaze to the sullen louts scuffing their feet in a loose ring around him. The Hondu had faded to rejoin the encircling crowd.

"Now," Retief said sharply. "Is the malefactor ready to step forward and receive his rebuke in good part?"

The entire contingent advanced a step, jostling each other and triggering a number of shoving matches which soon reduced the circle to a chaotic mob with Retief at the center.

"All right, students," Retief said heartily. "Recess is over. Class begins now. You." He pointed at a hulking lout with a jaw like a drag-line shovel. "Close your mouth, get that gut in, shoulders back, look straight ahead, and don't scratch!"

"Jeez," the pupil muttered. "This guy gives me five, no, seven things to do at once. "How'm I s'poseta . . . ?"

"Once more: Don't talk. One demerit," Retief said, and hit the loquacious fellow hard in the solar plexus. The reprimandee grunted and opened his snaggle-toothed mouth, then changed his mind and sat down abruptly.

"On your feet!" Retief snapped. "I said, 'Close your mouth.' Next violation is *two* demerits."

"He can't do it," a bystander remarked gleefully. "Old Snag only got one solar plexus." The heckler looked around for approval, but instead intercepted Retief's fist with his grin; he hit the pavement beside Snag, howling.

Snag put a hand over his bloody mouth and said. "Shh, Grinder, the nice man don't like yer voice."

"A-plus," Retief approved. "Snag, help Grinder up and both of you can stand at attention right over there. The rest of you can fall in on Snag and Grinder," he went on, as the two volunteer squad-leaders sheepishly took up their assigned positions.

"I hear you boys learned close-order drill back on Devilworld," Retief told his class. "Let's see if old Sarge Damon the Demon still knows his stuff. Left face!"

The squad pivoted left in an almost orderly fashion, but with derisive grins and slouched posture.

"Dress right, dress!" Retief shouted. The men did "eyes right," and each extended his right arm to touch his neighbor's shoulder, shuffling his feet to come into approximate spacing and alignment. Retief noted a wider-than-average space next to a gorilloid fellow addressed by his fellows, appropriately enough, as "Ape," but made no comment as he noticed that Ape's knuckles almost touched the ground as he stood erect, arms hanging at his sides, his beady eyes fixed on a point in space.

"Ape, fall out," Retief ordered. Ape complied without eagerness. "Jeez," he remarked *sotto voce*, as if wishing to avoid overhearing himself. "I wanneda be a *part* o' things, like the other fellows."

"So you are," Retief reassured the anthropoid. "In fact, you're platoon leader. Put your outfit through their paces and report to me."

Chapter 6

Ape did a snappy about-face and growled. "Ten-hut!" The squad dropped their extended arms and came to approximate eyes front.

"You, Buggy," Ape snarled. "Wipe that grin offa yer puss! This here ain't no playground! This here is war to the knife!" Ape did another about-face to look curiously at Retief. "I fergot to ast, sir, by what authority am I suppose to be taking orders from a civilian?"

"Actually," Magnan contributed, coming up just then, "Mr. Retief is a Battle Commander and chief of the armed forces of the Empire. He's only on detached duty to the Corps."

"Oh, par' me all to hell, General, sir," Ape stammered and brought up a semi-snappy salute. "Sir, I beg to report the squad is all at the position of a soljer!"

"Carry on, Lieutenant," Retief replied, returning the salute. Ape turned back to his command, stared at the front rank as if in disbelief, and bawled, "Lef-haa, fwut harch, hup-two, d'leflank, harch, hup-hoo, detail halt! Hand salute, two! You, Buggy!" he yelled at a gangly fellow with a thin neck and a lumpy, undersized skull. " 'Sloot' don't mean shade yer eyes like a hostile Injun lookin' fer settlers to scalp! Looky here, I'll show you one more time!"

"Fall 'em out, Lieutenant," Retief ordered, and beckoned his trainee officer close, putting the squad "at ease."

"Lieutenant Ape," he addressed the big-bellied man. "In three minutes, you're going to lead the charge in an assault on the rest of the crew of *Indefensible*. You'll want some disciplined troops behind you when you brace Big Ben Crmblnski, eh? So shape 'em up in a hurry!" He turned and walked away.

Ape motioned the at-ease squad closer.

"Jim," Magnan put in worriedly. "Do you think it wise to let that gang of recruits—?"

"Lissen," Ape addressed his clumsy troops. "You boys know how old Crummy is always blowing off his yap about how his own section's the sharpest outfit inna squadron. Well, in a couple minutes, we're gonna make him eat them words! So, do I get a little cooperation now, and no more klutz treatment?"

The men yelled "Yaaay!" and as if by magic flowed smoothly and re-formed in a crisp, rigidly aligned squad front, each man fairly vibrating with zeal.

"I guess Sarge Damon still has his stuff after all," Retief remarked to Magnan as they watched the squad deploy snappily into a line of skirmishers, re-form on command into a column of ducks, execute a flawless double-reverse flanking turn, and end at the spot from which they had begun, ready to assault the unsuspecting Second Platoon.

"Well done, Lieutenant," Retief congratulated Ape. "Now form up for an envelope on the next vessel in line. When you've got them in position, Sarge here will order the crew out."

"Wait just a minute," Powerful Pete objected as he

came up. "I thought I was in charge o' them vessels now. You said so yerself, Retief."

"True, Pete. But the crews don't know that; they'll respond better to Thrash right now."

"Oh, OK, but soon's we secure that tub, you'll make sure all hands get the word, right? If I hafta go in there cold, I might hafta bust a few guys, which I need all the crew I can get."

"Sure," Retief agreed.

Thrash came forward importantly. "Won't do you boys a whole lot o' good," he stated in a self-satisfied tone. "*I'm* the one got all the function codes right here." He tapped his warped frontal bone.

"Better give 'em to Pete," Retief suggested. "Or he'll reach in there and grab them."

"How *can* he?" the former commander jeered. "It's all inside my head, not wrote down nowhere!"

"Guess I'll just hafta open up yer head," Pete growled. "Less you wanta be reasonable, that is."

"Ha!" Sluggy snorted. "*That'll* be the day, you bullet-headed galoot!"

"Never mind," Pete said, and strolled over to the emergency exit hatch of the vessel in question. He studied the four-foot square laminated duralloy panel for a moment, then inserted his fingers under the edge and with a *screech!* of torn metal ripped it from its hinges. He threw it aside and came back over to Thrash.

"Now, what was that code again? I don't reckon a feller dumb as you would use more'n one access to the whole works. Spit it out!"

Thrash was still staring at the rudely removed hatch cover lying on the pavement bent almost double.

"That ain't *possible!*" he protested to the Big Umpire in the Sky. "That there panel tested ten atmospheres at the depot!"

"Think how your head will look," Retief suggested, "if you don't speak up *right now.*"

Thrash put both hands on the sides of his head and backed away from Pete, who reached out, took a casual grip on the sergeant's shoulder, and lifted him, at arm's length.

Thrash kicked his feet frantically, his face reflecting the discomfort in his shoulder. "You'll break it!" he yelled.

"Don't give me no ideas, Bub," Pete suggested. He dropped the stubborn fellow and turned to Retief.

"Reckon I oughta go aboard and operate on the panel," he said indifferently. "Take the numbers offa that sardine-can yonder, and plug 'em into the override system."

"Good idea," Retief seconded. "Meanwhile, I'll inform the crew you're the new admiral, so they won't get hurt."

Skunky began a protest, but a glare from Pete silenced him.

A cluster of unbeautiful faces were peering from the informally opened escape hatch. They shrank back as Pete came over, reached, and swung up and through the opening. A moment later a man leaped out, hit the ramp running, and yelled, "It ain't *nacheral!*" He scuttled up to Magnan, who received him in dignified silence, ignoring the excited fellow's babbling pleas for aid.

In the meantime, Pete descended and returned to Magnan's side, dusting his hands contentedly. "Nothing wrong with that tub a little discipline won't fix," he commented over the noisy complaints of the evicted crewman.

"Do shut up, my man," Magnan cut in. "You've just had the honor of meeting Powerful Pete, your new commanding officer."

"Not mine, he ain't," the refugee yelled, rolling his

eyes at Pete. "I ain't serving with no guy that can dump Heavy Bob on his butt withouten even looking at him, and bend old Bob's favorite flint-steel shillelagh into a pretzel with one hand! Lemme outa here!" He held his nose as if diving into a pool, and dug off. He had covered only a few inches before Pete's arm shot out, grabbed him by the collar, and hauled him back, bleating.

"Shaddup, Ratsy," Pete growled.

Ratsy fell silent.

"Pity these chaps are so undisciplined," Magnan commented. "Still, I'm sure you'll soon flog them into line, Pete."

"Say, Retief," Pete's hollow voice spoke up apologetically. "I guess I still got to explain a few thangs to them boys; seems like they had some feller name' Bob fer a captain, let 'em run wild. Back there, you!" he interrupted himself, lunging at Ratsy. "You know, I already said about I'll prolly hafta bend a few hard cases."

"Be my guest, Pete," Retief replied. "Just so you have the flagship ready to lift on full battle status in five minutes."

"But, Jim," Magnan protested. "The other captains—will they take orders from Pete?"

"By definition, Ben," Retief reassured his chief. He commandeered General Hish's all-wave talker, over the expostulations of the latter, and raised Admiral Foof, then handed the talker back to Hish.

"To go to full Pink Alert status at once!" the general commanded in the Court dialect of Groaci. "To prepare to receive the first units of our new allies, a formerly dacoit force known as the Cluster Defense Force. To lay on an honor guard, plus a reception line appropriate to the occasion, and prepare for inspection! To do it now!" Retief repossessed the talker, evaded Hish's grab, and switched to the Indestructibles' band.

"Foof is going to try something tricky," he told Pete. "When he brings his units up alongside and opens ports, you and your fellows are to invite them aboard. Welcome them as allies! We'll all be great pals! Got it?"

"Sure, Retief, we sucker the sticky-fingers aboard and then croak 'em! Neat! But why would they go dead in space and open up beside *us*?"

"Just a whim of Foof's," Retief explained. "Remember, Pete: No misunderstandings, now."

"Jim." Magnan clutched at Retief's sleeve. "I'm surprised at you! That is treacherous in the extreme! To decoy the Groaci aboard as guests and then do them in!"

"Not what I said, Ben," Retief corrected. "I told both sides they were pals now. Both sides plan to violate the truce, so that makes them even."

"Leaving us General Promo and the renegade Colonel Switchback to deal with, not to mention Wim Dit and the hostile factions here on the planet itself!" Magnan muttered. "Dear, *dear* me, sometimes one wonders if Galactic peace is worth all the fighting."

There was a heavy metallic *thud!* from above. The Groaci flagship, coming alongside *Unreliable*, had somehow managed to collide with its host vessel, accidentally wrecking the external antenna array deployed alongside the port side astern of the coil compartment. Angry yells clamored in Terry and Groaci from all talkers at once, until a deep bass cut through the clamor:

"OK! I get it. These five-eyed little sharpies are figgering on sabotaging my command here! But we're gonna show 'em that trick can work both ways. Watch that fore PC pickup blister o' theirs!"

All eyes went at once to the slight bulge in the

otherwise smooth curve of the forehull of the pride of the Groacian Grand Fleet, which housed the multiplex sensor array feeding data to all the external sensing systems of the high-tech vessel. It erupted in a spout of molten metal and incandescent gases.

"Ye gods!" Magnan burst out. "That's an act of war! An overt attack on a friendly vessel in the very act of paying a courtesy call! It's *your* fault, Retief! It was you who arranged the affair!"

"Thanks, Ben," Retief replied. "I can use the points back at Sector. Get set for some fireworks. We'd better ease over to the blockhouse."

Just as the vaultlike door closed behind the ill-assorted foursome, a giant clap of thunder shook the tiny structure to its foundation. At the external viewer, Magnan saw the tall Terran warship aflame from end to end, its keel batteries still spitting fire, while the Groaci vessel hovered a cable-length away, a pale violet aura attesting to the load its screens were under.

"They'll be—or have been killed!" Magnan wailed. "Poor chaps! And just when an armistice was within our grasp! If only Admiral Foof had turned the con over to an experienced space'n, and avoided that unfortunate collision! Poor Captain Pete took it amiss, and here's the result! I can't bear to look! Oh, look there, Jim! The poor devils are jumping—that's a hundred-foot fall to the pavement below, and—but it can't be!" He staggered back from the screen as a dozen suited crewmen leaped from the fore hatch, some beating out flames as they fell.

"Sure it can, Ben," Retief corrected. "They're wearing lift suits that'll let 'em down easy."

"But!" Magnan protested. "They're not—I mean—look, Jim! Instead of fleeing to safety, they're all clustering around the Groaci ship's ceremonial portal!"

"Right," Retief agreed. "They know Admiral Foof will be making a formal appearance there to accept the plaudits of the fleet or as much of it as was here to witness his clever handling of the dastardly sneak attack."

"You sound as if you were on *their* side!" Magnan whimpered. "Our poor lads never had a chance: there they were, all busy tidying-up and readying everything to greet their guests in style, and suddenly—disaster!"

"They got their batteries in action awfully fast for a bunch of fellows who were busy setting out party favors," Retief observed.

"Don't be cynical, Jim," Magnan sniffed. "It ill suits you."

"I was just quoting the Groaci standard Press Release #3," Retief pointed out. "The one they use whenever some tricky piece of business has backfired."

"Of course. 'In defiance of all civilized tenets of interplanetary relations, the conscienceless criminals opened fire, etc . . .'" Magnan quoted further from the same traditional source. "With both ships blind, however are they to straighten out this sorry contretemps?" he wailed. "If only Foof and Pete could compare notes calmly, a major disaster could be averted!"

"I guess it's up to us," Retief suggested. "We still have CD contact with both vessels. Let's see what we can do."

"Right on, Jim!" Magnan caroled, and grabbed for the talker. "Oh, Admiral Foof," he cried in a tone which combined Awed Awareness of the Presence of Greatness (1031-n) with Patience Tried Beyond Endurance (71-z). "And Captain Obtulucz, or maybe Pete, or both, and Sarge Thrash, you, too! I urge you all to do nothing hasty! This unfortunate misunderstanding can easily be rectified by restraint and goodwill! First of all, let's all you gentlebeings take a deep breath, and repeat: 'Groaci (or Terries, as appropriate) are just new friends I haven't hugged yet.'"

"How'm I s'pose to take a deep breath?" Pete

demanded, "when all I got to breathe is poison fumes from where my insulation's on fire, where the Commission never enforced the ban on poison-pro-ducing-when-burned stuff aboard all vessels under the jurisdiction of Space Regs?"

"Just hold your breath a moment, Captain, there's a good fellow," Magnan sang out.

"Ha! That's swell for Pete," Foof interjected. "But what I got here, to have every crew aboard out on his feet—barf-sick, you know, from that sneaky—"

"Yes, yes, we all know PR-3," Magnan cut in. "Just wait a few seconds and their Barf-nodes will have recovered from the momentary inconvenience. Then I want you to descend to the ramp, just as Captain Obtulucz will, and here, on the soil of the Free Port, under the sponsorship of the CDT, shake manipula-tory members!"

"Ha!" Skunky's outraged voice bellowed. "Me, shake manipulatory member with that five-eyed sticky-fingers!"

"*Cap*tain Obtulucz!" Magnan rebuked in a shocked tone. "There'll be no use of racial pejoratives! You be nice to Foof and he'll be nice to you!"

"To expect me to be nice to a treacherous Soft One, and even to touch his vascular-fluid-stained manipula-tory member?" Foof yelled.

"Now, Foof, what I said applies to you as well!" Magnan chided. "Characterizing Terries as 'Soft Ones' is hardly in the spirit of chumship! It's true we Terries lack your own handsome carapaces, but we have our points!"

"Am I to expect you, a Terry, to be unbiased in a dispute between Groac and Terra?" Foof demanded skeptically.

"To be unbiased is the great talent of the trained diplomat," Magnan replied jeeringly. "Just leave that part to me, Foof, and, I beg of you, descend at once!"

"You presume to order me, a Grand Admiral of Fleets of Groac?" Foof hissed. "You, a mere civilian, and a Terry one at that?"

"Get your skinny butt down here in two seconds flat," Retief interjected, "or I'll have to come up there and throw it down."

"To—" Foof started an impudent reply, but broke off with a hiss as the crewmen from *Unreliable*, drifting lightly in their lift-gear, plucked him from the open portal and swooped down, arriving just as Captain Pete in his lift-suit settled in beside Magnan. The enraged Groaci eluded Magnan's grab and aimed all five eyestalks at him in an Ultimate Expression of Revulsion (G-73-B). Magnan recoiled. "My *dear* Admiral," he expostulated, "I hardly think I warrant a Seventy-three, about a G, I imagine, under the present conciliatory circumstances! That's a ploy appropriate to the denunciation of a rapist/murderer caught in the act!"

"That was my C, Ben," Foof corrected, "and what's a trifle of forced copulation and strangulation compared with the violation of the most hallowed principles of civilized savagery? Eh?" The diminutive admiral relaxed his 73 and rearranged his ocular members in a somewhat mollifying 70 (Severe Disappointment in a Subordinate's Performance).

"Me? Your su*bord*inate?" Magnan yelled. "Why, the cheek of it! I'll have you know—"

"Later, Mr. Magnan," Retief cut in. "Listen." Magnan cupped an ear, and Foof deployed a single stalk from his dozen or so auditory organs to scan the sky above.

"About time," he muttered. "To have come perilously close to blowing the mission entirely."

"Who?" Magnan yapped. "What mission? Do you have anything to do . . ." His voice trailed off. He watched with horror as an *Overwhelming*-class super-dreadnought clearly of Bogan manufacture curved grandly into view above the horizon, like a rising moon. The billion-tonner approached, brushing aside units of both the CDF and Rex Promo's naval detachment, while the Groaci force bunched up and kept a wary distance from the intruding monster. The titanic vessel was descending rapidly, its turrets scanning left-right for suitable targets. Foof and Hish had gone into conference, ten eyestalks whipping in rapid sequences of Top Urgent symbolism.

"*General* Hish!" Magnan wailed, "if you've any influence over this atrocity, now's the time to call it to heel!"

"Not broody likely, Ben," Hish replied gloatingly. "Brag Gab has his orders—"

"Ha!" a coarse voice rang from the willy Groaci's lapel talker. "I heard that, Hish! It'll be a hot day on Ice Nine when *you* give *orders* to me!"

"Good Lord!" Magnan gasped. "Then the rumors were true: you're in collusion with the most notorious criminal gang in the Arm!"

Hish, busy reprogramming his talker to the privacy mode, waved away Magnan's plaint.

"Envy is a sorry spectacle, Ben," he hissed. "It's true that Freedom Fighter Brag and I have arrived at an accommodation. Look at them run: your vaunted Navy, as well as the ragtag dacoits of the CDF!"

"That's not the Navy," Magnan objected. "Only a mutinous detachment illegally intruded here by the renegade, Rex Promo!"

"Same thing," Hish dismissed the rebuke carelessly, "Just wait until Brag has his command at rest on-planet, and we'll see who's to dictate terms in Bloor City tonight!"

"If we live until tonight!" Magnan yelped. "That thing will crush the blockhouse like a glimp egg!"

"Not so, Ben," Hish corrected urbanely. Then, to

his talker: "Brag, I want you to pull back to five miles and shell the city and its environs, with due care to avoid any damages to the Customs shed where I have established my command post."

"I'll do what I please, you sneaky little bug!" the bandit leader yelled.

"Treachery!" Hish moaned. "Brag!" he yelled. "Remember the solid gold planetoid, the lifetime preferred membership in the Playtoy Club, as well as—"

"Skip it, Hish!" Brag bellowed. "I'm not settling for no handouts! I guess I know where the power's at here!"

"The rascal!" Hish wept. "After I supplied him with a dreadnought, and promised him the emoluments of a Groacian National Hero, too! He should have outdone himself to fulfill his part of the bargain—instead, he tries to hold me up for impossible demands!"

"Would you really have made him a GNH?" Magnan inquired. "I thought only—"

"Certainly not!" Hish snapped. "That's an honor bestowed only by the Council of Drones in solemn congress assembled! But he, poor unsophisticated creature that he is, had no way of knowing that! He should, according to the Manual, paragraph Nine-f, have gone along, naïvely dreaming of Imperial honors! It's not to be borne!"

"There's none so righteously indignant," Retief commented, "as a con man whose sucker slips off the hook after the gaff is set. All that hard set-up work wasted. Sad, isn't it, Ben?"

"To be sure, when one considers it in that light," Magnan commiserated.

"Bah!" Hish scoffed. "What do you oh-so-righteous Terries know of the trials and rewards of skulduggery raised to a fine art? I'll make Brag rue the day he turned on *me*!"

"You oughta learn ta switch off yer blab-box when

yer letting yer head-tendrils down," Brag remarked without rancor from the Groaci officer's talker. "OK, I don't hold no grudges, see? It don't pay. I'll just take care o' these here Cluster Defense bums, and then I'll hit old Buck Promo where he ain't expecting it, see, he don't know about the reinforcements here, and—"

"What?" Promo's irate voice blared from the open mike. "'The enemy of my enemy is my friend,' remember? And I'm here to neutralize the CDF, among other things! That makes us allies—or better yet, it qualifies you to place your force under my command!"

"That'll be the day!" Brag scoffed. "Tell ya what, Buck: you put yer little group unner *my* command! Then we'll hit old Pete where it hurts. I can nail the suckers onna ground! Whattaya say?"

"I never NEVER!" Promo yelled. "Chief Reilly, run out the aft battery; we'll give these bandits a whiff of grape, so to speak," he went on in an aside.

"Now whose mike's open?" Brag crowed. "Get set, boys," he told his own lapel talker. "Set up a Q and a half, we'll fake them Navy clowns outa position and hit 'em right up their stern-tubes! Do it!"

The group on the ramp watched as the naked-eye-visible spacecraft maneuvered smartly, each intent on crossing the other's T, while, from a distance, Switchback's fresh-from-maintenance force shifted into position on their flank. Meanwhile, the Indestructible force had split in two, and the two halves were moving to confront each other.

"Hey, Mister Magnan!" Thrash's hoarse voice blared from Magnan's defective talker. "This here wiper, this Obtulucz, is taking that phony title you give him serious! He's tryna take over command here. In fack, he's got my Second Division—"

"I know! You must give no provocation, Sarge! Let him think—"

"I'm the Grand Admiral," Skunky's voice came in. "You said so yerself! And don't start plotting against me, or I'll—"

"Uh-oh," Magnan remarked. "I fear there's to be carnage wrought here today, with Hish's command playing a role that will resound in the annals of betrayal! Look there, at Switchback's ships: they're easing around left-end. I'll bet Foof is going to hit Promo and Brag simultaneously, and deal with the Colonel afterward. And Thrash and Obtulucz are joining battle!"

"Sound tactics," Retief conceded. "Except that General Hish wouldn't like that, eh, General?"

He turned to the crestfallen alien, who was madly twiddling the controls of his command talker. "Foof!" Hish snarled, "I *command* you—and that's a direct order, mind—to drop back and take out Switchback's flagship as your first priority. The scamp has already laid his prime batteries on your command, ready to blow you out of space as soon as you go for Promo and the traitor Brag!"

"Hmm," Magnan murmured. "Hish is a better field commander than I'd suspected. Watch! He's—"

"Sure," Retief agreed, "and Promo is all set to do a Carousel and take him from below as soon as he lets fly with his first salvo."

"Brilliant!" Magnan exclaimed. "But disastrous for the cause of Goodness and Rightness! Promo is our only hope, Jim! If he retains any loyalty whatever to Naval discipline, he can—"

"Don't worry," Retief soothed. "Brag isn't about to be left out of the fun. He's pretending to be busy setting up a standard Ferris, but I'll bet you a fancy dinner at Mae's East he's going to—"

"You're right!" Magnan yelped. "There he goes! It's

all over for the Groaci, but Buck Promo won't take this lying down!"

"It matters little," Hish put in, "whether the notorious renegade Buck Promo lies prone or even supine: he's forestalled. You see, gentlemen, I anticipated the possibility of Brag Gab's defection, and detached a couple of special units disguised as tenders, to take up positions commanding his primary route of withdrawal, and— what's that! The miscreant Pete is spoiling everything!"

"Right, General," Pete confirmed. "I trusted you five-eyed little sneaks about as far as you can see with all five eye stalks tied in a square knot, which is what they'll be in about ten seconds, give or take a rearsquad action or two!"

"Ben!" Hish whispered. "You wouldn't let him . . . ?"

"I just might," Magnan purred, "unless you order Foof to envelop Switchback as soon as his first advance units reach NEV, and board his vessels and turn them against Rex Promo."

"Well," Hish temporized, "I suppose that in the really big pattern, it wouldn't hurt."

"Regardless of the proportions of the graphic representation," Lieutenant Ape interjected formally, "you better do like Mister Magnan tells you, Hish, or I'll do the job myself." So saying, he made a grab for the Groaci's neck, by which time the thoroughly cowed officer was barking commands to Foof as rapidly as he could inflate his throat sac to activate his vocal apparatus.

"—to do it smartly now, mind you, Foof!" Hish hissed. "Or you'll attend your court-martial with your oculars knitted into the form of a tea-cozy! Foof!" he snarled. "Do as I say!" then, to Magnan: "Ben, I call you to witness, the insubordinate rogue is deliberately defying me and laying into Brag's ragtag force!"

Averting his eyes from the scene of carnage developing

above, a swarming confusion of fire-spouting war vessels that boiled across the sky from horizon to horizon, Magnan moaned. "I never before grasped the fullness of the concept of chaos," he gobbled. "Promo is attacking Pete, Pete is savaging Switchback, who in turn is fully occupied with Foof's tricky feint, and Thrash and Skunky are going at it, even while fending off independent strikes by Brag and various units of all of the above! One hardly knows for whom to root!"

"To hope the scoundrels eliminate each other!" Hish remarked. "Look at that fool, ex-Admiral Foof! He's turned on Switchback's negligible force now, while he allows Pete to form up the CDF in a Knitsie enveloping his entire anterior quadrant!"

"We can't just stand by, Jim," Magnan said sternly. "We have to figure out which of the combatants represent the forces of G and R, and do what we can to aid them!"

"We can start," Retief suggested, "by letting General Hish call Foof out of the fray, eh, General?"

"Never!" Hish spat. "Or rather, to be a capital idea, Jim!" He proceeded to issue further orders to Foof, quite in vain, since the admiral had his grasping members full in attempting to disengage from Pete's violent counterattack. Meanwhile, Hish was hissing frantically into his CM.

Retief ripped the device from Hish's lapel and spoke into it: "Fun's over, Foof. Forget about the CDF, and ground what's left of your command soonest!"

Foof's faint voice came back, in a complaining tone: "Who are you, vile Soft One, to essay to command a Groacian flag officer?"

"Better tell him it's official, General," Retief recommended to Hish, "if you want to salvage anything out of this riot."

Hish obediently repeated Retief's orders, and the

Groaci units promptly disengaged and settled in, aligning themselves in a crude South Forty across the adjoining tundra.

As soon as the Groaci units had settled in they were followed by Brag Gab and the CDF.

"Debark crews and prepare for inspection!" Hish commanded harshly.

"Tell them to lie facedown, with tentacles extended," Retief told the general, who complied sullenly.

"A wise precaution," Magnan commented. "I've a notion the scamps were forming up for an assault on Gab's contingent."

"*Au contraire!*" Hish hissed. "The said Brag is, in point of fact, about to commit an act of aggression directed at Admiral Foof's disciplined command, who have trustingly cooperated with your illegal orders. Intercede at once!"

"Pete," Retief addressed the lanky pirate chief as he came running up. "Tell Lieutenant Ape to double-time his group around the perimeter of the port, to discourage Brag's reserves. They're getting set to blow the south fence."

"Let me at these local levies," Pete growled, and set off at a trot to marshal his captains. One of the latter, Yang the Execrable by name, had anticipated his order and was approaching Ape's platoon, which was standing at ease between himself and *Intolerable*, a battered cruiser sadly in need of maintenance.

"Hey!" Yang yelled, eliciting a curious glance from the lieutenant, who casually continued deploying his small force in preparation for advance through the spot occupied by the Groaci.

"Halt them at once!" Hish screeched. "Now it appears my trusting chaps are to be subjected to aggression on both flanks simultaneously!" He returned his attention to his talker: "Foof! Go into a zum-formation! Receive the Terries upon the bayonet!"

"What barbarity!" Magnan gasped. "Poor Ape doesn't stand a chance! Perhaps, Jim, we'd better—"

"Lemme have a word with that Yang character," Snag, who had been hovering nearby, grunted, and moved off toward the scar-faced Oriental, followed by Grinder and Buggy.

"That there," Pete contributed, "is Yang Shapiro, Genghis Ka Khan of all the Mongols. He'll use old Snag fer a penwiper." He looked at Retief. "Trouble is," he confided, "I don't know if that's good or bad. Old Yang's on my side, o' course, 'cept I got a idear he mighta made some kinda deal with that five-eyes name o' Foof; tricky, old Yang is. Then there's Sarge hisself. I got this hunch he's working fer that Brag Gab rascal. Buck Promo is siding with Ape right now, and maybe that's Big Ben Crmblnski conning *Indy*— if Chornt ain't staged a counter-mutiny. But Ape's going after the Indestructibles, and they're pals with Promo, looks like. The enemy of my enemy is my friend, but, I'll jest be fair with ya, Retief, I lost count. Who's the good guys—and why do I want to side with the good guys, anyways?"

"Just stick to self-defense," Retief suggested. "Right now it looks like Yang and Snag aren't hitting it off too well, so . . ."

"Yeah, and Yang's one o' my line captains," Pete supplied, "so that makes me against Snag, nyet?"

"Do be gentle," Magnan urged. "Poor Snag doesn't realize just what he's up against. And look out for Brag: he's a tricky devil."

"Ha!" Pete scoffed. "I eat them Brag-types fer afternoon tea!"

He strode across to where Yang and Snag had reached the "Oh, yeah?" and shoving stage. He grabbed Snag carelessly and yanked, and the latter yelled, "I ain't even *seen* you!" He swung wildly, and collapsed.

"Jeez, pal," Pete said contritely. "I di'n't know you was sick!" He turned to look mournfully across at Magnan. "Whyn't you tell me the guy was one o' them invalids?" he demanded. "Coulda hurt the pore feller."

The remainder of Pete's plaint was lost in a roll of thunder as Ape's small contingent of condemned space-vessels swooped low over the field, sending up roiling clouds of gritty dust. Hish, threshing his eye-stalks in evidence of Dire Distress (G-12-a), clutched at Magnan's sleeve. His voice, never strong, was almost inaudible:

"Ben! Let's deal! Call off that gang of criminals and I'll turn Foof's command over to you to do with as you see fit! Foof's overdue for the Retired List anyway, and definitely out of favor with the Council; it wouldn't do for me to be too closely identified with his probably illegal activities here!"

"*General* Hish!" Magnan gasped. "You'd sell out your very own subordinate commander? Shocking! Anyway, *I* have no control over Ape! He's acting Grand Admiral now, you know. Why he dragged the field, I don't know . . ." Magnan paused to bat ineffectually at the settling but still thick dust. "Just boyish spirits, I suppose." He fumbled for his talker, and barked: "Lieutenant and Brevet Grand Admiral! Ground your command at once, just beyond the Groaci units. Don't buzz the port again! Over and out!"

"Are-Roger, Field HQ," Ape's drawl came back. "Sorry about that. I tole the boys to pass in review and I guess they forgot to bleed off relative velocity first. Won't happen again. By the way, before I go outa the pirate business, you fellers want me to neutralize the assault force I just picked up on a hard-contact veck? Looks like it might be them rogue units outa Blinch. Colonel Switchback's bunch."

"By all means!" Magnan yelled. "But don't precipitate a war with the Navy!"

"Jeez," Ape moaned. "The burden o' command is never so heavy as when a fella gotta figure out how to do the impossible. 'Hit 'em, but don't hurt 'em,' the guy says. How'm I s'pose to do that?"

"It is precisely such thorny questions to resolve which you received your promotion," Magnan snapped. "Hop to it! I can see the Colonel's lead units already!"

"I'll pull a bluff," Ape announced, and at once yelled, "Sarge! Get your rust-bucket in line abreast on my left flank. Soonest. Brag," he went on, "you got maybe a kinda chance if you can get that gang o' Yahoos o' yourn under control long enough to get in echelon coming up my right flank! Hish," he addressed the once-arrogant general, "if I let Foof lift off, will you order him into line astern o' me?"

"What? Act as an escort to a Terry corsair?" Hish shrieked. "Never! To be astonished at your impudence!"

"Then I guess I'll hafta blast 'em where they set," Ape remarked, even as he re-formed his strike force in an all-enveloping Omar and executed a smart wham-reversal to approach the grounded Groaci task force at strafing level.

"That is to say," Hish gobbled, "on more mature consideration, to feel that perhaps—"

"'Perhaps' don't cut it, Hish!" Ape interrupted. "Are you in, or out?"

"In, by all means!" Hish gobbled. "I'll have these fellows in position before you can say 'Treason to the Autonomy'!" He switched over to Foof's channel and issued crisply conflicting orders. The Groaci flag vessel lifted at once, followed, rank by rank, by the rest of the command. When the dust cleared, the tight Groaci formation could be seen rapidly overhauling Ape's somewhat dispersed units, which abruptly split into a fountain as each echelon curved out and back to come alongside the approaching aliens.

"Retief!" Ape's voice shouted from the overused

talker. "These here Five-eyes are trying to pull a fast one! When I wasn't looking, they done a sneak maneuver which they're abaft my beam-ends, coming on balls to the wall. OK if I rake 'em good?"

"Hold your fire, Lieutenant," Magnan cut in quickly. "They're trying to rendezvous with you to escort you past the Navy and the Indestructibles, just so there'll be no misunderstandings."

"Hah! what I'm worried about—not that I'm worried—is *under*standing! Th boys sees me in formation with a bunch of Groaci, look out! Uh-oh, sorry about that, fellers, seems like my gunnery officer got a little previous and taken out the Gruck flagship! Now I better—" His voice cut off abruptly at the same moment that his vessel, *Irresolute*, exploded.

"Oh, dear!" Magnan wailed. "General Hish, you shouldn't have—" He broke off as the remainder of Ape's force broke formation, each ship diving directly toward the nearest vessel of the putative escort. Magnan yelped and began gobbling contradictive orders to both Buck Promo and Colonel Switchback to intervene at once and separate the combatants and by *no* means become involved themselves.

"How'm I s'pose to do that?" Switchback grumbled. "I and Buck Promo got a bone to pick, anyways. *Can't* cooperate with the sumbuck, which he's not a feller to stay bought!"

"You'll have to," Retief told him. "Or Brag Gab will neutralize both of you, if Pete doesn't do it first."

"You just say the word, Retief," Pete's growling voice cut through the chatter. "I can take out Promo's flagship, and the rest of his gang won't know whether to spit or go blind!"

"Hold it, Pete," Retief cautioned. "I need you to stand off and monitor the action, and then step in to pick up the pieces."

"Jim!" Magnan rasped, his eyes narrowed as he listened

intently to his right-beam talker, linked, Retief knew, directly to the Embassy Coderoom.

"We have to clean up this little misunderstanding at once!" Magnan gasped. "Of all times, the Sector Inspection Team has chosen now—this day, this hour—to stage a surprise inspection. The Ambassador is furious! He demands we show the Team a pacified Bloor. They'll be here in half an hour."

"Nope," Retief replied. "They're here now."

Magnan turned to follow Retief's wave, and saw a VIP-converted heavy cruiser on final approach at the far end of the debris-littered port.

"Heavens!" Magnan moaned. "Whatever are we to do, Jim, to show them the true peace and harmony that rule here, somewhat disguised at the moment by the apparent disorder now seemingly in progress?"

He paused, then: "I have it!

"Let's tell 'em it's Reverse Peace, an old Bloorish custom," he proposed earnestly. "In honor of all the joy of halcyon coexistence, they stage a mock Battle Carnival to remind each other of what they're missing. The inspectors are generally a dull-witted lot. They'll believe anything that will cut down on their paperwork!"

"Magnan," a stranger's voice came from the talker by his ear. "I'm FSO-1 Snail, Chief Inspector, TFS. You really ought to watch that open mike. A fellow could get in deep stuff thinking aloud on the all-band."

"Yipes!" Magnan exclaimed. "I didn't even—I mean I only meant—"

"Jim," Magnan groaned, "that's Pokey Snail, the demon inspector! How honored we are, to receive his personal attention!"

"Sure, Ben," Snail came back. "Say, what was that you were saying about cutting down on the paperwork? A carnival, you say? Glad you mentioned it. Captain Muldoon here was getting nervous."

Magnan paused to switch off his master communications box before remarking to Retief:

"Did you hear that, Jim? It's mind-boggling! Po— the Chief Inspector himself said he'd overlook any irregularities here in the interest of simplifying reportorial procedures, in return for which I'm to supply appropriate documentary proof that this mess is really a festival, to cover him in case anyone actually checks up!"

"Meaning," Retief interpreted, "if we can give him an out, he'll cover up the whole thing, to avoid having a blot on his chumship record. I admire your ability to interpret triplespeak, Ben."

"One must, in order to survive," Magnan dismissed the tribute. "Now, all we need to do is prove this is all in fun; and—"

"Good idea," Retief approved. "And if we can sell the idea to Brag Gab, and maybe Buck Promo . . ."

"We'd have to have Switchback's cooperation as well," Magnan contributed. "But if we can convince him it's a trick to take Promo out of the picture . . ."

"And just how," Hish cut in, "do you propose to convince *me* that this full-scale battle is a joyous carnival?"

"That won't be too hard, General," Retief remarked to the ill-tempered Groaci, at the same moment that he brushed aside the alien's jewel-encrusted VIP eyeshields and grasped his twitching eyestalks. He gave the sensitive oculars a half-twist to the left and paused.

"Ready to give Foof his orders?" he inquired artlessly, "or shall we go for a full one-eighty?"

"Oh, Admiral Foof!" Hish gobbled into his talker. "To have forgotten to mention it, perhaps, but our participation in this festival doesn't include the actual symbolic discharge of live ammunition. So *do* be careful not to give an erroneous impression!"

" 'Symbolic'?" Foof hooted. "I've got hot loads

programmed in all batteries, Hish, and I'm raring to go! What festival? You mean like a turkey-shoot? Whee! Commence firing!"

"To be too late," Hish moaned. "To have sprung this piece of fakery a trifle earlier, to have been better, Ben!"

"Yes, of course," Magnan gulped. "But under the circumstances—" His voice trailed off; above, six gung-ho fighting forces converged, intent on clearing space of lesser rascals.

"What's a general officer to do?" Hish wept. "If Chief Inspector Whilsh arrives here and sees Groaci units engaged in open combat with Terran-manned units—no matter they started it—well, Ben, *both* our careers will lie in ruins, *and* I daresay the Terry Peace Enforcers now conducting exercises off Floon will feel called upon to intervene, as well. Ghastly! Do you suppose if I order Foof . . . ?"

"Without doubt that will defuse the situation," Magnan enthused. "Just tell the scamp to pull back ten thousand miles and take up a #1 Siesta, and await my further instructions as to their participation in the festivities!"

"'*Your* instructions,' indeed!" Hish sputtered. "Foof!" he yelled into his talker. "Disregard Ben Magnan's impudent 'order'! You can just retire ten nards and go into a single-lobed Siesta formation and stand by to execute kill order! Over and out!"

"Gee whiz! General Hish, sir," Foof temporized. "Won't that leave my flank wide open to old Pete?"

"I meant of course, Admiral," Hish came back hotly, "that you will carry out your strategic withdrawal *after* you've raked Pete's garbage scows stem to stern with yum-radiation! Do it!"

Pale green halos appeared along the port flanks of Foof's vessels—the side facing Powerful Pete's CDF units. The latter at once went inert, as indicated by the abrupt cessation of the carrier wave that had been droning from Ben's talker. Suddenly the massive, heavy vessels dropped from formation, falling through and past the Groaci picket-line.

"Yipes!" Magnan yelped. "They'll crash right where we're standing!"

"I doubt it," Retief corrected. "Watch: as soon as his last unit is clear of Foof's control-zone, they'll—" He fell silent as the wildly tumbling warships righted themselves, assumed a battle-front formation, and returned to the ready-line.

"Smooth as Ziz-silk!" Magnan breathed. "I didn't think Pete's irregulars had it in them to pull a China that way!"

"Fire!" Hish yelled. "Fire all batteries *now*, you idiot!"

"The port batteries to bear on emptiness!" Foof objected.

"I meant fire all effective batteries, of course, you cretin!" Hish sputtered. "Have you no intellect whatever?"

"Not much," Retief supplied, "or he'd be cutting space for shelter on the far side of the satellite, before Pete gets annoyed and swats him."

"To do so at once, and that gladly!" Foof gobbled. "Thank you, General! To meet again in the Bad Place, perhaps!"

The Groaci vessels executed a smart end-for-end and made a beeline for a point on the far side of the scene of carnage.

"Smart fellow, Admiral Foof," Magnan remarked. "Congratulations, General, on saving your fleet."

"Mutiny! Treason!" Hish yelled.

"No thanks," Retief spoke up for all present. "We'll manage with what we've got. The inspectors are here, you know."

"Able Space'n Foof!" Hish shrieked. "To keep a

pair of oculars cocked for a Terran sneak-up from the direction of Bloor City! To capture said vessel, more or less gently, and escort it here."

"You mean that *Goliath*-class that's rising like a moon half a nard due east?" Foof yelped. "No fair!"

"Hish! You wouldn't!" Magnan gasped. "Chief Inspector Snail is not known for his patience with unwarranted interference!"

"This is warranted, Ben," Hish replied coolly. "To give you a few seconds to rearrange *your* scenario, too."

"There *is* that," Magnan mused. "But how in the world am I going to convince these hard-nosed snoops that a war is a carnival?"

"That's your problem, Ben," Hish muttered. "You were the one who thought of it, remember?"

"Certainly!" Magnan agreed. "I was inspired! But it's in both our interests to prevent unfortunate reports of carnage on a planetwide scale reaching Sector, or Groaci Sub-central, either!"

"To take it easy, Ben," Hish soothed. "Imagine Pokey's delight when his transport is met and escorted in by an interplanetary honor guard including sophisticated Groacian peace-keeping vessels, patently devoted to safeguarding his well-being!"

"You mean . . . ?" Magnan gasped.

"Precisely," Hish confirmed. "Foof, you heard that. Now, do Groac proud in your role of emissary of Interbeing Goodwill. Fall your command in on Pete's. There's a restoration of rank in it for you if you put Pokey down in a good mood."

"Then," Foof expostulated, "to not get to fire these starboard batteries after all? To have them all laid and ready to go! My chief gunner will be furious!"

"Stay your grasping member," Hish ordered. "The reputation of fair Groac depends now upon the subtlety of your approach. Run those guns in! To display more bunting than a used-car lot on a slow Saturday!"

"That was close," Magnan sighed. "What if Foof had accidentally blown the inspection team out of space! Why, the scandal! And some busybody at Sector would probably have considered it an attempt at a cover-up and dispatched a full double-X emergency team in to find out what was being covered up!"

"Yes," Retief soothed, "but that didn't happen. All we have to deal with is Pokey's team. That's relatively easy, eh?"

"I shall attempt to regard the situation in that light," Magnan moaned. "Look!" he interrupted himself. "There it is now! Old Pokey's got himself one of those converted cruiser-cum-superdreadnoughts as his private play-pretty! Huge thing, isn't it? Foof's vessels look like flies around an elephant. But why are they . . . ?" He broke off and stared in horror as first one, than a group of three, then the entire Groaci squadron opened fire on the Terran behemoth.

"The fools!" he yelled. "When they return fire—"

"She's been decommissioned, Ben," Retief reminded him. "That means the battle-board stays dark. Unless . . ." he mused.

"That's *almost* a pity," Magnan sniffed, "when one considers the effrontery of Admiral Foof in attacking her. *He* didn't know her batteries are silenced."

"Gutsy little fella," Retief commented. "Let's find out *how* gutsy." He turned and plucked Hish's talker from his lapel just as the general was launching into an excited speech.

"—to be dead in space!" Hish made a fruitless grab for his property and subsided.

"Look yonder!" he spat at Retief. "Now see the cowardly Terries have refused our challenge!"

"Skip it, Hish," Retief rebuked the excited Groaci. "You know as well as I do she's disarmed. I guess that's why Foof fired on her. That's hardly in the spirit of Gorm Festival!"

"That happens to be Groacian naval property you're sequestering!" Hish hissed, making another grab for his talker. "To gimme that, at once!"

Retief pushed him away. "Better put the general in irons, Ben," he suggested. "I'm going to be too busy to bother with him."

"As you well know, Jim," Magnan countered, "I don't have any irons in my pocket!"

"That's all right," Retief comforted his agitated chief. "Just turn him over to the black gang to watch."

"Capital notion!" Magnan agreed. He beckoned to one of the surly malcontents from *Indefensible* standing by watching the large vessel on final approach. The name *Corruptible* was legible now, blazoned across her bow.

"Pity the '*In*' was shot away," Magnan muttered. "I suppose I'd best get over there quickly, to orient Pokey properly, before he forms an unfortunate impression of the state of affairs here."

"Sure. Come on, Ben," Retief agreed, as he took the driver's seat of a line-cart parked near at hand. Pulling in under the still-hot and reeking stern-tubes was like probing the flanks of a live volcano. Magnan craned his neck to scan the curve of the vessel's mighty hull.

"I wonder what the delay is?" he muttered. "Usually Pokey is egregiously prompt in debarking. He hates space travel, you know."

"Who wouldn't?" Retief inquired. "Weeks on end boxed up in a metal labyrinth full of stale air and complaining passengers. Planetfall is always a welcome event."

"Ah, there he is now," Magnan caroled as if in delight, as the VIP balcony deployed from a point a hundred feet above them. A short, plump man in full

early midmorning ceremonials gripped the rail and
stared down at his welcoming committee, now con-
sisting of not only Retief and Magnan, but a dozen
tube-sweepers as well, who had followed the cart to
gape.

"Ah, there, Magnan," the Chief Inspector's fruity
voice echoed clearly along the hull. "I *do* appreciate
the welcoming display your chaps are putting on, but
firing live ammo at me—isn't that a trifle beyond the
limits of good taste?"

"It's Gorm Festival," Magnan lied like a trooper.
"Your timing is impeccable, Pokey! You've arrived pre-
cisely at the climax of the ceremonial mock battle!
Striking spectacle, isn't it, sir?"

"Spikking striking," Pokey returned, ducking shell
fragments, "that one struck maybe ten feet from my
person. Those are hardshots, Ben!" The paunchy
inspector turned back, to motion his staff out beside
him.

Retief released Hish, who stooped to recover his
VIP eyeshields.

"Oh, looky!" Magnan urged Retief. "He *loves* it!
He's urging his toadies—ah, staff, that is—to come
out and watch with him."

"I don't think Foof is as expert at near-misses as
could be desired," Retief pointed out. "He's lobbing
those frags in there a little too close for comfort."

"I appreciate your chaps' zeal for verisimilitude,
Ben," Pokey called, "but I fear for my people here.
I'd best descend at once. You may tell them to stop
firing now."

"It's working fine so far," Magnan told Retief confidentially. "But what's going to happen when he finds
out I can't stop the firing as he so lightly proposes?"

"That won't be a problem, will it, Hish?" Retief
inquired of the literally crestfallen alien, at the same
moment taking a new grip on the general's eye-stalks

with his left fist and handing over the talker with his right.

"You'll know just what to say," Retief suggested gently.

"To leave go my oculars!" Hish wailed. "They're still a little out of focus from last time!" Then into the talker:

"Foof! You stop that at once, do you hear?"

The Groaci ships began peeling off and streaking for the stratosphere as Hish spoke rapidly to his subordinate. When the last Groaciship had withdrawn, Retief repossessed the talker. Pete's irregulars moved in to escort the mighty warship.

"Nice work, Admiral," Retief said. "Now, for an encore, just put your command down, in formation, on the parade ground to the east. I'll see you in person on the ground in a little while."

"Look there!" Magnan yelped, and pointed upward. A small, maneuverable skiff had emerged from *Corruptible*'s cargo hatch just forward of the coil compartment, and was dashing after the retreating Groaci squadron.

"Ben!" Pokey's distressed voice came in echoey, on ten bands at once. "I thought it would be like my yacht, but it's got all these thermometers and clocks, instead of comforting green lights! I don't know if you can hear me or not. If you can, wave both arms."

Magnan immediately semaphored, peering upward at the skiff, which was now turning back toward its mother ship.

"Yes, that's it, Mr. Snail!" he cried. "One mustn't interfere with the rituals, of course. *Do* ground your skiff and we can have a nice drive back to town for the welcoming banquet."

"Look there, Magnan!" Pokey came back hotly. "The vandals have shot the '*In*' off my prow, so that it appears my vessel is '*Corruptible*'! Disgraceful!"

"I don't think anyone will notice, sir," Magnan gobbled, "if you'll withdraw her to the periphery of the carnival."

"I can't work that one, either," Pokey snapped. "My captain is incapacitated at the moment: poor chap was holding a bottle of some kind to his lips when the first salvo struck. He quite naturally jumped in startlement, and broke a tooth. The pain must be unbearable. Quacky gave him a shot, but it reacted badly with the .7 alcohol level in Cap's blood. He's unconscious, though still on his feet, swearing some perfectly *dread-ful* oaths! What's a 'gaboochie'? Pardon men if it's an obscenity I hadn't encountered before. This scamp ignores my orders, and insists we're under attack! Isn't that ridiculous?"

"That's pretty funny," Magnan agreed. "But if you'd just put that skiff down over here by the Customs hut, we could explain all the fine points of Gorm Festival to you. It's considered bad form actually to kill anyone, so you'll be safer here."

"I don't follow your reasoning, Ben," Pokey snarled. "Still, I'll try if I can figure out how to slow this thing down."

The group on the ground watched as the tiny ship-to-shore boat circled the port at high speed, then slowed and swooped in for a creditable belly-landing.

"Oh, dear," Magnan sighed. "I *do* hope he hasn't broached his hull-integrity with that in-violation touchdown."

Chapter 7

"I'll go see," Retief volunteered. He drove the line-cart back over to the still-hot *Goliath*-class, which seemed much bigger at rest than it had darting among the space leviathans still maneuvering above.

Retief rapped out an emergency-open code on the hull, and a circular hatch rotated, spun, dropped a ramp, and fell away. He climbed the access ramp and stepped inside. Magnan was trailing hesitantly. There was a rank odor of unwashed space'n and denatured alcohol. The passage was littered with issue gear, good scraps, and snippets of wire and tubing from what appeared to be hasty emergency repairs. A burly space'n in soiled whites with J. BLATSKI on the pocket emerged from behind a data-bank, and said:

"Who're you, sir? No unauthorized personnel authorized back here inna utility deck." He looked dubiously at Magnan.

"That's all right," Retief told him easily, returning a sloppy salute. "I wasn't planning on bringing anyone unauthorized."

"Oh, OK, just hadda say it," Blatski explained. "Doin' my job. Say, what's going on around here, anyways?

Looks like a war we stepped into, but the word is, it's just some kinda celebration. If it was me, I'd choose a clear lane and give the whole crew liberty."

"Good thinking, Chief," Retief agreed. "Let's start by pacifying Captain Muldoon. Where is he?"

"Him?" the husky CPO scoffed. "Ain't nobody gonna pacify Typhoon Muldoon when he's on a bender! Listen!" he cupped an ear dramatically. Retief heard distant yells and sounds as of things breaking.

"Anyways," the space'n went on, "I don't guess it's my job to say where he's at." He planted himself in the entryway as if to block it. His massive arms hung at his sides, and his vague expression had tightened into a scowl. "I ast you who you was," he reminded the civilian intruder. "I figgered maybe you was some kinda local big shot, reason I open up fer ya."

"You did just right," Retief assured the man, and socked him in the gut hard enough to bend him double, retching.

"Jeez," the victim groaned. "I never seen that one coming. And me a ex-fleet champeen."

"How about this one?" Retief inquired genially, and right-hooked the big fellow back into the space from which he had emerged. Retief stepped over him and went toward the sounds of carnage.

As Retief reached the compartment where the riot was in progress, Powerful Pete was dusting his hands and looking around. A burly rock-miner from Dobe, to judge from the dust that exploded from the seams of his aged overalls when he impacted, was in the act of tackling the lanky chieftain. Pete glanced down in annoyance and kneed the attacker's already well-battered face.

"I tole you, Bennie, I tole you and I tole you, don't do that flon tackle on nobody ain't asleep on his feet! Don't work good, *and* it smarts you some when you get the knee in the mush. Go clean yerself up, now, and come back here and do right!" Pete glanced apologetically at Retief. "Old Ben means good," he explained. "He just ain't real bright, is all. You got to excuse a fella can't learn nothin'."

"Such are the burdens of leadership, Pete," Retief reminded the discouraged boss-pirate.

"Sometimes," Pete confided, brushing a tooth fragment and a dust spot from his pants leg, "I get kinda discouraged. You try to teach yer fellers a few pointers, but they just ain't listenin'!" He ducked slightly to allow a booted leg to pass over his head, then half-turned to grasp the proffered member and upend a mountainous tube-scraper whose lumpy skull struck the stone floor with a dull *thud!* He subsided, snoring.

"Like poor old Maffy here," Pete continued. "Tried to cure him o' that, but he's still determined to get his two guck worth outa the mail-order ai-itchy-gugg course he sprung for."

"It's a nuisance," Retief agreed, as he sidestepped a haymaker thrown by a living testimonial to the relationship of man and gorilla. Pete back-kneed the fellow and said, "Excuse me, Retief. Don't mean to meddle none."

"It's quite all right, Pete," Retief assured the earnest ex-naval officer, over the din of battle. "What's it all about?" he inquired, glancing at the melee, which seemed to include not only local Insupportables and their sworn enemies, the Reprehensibles, but also stragglers from Promo's detachment, plus some refugees from the Indestructibles, a few of Colonel Switchback's irregulars, and a smattering of CDF personnel.

"Well," Pete drawled, "one o' my boys was talking into some rating offa Buck Promo's tub, and along comes a local name of Jum Derk, said he was in charge o' pacifying the area, an' he laid a han' on Dirty

Bimbo, that's my guy, and along come some guys looking fer some Sarge Thrash, and some way one of 'em accidentally tripped or like that, and right away them two locals jump him, and that's when I and my boys taken a hand. Trouble is, I don't remember who's on what side. Take this here loser, fer example." Pete indicated a three-hundred-pound half-bull/half-man diving from the affray directly toward him. He snap-kicked the snarling face, and Retief stepped back to allow the hurtling body to pass between them.

"He shoulda knowed better'n that," Pete commented sadly. "Another learnin'-impaired case. Say, Retief, you wanta excuse me a second?" With that, Pete waded in, caught a spidery little bronze-belt by his wide metal buckle and threw him aside, affording access to a pair of muscular bluish gnomes locked in mortal combat. Pete plucked them apart, held them at arm's length, and spoke sternly:

"Cheesy, and you, too, Peanut, you boys are both s'pose to be pulling for the CDF. I got a good mind to ship the both of ye back to Goblinrock in arns, that's what I got a good mind to!"

"Not that, Chief," Cheesy wailed, grabbing in vain for Peanut's groping arm. "Gimme one more chanst, and old Peanut too, and we'll show ya we're true-blue! Honest, we was just funnin'!"

"Funning, was ye, with work to be did?" Pete yelled, and threw the combative pair back into the riot. He sighed. "I dunno, Retief. Sometimes I feel like—"

"I know, Pete," Retief commiserated with the distraught pirate chief. "But you just get this little party quieted down, Pete. I've got an idea." He fended off one more attempted murder and turned back to tell Ben Magnan he was going to report to Inspector Snail.

"You propose to confront the Chief Inspector in that state of disarray?" Magnan gasped. "He'll suspect you've been personally involved in some sort of violence! It won't do, Jim! You know very well a Terran Foreign Service officer is supposed to be above such behavior! Still, if you're determined . . ." He dusted at Retief's lapel.

"I think it's best," Retief told his chief. "Otherwise he'll get excited and start giving orders."

"But whatever do you hope to accomplish?" Magnan persisted. "It's well-known that Pokey Snail is not amenable to reason!"

"That's what I'm counting on," Retief replied. "Any reasonable person would understand at once that we're in the middle of a couple of wars here. But old Pokey is primed to listen to any explanation that would let him off the hook. He doesn't like the idea of trying to report a war in his jurisdiction in a way that wouldn't make him look good."

"True," Magnan conceded worriedly. "But I still can't—"

"I'll be back in half an hour," Retief said. "With my shield or on it."

"Don't do anything *rash*," Magnan admonished.

"Right now," Retief reassured the anxious Magnan, "I can't think of anything that would qualify as rash, under the circumstances."

Magnan shied as the flaming wreckage of a two-man side-boat slammed into the hull nearby, causing a damage-control bulkhead to slam shut.

Retief waited until the centroid of violence above had passed on a few yards, then went to the nearest hatch.

He rapped out a GUTS priority tattoo on the duralloy panel, and after a few seconds it opened to reveal a sergeant with a squad of armed Marines awaiting his next move. Retief ushered Magnan in ahead of him.

"Oh, hi, Mr. Retief," the sergeant said around Magnan.

"What's up? Looks like that war we're s'pose to be preventing is already started without us."

"Not yet, Bill,' Retief replied. "They're just choosing up sides. I need to talk to Pokey. Where can I find him?"

"Cohen, you take the squad," Bill ordered the rangy corporal standing beside him. "Come on, Mr. Retief," he added. "I'll show you the way. This here tub has got more dead ends than a platoon o' Chinese Marines."

"Retief," Magnan stage-whispered, "you must never, *never* refer to Mr. Snail as 'Pokey' in the hearing of enlisted personnel!"

After following a meandering route from the stern to officers' country amidships, Bill indicated a bleached teak door. "He's in there," he told Retief, "if you really want to talk to him. But he's not in his normal jovial mood, I'll tell ya," he added. "You prolly noticed some o' these clowns are pulling live-ammo practice, practically in port, too. Pokey's pissed about that."

Retief thanked the sergeant and tapped at the door.

"You, too, Bill," Magnan rasped. "Never let him hear you call him 'Pokey'!"

A snarl came from within. Taking this as an invitation to enter, Retief did so, Magnan at his heels.

The paunchy Chief Inspector was sitting sunk deep in an Imperial-model Hip-u-matic chair behind a desk like a mahogany tennis-court. He looked up at Retief as if astonished. "Who the devil are *you*?" he demanded, not in a tone which suggested that it mattered.

"Retief, FSO-3, sir," was the reply. Pokey frowned, an effect like a near-space view of the Sierra Nevada. "Didn't you hear me say I was busy?" he growled.

"Nope, I must have missed that one, Pokey," Retief replied in a tone devoid of awe. He swung a chair around and sat in it.

"Ben Magnan's idea to come here?" Pokey barked, fixing a cold eye on the latter.

Retief nodded. "Not precisely," he said. "That is, he didn't actually forbid me to come."

"Well, I . . ." Magnan faltered.

"Humph!" was the chief inspector's response. "What's going on here?" he muttered. "Looks like a full-scale shooting war."

"We call it Gorm Festival, sir," Retief said casually.

"It can be quite disturbing to anyone not familiar with local customs," Magnan added comfortably.

Pokey slapped the blotter before him with enough force to cause his genuine plastic and solid gold pen-set to fall over. When the ill-tempered inspector had retrieved the last of the writing utensils from the carpet, he gave Magnan a withering look. "Are you suggesting," he demanded, "that I am not well-informed on the *mores* of the worlds falling within my jurisdiction? Why, only this morning I was rereading the section of the Post Report relevant to Gorm Festival! A joyous occasion, indeed! But I fear some of the celebrants are overenthusiastic! Colonel Wishbone, my armaments man, has informed me that, as I suspected, a number of actual hits have been scored directly on the hull of *Incorruptible*! Most careless! Is no one supervising the festivities?"

"Certainly, Pokey," Retief informed the increasingly wrathful FSO-1.

"But," Magnan put in, "as it happens, Pokey, the cap once had a bad experience with a Terry battle-wagon, so he's slipping in a few aimed shots."

"What's the idea calling me 'Pokey'?" the inspector yelled. "That's the kind of insolence with up which I will not put!"

"Sorry, sir," Magnan whimpered. "It's just an affectionate nickname, used by those who're privileged to serve with you."

"I don't need affection, Ben!" Pokey barked. "What I need is discipline!" Pokey rose to pace the width of the spacious office and return to confront Retief. "Now, you—Mr. Retief, isn't it? I expect you to put an end to this nonsense instantly! Do whatever's necessary, but stop it. Sector wouldn't understand!"

"Do hurry along and attend to that, Jim," Magnan encouraged. He offered Pokey a frail smile. "*So* high-spirited," he murmured indulgently.

"Refurbishing *Ruppy*'s hull will cost the corps a couple million guck, minimum!" Pokey barked. "There goes the fun-pit I'd slipped into my '89 Public Works Program! You should have read my Justification, Ben," Pokey enthused. "It was a masterpiece of subtle misdirection. Those silly chaps on the MCP review board were probably weeping by the time they finished reading it. Only half a million guck, too. But that's out of the question now. I must struggle along with the paltry quarter-million-guck facility already in place. Outrageous!" Pokey used a VIP-sized hanky to dab at his eyes. "Now back to business!

"Are you still here?" he demanded of Retief. "I thought I told you—"

"He was just going, P—sir," Magnan stammered. "Weren't you, Jim?"

"First," Retief stated firmly. "I need a document giving me full powers aboard this vessel."

"Preposterous!" Pokey yelled. "Why, that would mean, in effect, turning over command to you—right over Captain Muldoon's head, too! It won't do! Magnan!" The irate inspector turned on the shocked FSO-2. "See to this! Give him some sort of paper, short of resigning my commission! And keep Typhoon happy! Hurry up! The bombardment is growing more intense!"

" 'Full powers,' " Retief repeated. "Otherwise I couldn't order a mess-boy to empty an ashtray."

"Why in the world would you want to bother with

ashtrays at a time like this?" Pokey thundered. He ripped open a drawer, pulled out a stack of elaborately embossed forms, entered *Retief* and *Full Powers* in the appropriate spaces on one, embossed a seal and handed it over.

"Jim," Magnan quavered. "You *will* be prompt, I hope, and careful?"

"My idea exactly," Retief returned cheerfully. He left the cabin, passed through empty passages, rode the lift down to Power Deck, and collared a burly rating who was buckling on a sidearm.

"You won't need that, Chief," Retief told him, tossing the weapon into the recycler. "All in fun, you know. Our job is to show a little muscle and convince them it's time to pack up their toys and go home."

"I seen Buck Promo's outlaw outfit in there," the noncom replied. "Neat, huh? 'Outlaw *out*fit.' But he ain't the boy to take no orders from a CPO."

"I'll take care of that part," Retief said easily. "Just get your PE up to a quarter-gen and I'll take it from there."

"A quarter-gen!" the space'n repeated. "Jeez! That's what the Manual calls for 'Stand By for Class Four Action'! Cap Muldoon—"

"The captain is indisposed," Retief mentioned.

"Yeah, I heard him," Muldoon's voice barked from the squawk-box. "Now hear this! This here's the captain, you deck-apes! I got a idea we're in a ambush, you can bet your left hind gaboochie on it!"

"Keep alert," Retief reminded the chief, and went on to Secondary Control.

The duty NCOIC was sitting at a desk, sneaking a lavender Groaci dope-stick and gazing mournfully at his desk console. He looked up as Retief entered, dispensed with the butt and got to his feet. His nameplate read S. BLATSKI—a relative, apparently, of the sloppy space'n on the utility deck.

"Don't allow no civilians on Secondary," he grated.

"Right!" Retief agreed. "Glad to see you're doing a job, Blatski. I'm just checking to make sure everything's in order here."

"Sure is, sir!" Blatski gobbled. "All loads homed and locked and all circuits deader'n a Floorian mud-eater in air! I been with *Ruppy* since she was launched. Was in the scrap off Coldcock where we done the rebels brown; and I taken part in that there invasion of Goblinrock, too. She never lost a rumble, and now some civilian—no offense—gives orders for her to go into action with her board dead! It ain't right! I gotta good mind—there! Another hit astern! Good thing them Groaci don't know how to handle hard stuff or she'd be holed by now. All they'd have to do is pour concentrated Class-two fire into the weak spot aft of the fore lazaret."

"Easy, Blatski," Retief urged. "It's not just the Groaci; in fact Admiral Foof is only doing a job of ceremonial escorting. *All* these fellows are lobbing shots at this tub."

"What for?" Blatski demanded. "We're—well, we're on this here peacekeeping mission and all. Ain't hardly fired a shot in anger at nobody! Can't. She's decommissioned! Looky here." The aggrieved Blatski led the way to a massive yellow-painted panel secured by a loop of wire with a deeply embossed plaster seal. "Closed off tight," he carped. "If I could get at them stern battery controls, I'd show them hillbillies it ain't a good idea to fire on *Ruppy*, even in fun!"

"What do you mean 'closed up right'?" Retief asked.

"Lookit this here," Blatski grumbled, fingering the garish orange-colored seal. "Says, 'Use of this installation interdicted by order of the Council. Paragraph 12–2 applies.' Jeez! That's where it says anybody messes with it gets a DH and two hunrit years on Judson's Hell. Meaning you get buried there." Blatski, impressed, stepped well back from the forbidden panel.

"Funny fellows, those paper-pushers back at Sector," Retief remarked. "They think a piece of paper and a blob of plastic are as effective as a fleet of heavy battle-wagons."

"Take that to put *Ruppy* out o' action," Blatski agreed. "But—" He uttered a strangled cry as Retief's hand went to the seal and ripped it away. An adjacent red glare-strip lit up, blinking EMERGENCY.

"Chief," Retief addressed the astounded gunner. "Lay a trajectory through that madhouse out there that will give all of 'em a good look at a Terry dreadnought with her battle-board lit up."

"Sure would love to," Blatski replied doubtfully. "But Cap Muldoon—"

"The captain is having French fits at the moment," Retief told him. "I'm handling the con right now."

He showed the document signed by Snail to the non-com, who at once snapped-to. "Permission to man the fire control box, sir," he said eagerly.

Retief said, "Do it."

Magnan came rushing in at that moment. "There you are!" he cried. "Jim! See here—I've been looking all over for you, but . . . things are chaotic aboard this vessel!" he declared. "It's disgraceful. And that Captain Muldoon! I do declare he's been drinking! Oh, as you were, Space'n!" he addressed Blatski, having just noticed the big fellow busy at the forbidden panel. A low-pitched rumble caused the deck plates to vibrate.

"Jim!" he yelped. "If it weren't so ridiculous, I'd think that was the coil start-up! You know how the accelerator rumbles as it bleeds off torque!" He grabbed for support as the deck tilted underfoot. "Help! Jim! That drunken captain is lifting off with me—us, that is—still aboard! And there's a battle raging—"

"Gorm Festival, you mean," Retief commented. "Let's strap in." He led the way to the shock-mounted bench provided for redundant personnel during maneuvers.

S. Blatski joined them. "Old Chief Hoon in Power is right on the ball, I gotta give him that," he grunted. "Had the pre-coil hot and ready to go. Seems like the paper that desk-johnny stuck in it back at Depot musta fell off someways. I got a good course punched in, Mr. Retief. Oh, hi, sir," he said to Magnan, and offered a callused hand. "I'm Gunner Stan Blatski. Glad you boys changed yer minds."

"To be sure," Magnan murmured. "So glad to be here, Mr. Blatski. But just what's happening? I understood . . ."

"Well, I gotta get set to show them locals boys where the power's at," the gunner replied. "We're just taking up a position where I can command all the excape trajecks, and then I guess Mister Retief here has got a few words to say to them rebels, or dacoits, or guerrillas, or whatever you wanta call 'em. Buck Promo, too. He messed up bad; he's busted all the regs they got, and picked the wrong side, too. Par' me, I gotta have a word with Hoon. He's only a Hoogan, got to give him his orders kind of in detail, if you know what I mean." He released his shock frame, rose hurriedly and went to the action board and began poking keys and yelling, "Breaker for Hoon!"

"Jim," Magnan addressed his colleague in a confidential tone. "I fear the chief may interpret your remarks as authorizing him to take offensive action directed against the revelers!"

"Don't start believing your own alibis, sir," Retief suggested. "It's only a matter of time before one of those boys realizes he only has to concentrate fire on the fore ballast bay, where the hull armor's broached for the cable conduit. They'll crack her wide open. We have to *do* something, fast!"

"Well, if you really think . . ." Magnan offered, edging away as if to disassociate himself from such unruliness in the eye of an omniscient observer.

Retief went to the locator panel and studied the disposition of the swarming vessels through which *Corruptible* was now moving ponderously. All units had prudently drawn back, with the exception of Promo's little detachment of Navy sideboats and tenders.

"Better shave about an inch off the prow of that tanker," Retief told Blatski. "Just a graze, now. Can you do it?"

"Me? Gunner Blatski?" the super exclaimed as if amazed at the query. "Look, pal, I don't know nothing about the calculus, not even why they say 'the,' instead of just 'calculus,'" he declared, "but when it comes to laying down the fire, boss, I does *that* thing!" He went to work, deftly spinning dials with his left hand, reading LEDs, correcting, reading again, while his right hand played the keys of the fire control board like a Sunday School organist trying out with a Rocky Mountain combo.

Retief stood aside and watched the DV panel. Magnan fluttered like an anxious mother bird whose nest is being disturbed. At last, Blatski turned to Retief and said, "Fire in the tube, sir!"

Retief responded by playing a tune of his own on the keyboard. Blatski uttered a grunt. "Geeze, I didn't know you was a gunnery officer, sir," he blurted. "Academy, too, I guess: You fined that down to a RCH. Closer'n I woulda done. Let's just hope—!" He darted to the target observation screen to watch as a burst of false-color flared at the prow of the zillion-tonner Retief had designated.

Retief, meanwhile, had activated the needle-beam talker and focused it amidships on the tanker. "Heave to. The officer in command will report to me at once, via fat beam."

"Uh," came the hesitant reply. There was a penetrating _zing_/ing in the background. "I can't hear good," the voice went on. "That damn graze got my whole command ringing like a cracked bell! Wait a minute, I got to—"

"Pull that bladder out of formation, and fall it in on my starboard bow," Retief ordered. "The next one will be a little closer." Blatski started to protest, but thought better of it and hastened to issue the appropriate order.

"Hey!" Powerful Pete's voice cut through the clutter. "That's you, ain't it, Retief, conning old _Ruppy_? What's up? My boys are getting spooked: looks like yer taking up the Hot Spot, got everybody under yer guns and vice versa!"

"You got that right, Pete," Retief confirmed. "I have to make it clear to all hands that I'm not making suggestions when I tell them to fall back and revert to Status White."

" 'White'?" Pete echoed in a horrified tone. "That means go to standby power, close down the battle circuitry, open all screens and stand by!"

"Right again, Pete. I'm counting on you and your command to set a good example. Now!"

"I ain't got what you'd call a command, except for old _Cockroach III_ here, o' course," Pete protested. "The Cluster Defense Force is a voluntary association of independent ship-owners! I can't _order_ these boys!"

"Try it," Retief suggested.

"Well . . ." Pete's voice hesitated. "Dirty Bimbo," he resumed, "you can pull back ten miles and go dead in space."

At once, a shabby, partly black-painted garbage scow still baring the faintly visible legend "_New York_

Sanitation Dept.," fell out of formation and streaked for deep space.

"Worked pretty good," Pete commented. "Now, Nasty Jack! You do like old Bimbo, and do it snappy!" Pete proceeded to contact Yang, Ma Cutthroat, Princess Sally, Boss Nandy, Tinkerbell, and a few other of his most trusted captains, then declaimed a general order to the rest of the CDF, which responded promptly.

"Form them up in an Oort, using a Standard Number Nine coverage," Retief directed.

"Hey, Retief," Pete protested. "You know I don't know nothing about textbook tactics!"

"I know you were third in your class at the Academy," Retief reminded the superficially uncouth space tramp. "Let's get this show on the road."

"Aye, sir," Pete mumbled, and returned to his duties. There was a stir at the entry lock and Superchief Blatski sprang to his feet and yelled, "Shunt!"

A bleary-eyed man of middle age, dressed carelessly in a blue-baker officer's blouse, white space'n's bell-bottoms, and an old Marine campaign hat staggered into view, waving an almost empty bottle. "What's going on here?" he roared, and hiccuped. "You can't fool me! My command here is clearing for action! My battle station is on the bridge, of course, but first I got to see— Oh, hi, Chief," he interrupted himself. "Glad to see you're in charge, but who're these civilians?"

"Captain Muldoon, sir," Blatski managed, his rigid posture of attention almost locking up his breathing. "This here's one o' them diplomats you invited aboard. He's stopping a little war, it seems like."

"Oh. That's swell," Muldoon replied. "That way I don't hafta bother. What's all the excitement about, anyway? Somebody's lobbing ineffective fire at us, did you know that? Amateurs, don't know what they're doing, bouncing Class-four stuff off *Ruppy*'s stern-plates. Waste o' time and ammunition. You boys fixing to blast 'em out of space, or what?" The captain, not so drunk after all, wandered over to the DV screen and nodded.

"I see yer setting up a Oort, eh? Good idea. We can clear 'em out like a dose o' salts does a case of spaceguts! About ready to open fire, are you? Good! I like to watch old *Ruppy* in action. Usually can't see much on that little screen on A deck. This one's better. Got scope! Boy, oh, boy, look at that Groaci gunboat go! He's hightailing it for dirtside! You going to let him go?"

"Absolutely, Cap'n, sir, good idea," Blatski replied. "What I'm tryna do here, I'm tryna get all these freebooters—Promo, too—to line up orderly and—"

"Easy, sir," Blatski interrupted himself. "Why don't you just set down here, Cap'n, and we'll take care of everything, just like you said."

"Chief Blatski!" Muldoon roared. "Now hear this: I've got important orders." He paused and yelled impressively, "Splice the main brace—all hands, mind you!"

"What in the world does he mean?" Magnan queried.

"Means 'issue a tot of rum all around,'" Retief supplied. Blatski went to a double-padlocked wall-locker, opened the door with a deft twist, leaving the big Yale in place, and took out a blackish bottle.

"Hey, you!" Muldoon roared. "What's the idea, Stan, messing with the classified supplies? Bring that here!"

"Sir," Blatski offered, "you said to splice the main brace."

"Sure I did!" the captain agreed readily. "Start with me; I haven't had a snort for five minutes!"

"Jim," Magnan said anxiously, "we have to *do* something, *now*, before he gets out of hand and starts ordering the troops into battle!"

Retief studied the big all-around screen, which afforded a view of a ten-mile sphere of space, centered on the AR transmitter aboard *Ruppy*. It showed the formerly freely-darting vessels of the four mutually hostile task forces arranged in a twenty-mile sphere with *Corruptible* at the center.

"Ye gods!" Muldoon yelled. "We're in the hot spot! They've pulled off a textbook englobement! They can pour concentrated fire into us from all quarters at once! Abandon ship!"

"Easy, Captain," Retief urged. "It also means we can fire in any direction and hit pay-dirt. Hold the panic button. I'll have a word with them."

"This is no time for diplomacy!" Muldoon declared wrathfully. "The time has come, gents, for action. Chief Blatski: fire all batteries at will!" Muldoon sank back to his stool and resumed splicing his main brace.

Retief spoke into the all-band talker. "Attention all captains," he called. "You're under *Ruppy*'s guns, as you can see, but I'll try to persuade the captain not to use them, if you can ground your vessels in good order, due east of the port. Pete, you ride herd on this maneuver and see they set them down in orderly rows, prow-to-stern."

"You heard Jim Retief," Pete's voice growled. "Now, do it, you miserable space-sweepings, before I get my dander up and start squirting low-R nukes right up yer tailpipes! Go!"

The dispersed vessels coagulated into neatly ranked formations and dropped toward the broad plain far below. They slowed on entering atmosphere, a few prows with inadequate shielding glowing white-hot for a few moments as they dropped lower and went over to airfoils. They spread out, took up parking formations, and settled in, rank on rank. At high-M, Retief could see crowds of people streaming out along the roads from the city and forming up in an immense mob along the security fence of the port.

"Jim, we've got to get down there fast," Magnan blurted. "Before there's another unfortunate misunderstanding."

"Look here, Mr. Retief," Pokey's harsh voice rasped from the squawk-box. "What's going on here? Something seems to have disrupted the festival, and before I got video footage of the hijinks for my files, too!"

"It's quite all right, sir!" Magnan caroled. "The carnival will resume as soon as the crowd reaches the debarking crews!"

"Pete," Retief called, "you'd better look for a fellow named Wim Dit: He's handling the ground-based phase of the festival down there. Keep him calm and tell him there'll be a fresh distribution of play-pretties as soon as he's shown me a properly organized welcoming celebration for all his new allies. He'll be notified of the location of the handout as soon as I see the lion lying down with the lamb."

" 'The Insupportable lying down with the Unspeakable' would be more to the point," Magnan sniffed. "Jim, do you really think . . . ?"

Chapter 8

With a clatter of polished boots on unpolished deck-plates, Chief Inspector Pokey Snail appeared personally on the scene. When an elaborate, stagey throat-clearing failed to elicit an instant response, he declaimed, "Ah, Ben, it just occurred to me—silly idea, of course, that vessel being as it is decommissioned—that some hothead among the celebrants might somehow receive the impression that *Incorruptible* might in some fashion represent a threat, and thus inspire retaliatory action in advance: an attack, that is. So wouldn't it be prudent to offer our immediate surrender, so as to defuse such a dreadful potentiality before the fact? Now, a simple document would be best, I think: something along the lines of, 'The Chief Inspector in charge of the VIP Transport (ex-battlewagon) *Incorruptible* requests an accommodation with all groups now engaged in the celebration. While it is true that certain trifling regulations have been broached by the inattentive among you'—here I refer to the bombardment to which I was subjected—'I understand that it was all in the joyous spirit of Gorm, and I give assurance—'"

He broke off as Magnan interrupted: "Oh, sir. Is this the *simplified* form of your proposal?"

"To be sure, Ben," Pokey replied affably. "Perhaps I was getting a bit carried away, but I'm sure you get the idea: we come on like a bunch of boobs and con these hillbillies into grounding their vessels where they can do no more accidental harm—then we move into zenith and show them where the power is. I suspect a prize court would settle a respectable sum on those responsible for such a coup, in addition to the pleasing glow of satisfaction we'll all experience at having escaped alive from this ridiculous contretemps: barging into the middle of carnival time, as if—at *your* insistence, Ben—as if we had no conception of respect for the quaint native customs of emergent, ah, developing, er, inferior, that is, peoples."

"Do you think they'd go for a simple-minded gambit like that?" Magnan inquired of Retief, who shook his head.

"Let's ask them," he suggested, then, to the talker, "Pete, how does it sound to you?"

"Oh, that darn off-key again!" Magnan complained. "Do you suppose the uncouth fellow heard the whole thing?"

"Damn right, Ben," Pete replied promptly. "And unfortunately for hopes of pacification of the unruly element, so did the rest o' the boys."

"But they *do* understand," Pokey put in quickly, "that I'm offering unconditional surrender?"

"That's cool," Pete acknowledged, "but the part about the prize court sounds a little crafty. But anyway, if you wanna surrender, go ahead. Close them gun ports and set her down nice. I'll try to keep the boys in line. The Groaci, too—and even Buck Promo. Remember, Retief, I got no control over them auxiliaries."

"I'll bet you could think of something, Pete," Retief encouraged.

"Damn right," Pete muttered, and flipped keys.

"All right, you volunteers!" he boomed. "I got no objection you wanna get in on the fun, but *I'm* War Chief around here! That means you, too, Buck! I know you useta be a admiral and all, but you quit yer job, remember! Now, lay offa the tough stuff and hit the deck, right now, or I'll hafta—" He broke off and punched another button. On the screen, a blue-white fireball appeared adjacent to Promo's flagship. The cruiser did a snappy vertical one-eighty and dropped away, its subordinates in line astern.

"Hey, you, Admiral Foof—yeah, I reckernize you, you five-eyed little ulsio! I'm giving you one chance: get outa this *now*, and put down east o' the rest o' the boys! Get going, or—"

"To stay your hand, Pete," the Groaci's breathy voice came back. "To see that blister you raised on Buck Promo's favorite play-toy! I'm going! To just take it easy!"

"Hey, you, Brag Gab—back off, there!" Pete yelled. "No fair tryna sneak up on them Five-eyes whilst they're in compliance!" Pete continued, muttering: ". . . dumb swabbie! Shun't have command of a GI mop, much less a attack group! But no use griping: I got work to do, getting out o' this without starting a war right under Pokey's nose!" He turned his attention to Retief. "Whattaya think, Retief? Can I trust that long-nosed pencil-pusher?"

"Not on your life," Retief replied promptly, as Magnan bleated:

"Would you impugn the integrity of a CDT inspector-general?"

"Sure would, Ben," Pete confirmed. "You heard the little weasel good as me."

" 'As well as I' would be the preferable formulation! Magnan countered sharply, "the first-person pronoun being as it is the subject of the verb 'to hear'! Still, I grasp your meaning. Pokey did, indeed appear to be suggesting a highly questionable course of action, eternal-chumship-wise!" He appealed to Retief: "Jim, can't we *do* something to prevent Inspector Snail's betrayal of all the poor fellows who repose confidence in his assurances?"

"I don't see any sign of anybody reposing any confidence in his assurances," Retief pointed out. "All participants in the carnival are still Gorming away as if he hadn't lied to them at all."

"That's *some* consolation," Magnan breathed. "But Pokey will be furious. Won't you, Pokey?" he appealed to the glaring inspector.

"Indeed I am, Ben!" Snail grated. "I fear your excessive squeamishness is likely to have interfered with the harmonious exercise of my professional peacemaking virtuosity! Kindly keep out of this! Now, you, Chief Blatski, I want you to run out the battle flag, just to shake these fellows up a bit, you understand; they don't know our battle-board is sealed."

"Ha!" Blatski exulted. "Watch this, fellows!" He slammed home a big red-striped knife-switch, at which the dim-lit battle-board lit up in a blaze of cherry idiot-lights. On the external-inspection screen, *Ruppy's* battle colors were now glowing in a bright pattern all along her mighty hull.

"Looks great, don't it, Cap?" Blatski shouted.

Muldoon was waving his empty rum bottle and yelling: "That's a glorious sight, Chief! Never thought I'd see it again! That's why I took to boozing!"

He glared at the flask in his hand and threw it from him. "From now on, it's straight Battle Procedures all the way, right out of the Manual!" he declared in a ringing tone.

"You got to hand it to Cap," Blatski confided loudly to Magnan. "He got a iron gut on him: he can swill

that Groaci near-rum all day, and straighten up in a
second when old *Ruppy*'s board lights up!

"Aye, sir!" he continued. "All batteries laid and all
personnel at action stations. Just like it says in Section
I: 3a!"

"Hold your fire, Chief," the captain growled. He
glared at Magnan as if seeing him for the first time.
"What are these civilians doing here at such a
moment?" he barked.

"What sort of moment was that, Captain?" Magnan
inquired earnestly. "We're from the Embassy; we're
observing Gorm Festival, of course. Quaint native customs are one of my chief subsidiary interests."

Muldoon jerked his rumpled tunic straight and patted his braided lapels, glancing at the array of screens
showing war vessels on all sides.

"Looks like an ambush to *me*!" he barked. His eyes
went to the battle-board. "She's lit!" he yelled. "I don't
know how, but old *Ruppy*'s ready to take on all com-
ers! Start with that yellow Groaci Thousand-tonner
doing a sneak away from the field of Battle, Stan," he
ordered.

Blatski hesitated, looking uncertainly at Magnan.
"But, Cap'n, sir," he bleated. "Mister Magnan said—
I mean, it's not what it looks like! The Groaci are
our chums now! They're helping us celebrate Gorm
Festival, like Mister Magnan said! I'd hate to be the
one—"

"You'll hate to be Superchief Stanislav Blatski if you
don't get on the ball, you damn fool!" Muldoon told
him harshly. "Do it, now! Are you a trained fighting
man, or what?"

"You bet, Cap'n sir," Blatski confirmed eagerly. "I
been through the old NCO school at Annapolis and
everything! Flunked chumship, though," he confessed.
"That's why I'm not a admiral now."

"Lucky," Muldoon dismissed the plaint. "Admirals—

and captains, too—hold responsibilities that the rank and file never dreamed of! Like me: I've got to figure out how to keep *Ruppy* in one piece, and at the same time pacify that Embassy Johnny who was bugging me a moment ago!" He looked left and right. "Where'd he go?" he yelled. "I'd like to give that damn bureaucrat a piece of my mind! I'll—"

"He's standing right behind you, sir," Blatski got in hastily. Muldoon spun and stared down at Magnan.

"Don't pussyfoot around my power deck—if you don't mind," he amended more temperately. "I've got too much on my plate, right now, to be trying to keep up with snoopers poking their noses in where— Shaddup!" he ordered his mouth. Magnan was jotting busily in a spiral-bound pad; he looked brightly at Muldoon.

"Pity," he murmured. "I didn't catch that, Captain. The noise from the screens, you know."

"That's OK," Muldoon assured him. "Just highly technical stuff a da—civilian wouldn't understand. Now, Blatski," he breezed on. "Just ease *Ruppy* over among those garbage scows there, and—"

"That's the Cluster Defense Force, sir," Blatski explained. "Meanest bunch o' privateers in this or any Arm."

"Tell 'em to heave to," Muldoon grunted. "If they hesitate, take out the one with the big red Coke ad on the side. Damn stuff gives me gas!"

"That'd be the flagship, sir," Blatski informed his captain. "Fella name o' Powerful Pete aboard her. He ain't noted for his patience."

"Bother his patience!" Muldoon bellowed. "Hit him hard!" Just then the putative target did a neat one-eighty and swelled on the screen, coming close to *Ruppy*'s mighty flank. Muldoon motioned urgently to Blatski.

"Oh, I wouldn't, sir," Magnan twittered.

"Sure you wouldn't!" the captain agreed. "But you're not Clarence (Typhoon) Muldoon! Stan! Do your duty!"

"Well, sir," Blatski replied as if unwillingly, "I can't see her on my screens right now. Whereat is she?"

"She's got in my dead space!" Muldoon yelled. "Can't get at her with the main batteries, and too high for the anti-personnel charges to clear out! We've got to do a snap-roll. Blatski, order all hands to secure for a Fido!"

"Jeez, sir!" Blatski protested. "That's liable to mess up everything! Last time you did that, Chief Ying never did get the chow sorted out again. Spaghetti and lobster sauce ain't too good, sir!"

"Blatski—!" Typhoon started.

"Bob Ying's the best cook inna Navy, sir," Blatski reminded his captain. "How's about we just skip the Fido?"

"Well, I was only kidding," Muldoon relented. "We'll do a dead slow instead, and blast 'em when they scoot out ahead of us!"

"That's some better," Blatski muttered, "but when I brake, all the loose gear aboard is gonna hit the bulkhead like a avalanche."

"Got to do *something*," Muldoon pointed out, "or they'll have a prize crew aboard here before you can say, 'Man the lifeboats'!"

"Uh-oh," Blatski said hoarsely, cocking his blunt head to watch a series of yellow lights flashing on the Hull Integrity panel. "They're aboard, sir! What'll I—?"

"Just step back away from that battle-board, Chief," the rasping voice of Powerful Pete supplied.

All heads turned. The rangy CDF chief was standing in the entry, holding a 2mm casually aimed at Muldoon's knee. "Cap," he addressed Muldoon, "you better go lay down on the Duty NCO's cot. I got to have a few words with Blatski. Hi, Retief," he interrupted himself. "Sorry if I'm butting in, but—"

"No problem," Magnan assured the dacoit. "We—Jim Retief and I—were just doing a little job of salvaging a Chief Inspector's career, nothing important. Now, what do you think we should do, to prevent these fellows from savaging each other—and us, too, in the process—to the detriment of peace and order here in the System?"

Pete's eyes went to the battle-board. "Lit up like Macy's Christmas tree," he murmured. "I heard . . . What you waiting for, Chief?" he demanded of the Master Gunner.

"Well, these fellows"—Blatski indicated the civilians—"said—"

"Don't pay no mind to Ben Magnan," Pete growled. "He's only interested in saving water while the house burns down."

"We got plenty water," Blatski blurted. "Tanked up to the max back at depot!"

"He's not talking about water, Stan," Muldoon contributed. "What he means is, *Ruppy*'s board's lit, and we've got ideal targets out there, and you're qualified as a Master Gunner! So . . . what's the delay?"

"Hold it!" Retief said as Blatski turned to the fire-control panel. "I'm going to talk to Buck Promo." He went to the com cubicle with its array of lighted dials and selected Promo's frequency.

"Admiral Promo," he called. "This is the flagship talking. I want you to form your command in a space'nlike manner and escort Colonel Switchback's units to the designated parking area."

"Yeah, I hear you," Promo came back. "That *is* you, Muldoon, I guess. Well, *I'm* admiral here, and I say—"

Retief punched a red button on his panel, and broke off as a thunderous detonation drowned Promo's voice.

"What—?" the admiral blurted when the echoes had faded. "Hold on, Typhoon!" he yelled. "I'm doing it, as fast as I can, ain't I!"

"Heavens!" Magnan twittered. "What do you suppose—?"

"I just used the special-effects circuit to startle him a little," Retief explained.

"That man's a deserter!" Muldoon barked. "But he's still trying to come on like an admiral! I ought to put him under arrest! In fact—"

"Later," Retief suggested as the now cold-sober captain opened his mouth to precipitate disaster.

Muldoon subsided. Then, "Don't let him get away, now I've got him under my guns," he muttered. "The rest of these jaybirds, too! I can round up the lot of 'em and make points at Headquarters!"

"The matter is well in hand," Retief soothed. "Just lie down, now, sir, and let Chief Blatski get on with his work." He led the confused officer to the alcove where the Duty NCO cot waited, and the portly skipper flopped on it and went to sleep.

"Well!" an irascible voice spoke up from the direction of the union-mandated coal bunker. "I *do* declare! Such a scene of disorder I've never witnessed." Heads turned; a small, not to say stunted fellow in a pale puce CDT early late mid-morning dickey-suit was advancing, brushing coal-dust from his seat. "Just look at that screen there!" he squealed. "It's war, open and notorious! What are you going to do?" His remarks seemed to be addressed equally to the chief inspector, the diplomats, and Chief Blatski.

"It's Reggie Mascot," Magnan whispered audibly in the mounting silence. "Jim, he's known even to his fellow sneaks in the Division of Inspections as an insidious nosy parker and tell-tale!"

"Indeed?" Reggie chirped. His eyes went to Pokey.

"And what have *you* to say to that assault on our noble division, sir?" he demanded.

"Easy, Ben," the chief inspector urged, advancing toward Mascot. "Why, Reg, old boy, whatever were you doing in the coal-bin?"

"Not in compliance," Mascot muttered. "Almost empty." He jotted further, mouthing the words, "Chief Inspector indifferent to slurs cast on revered Inspector of Inspectors . . ."

"We don't use no coal," Blatski pointed out defensively. "That's just the union . . ."

"The Union," Mascot declared loudly, "has a well-financed lobby, which has secured legislation requiring not only a coal-bin and coal, but a coal-heaver aboard all capital ships of the Navy!"

"Everybody knows that's just for the union," Blatski muttered.

"Chief Inspector countenances breaking of regs, as well as offering insult to the Inspector General," Mascot muttered as he jotted.

"That's a damn lie!" Pokey yelled. "I never said word one about that old basilisk!"

" 'Old Basilisk,' " Reggie scribbled and closed his notebook with a brisk *snap!* He looked around greedily, like a canary-fed cat looking for his next snack. "You, there, 'Blatty' or whatever that name-plate says," he barked. "Now you get over there and rearrange that anthracite. It's untidy in the extreme!"

Stan looked mournfully toward the alcove where Muldoon's snores had ceased abruptly.

"No damn civilian is going to put my master gunner on detail!" the captain's voice roared as he thrust out past the stiff GI canvas curtain shielding the cubbyhole.

He stamped across to thrust his face into Mascot's. "And who in nine hells are *you*, Mister?" he shouted.

Reggie retreated like a paper cutout caught in a sudden gust. "Why, as to that," he squeaked, "I'm

Reginald P. Mascot, CDTO-1, working directly out of
Sector, and I'd like—"

"Stan," Muldoon addressed the non-com, "put this
little pipsqueak in irons, if you've got any irons; I don't
know what the union has to say about irons."

"Says we got to have 'em aboard, sir," Blatski supplied. "But Navy regs say they hafta be locked up in
the captain's safe, sir!"

"Oh, yes, I remember seeing them last time I had
to splice the main brace," Typhoon agreed, nodding.
"I'll go get them."

"Sir, permit *me!*" Blatski offered.

Muldoon shook his head. "You don't have the entry
codes, Stan," he reminded his subordinate.

"Sure, I do, sir!" Blatski corrected. "After all, us
crew got to splice the main brace once in a while,
too!"

"I thought the classified supplies were dwindling a
little faster than personal consumption could account
for." The captain nodded. "OK, you go get the irons,
Stan, and I'll try to find out what this nosy little sucker
is doing on my Secondary Command deck in the middle of a ba—Gorm Festival," he offered.

" 'Gorm Festival'?" Mascot blurted. "Do you mean
to suggest that this war is only—"

"Steady, Reg," Snail put in quickly. "We wouldn't
want these good people to gain the grotesque impression that we, as inspectors, are inadequately briefed
as to local customs."

"Local customs?" Mascot asked in a tone of Total
Disbelief at the Impossible (1091-b).

"Am I to understand," Pokey Snail demanded in a
tone like the Würm Glaciation, "that you intend to
imply that a Special Observer from Sector is unac-
quainted with the colorful *mores* of the peoples falling
within his interest cluster?"

He turned gravely to Magnan. "The captain has

seen fit to place this officer under arrest," he recapitulated. "And I see no reason to interfere. Where the heck is Stan with those irons?"

"Right here, sir," Blatski responded as he arrived, puffing. He displayed a chrome-plated restraint, VIP, for the use of. "Cun't find the delocker," he reported. "Once on, they stay on till we get the sucker back to Sector."

"By the way, Ben," Snail remarked, "I've been thinking: a word in the ear of Grand Inquisitor Wim Dit at this point might be advisable. He can assess the grounded fleets with port charges, landing fees, debarkation licenses, usage tax, and a few other little surprises I'll think up for him. Ten percent will go to the CDT Foundation's sinking fund, of course—"

"But, sir!" Magnan protested. "They wouldn't sit still for it! They'd defy Dit and probably open fire on his mob! The mob would respond in kind, and—gosh, sir, I can hardly bear to consider consequences!"

"I read you five by five," Wim Dit's gluey voice came from the G-to-S talker. "Good notion! Plus they been piling up demurrage fer three days! I'll squeeze the suckers plenty!"

"Oh, sir," Magnan wailed. "The fat's in the fire for sure!"

"Pity and all that," Pokey replied coldly. "You heard me, Ben! Otherwise you wouldn't be whining in that peculiarly irritating fashion. Do it! Get this Dit fellow on your talker again, and confirm the order! Judging from the data from the scanner, that army, or crowd or whatever he has with him is big enough (ten thousand, the analyzer estimates) to make even half-a-dozen combat teams pay attention. Good job they're not armed! Or perhaps they are by now: I noticed on the hot-line that a shipment of handguns destined for the constabulary on Krako 8 was hijacked just hours ago."

"Disaster!" Magnan yelped. "Pokey! Or, 'Sir!' I mean! Do you realize that once the Abominables have access to weapons, they'll embark on a program of genocide, starting with Objectionables, then their Special Enemies—the Insupportables—and the Viles will come in to support the Insupportables—"

"Contradiction in terms, Ben," Pokey put in impatiently. "And by the way, it's most unprofessional of you to refer to these deserving local groups by the unflattering epithets you've employed!"

"Oh, no, sir," Magnan whined, "that's their real names—they're proud of being Execrables, or Abominables, and so on!"

"Excuses, Ben, excuses," Snail intoned, jotting. "Let's get this show on the road, Magnan."

"Oh, you already did, sir," Magnan hastened to assure the senior official. "You see, we have this bad TALK switch, and, heck, a fellow can't keep a secret if he wanted to!"

"That's cool, Ben," Pokey approved. "My conscience is clear. Now, as soon as this General Wim—"

"He's a civilian, sir," Magnan put in. "Grand Inquisitor, actually."

"As I was *attempting* to say, *Mis*ter Magnan," Pokey resumed grandly. "When General Dit has completed the collection of port fees, we'll set *Ruppy* down and confiscate and take! Is that bad switch open?" he concluded.

Magnan nodded eagerly.

"Don't look pleased, dammit, Ben!" Pokey snapped. "If they know the game plan, they might prove obstreperous. It will be better to keep it low-key until the moment when we drop the mask and show them the naked power of Terra!"

"Sure, sir," Magnan replied, trying the OFF key hopefully. The idiot light showed ALL STATIONS COPYING. "Damn!" he exclaimed. "That means Dit is going to come waltzing up to Sarge Thrash and demand his exorbitant fees. Thrash will throw him out, and the mob will close in on the heavily armed pirate crews just debarking, and Armageddon will result! What are we to do?"

"Don't ask me for substantive guidance in the performance of your duly assigned mission, Magnan!" Snail snapped. "I am here solely in the role of Official Observer!"

"But it was you that thought up this diabolical plan and then spilled the beans to not only Wim Dit and his army, but to Switchback and Buck Promo and the rest, as well!" Magnan wailed.

"Critical," Pokey noted in his pad, then scratched it out and replaced it with "Stubborn. Rejects Corps policy: hesitates to perform duties! Openly accuses superior of criminal incompetence." He snapped the book shut. "I guess that's that," he commented. "Well, Ben, it was an interesting career while you had it, eh?" He neglected to offer to shake hands before he strode from the Power Deck.

"Jim, did you hear that?" Magnan quavered. "He spoke of my career in the past tense! But surely, even as slimy a little rat as Pokey Snail wouldn't deliberately stir up a hornet's nest and then—"

" 'Slimy little rat,' did you say, Ben?" Pokey's voice sounded from the intercom. "Yes, I heard that. I had merely withdrawn a few feet to pray and contemplate before finalizing my report," he went on contentedly. "Hadn't quite decided whether to credit you with bringing in some much-needed revenue to the Fund, or lay this whole sorry Gorm Festival business squarely at your doorstep; your unguarded remark helped me decide. You really ought to get that switch fixed, Ben. Ta."

Chapter 9

Half an hour later, Magnan sat glumly contemplating the Z-screen, which showed him the six grounded fleets arranged in circle-the-wagons style, and the immense mob deployed from the city enveloping *them*. Already the bright flashes of small arms were twinkling along the interface. The hijacked weapons had arrived, it was evident.

"Stop!" Magnan yelled. "All personnel, local and out-of-town, cease hostilities at once!" His command was ignored.

"We'll have to act fast, Stan," Captain Muldoon remarked, "if we're going to put a stop to that Donnybrook."

"Right, sir," Blatski replied eagerly. "I'll get on to Hoon in Power Section and tell him to take a heading on Altair and go to full gain, pronto!'

"What, flee the scene of action?" Muldoon roared. "No, by Godfrey! I'm taking her down! Stan, let's see you explain to Nav Section that I want this vessel to put down on that ridge on which both sides are converging so as to command the entire battlefield!"

"Oh, Jim," Magnan gasped. "If he puts *Ruppy*

down, he'll lose the advantage of maneuverability. Every gun in all the grounded fleets will be laid on that ridge, and I can see Dit's skirmishers already infiltrating along the south slope. He'll be in the middle of the most violent confrontation it's ever been my misfortune to observe!"

"It occurs to me, Mister," Blatski remarked, "that your job right now, as diplomatic observers, is to use the lifeboat to withdraw a few miles into space and record the action."

"Good notion," Magnan gobbled. "But don't you think running away—"

"Not running away," Muldoon corrected. "Just moving back to optimum observational range. You'd better get moving."

"Consider that an order, Ben!" Snail's voice rasped from the squawkbox on the bulkhead. "In the performance of *my* duties, I will observe from here."

When Pokey fell silent, Muldoon gave the appropriate commands, and *Ruppy* started her majestic descent into the center of the battle raging below.

"Jim," Magnan gasped. "Pokey doesn't know what he's doing! He's used to destroying the opposition by an equivocal hint, or an inconclusive report; he has no experience of the persuasiveness of actual gunfire!"

"The irregulars aren't likely to do *Ruppy* much harm," Retief pointed out. "They're accustomed to dealing with territorial levies as badly equipped as *they* are."

"Wim Dit—he'll be massacred!" Magnan groaned. "Those poor chaps are accustomed to fist-shaking and garbage-throwing! Even with handguns, up against Promo's firepower they haven't a chance!"

"Never mind," Retief soothed. "Pokey Snail doesn't know how to make use of what he's got."

"But, Retief," Magnan moaned, "its utter failure! When we arrived, the local factions were hostile, but impotent. Now, goaded by Pokey's arbitrary taxation, they're armed and confronted with overwhelming invading forces! And both groups are implacably hostile to *Ruppy*, thanks to the incautious remarks of Chief Inspector Snail! When they clash, it will be too late to salvage anything!" He stared in horror at the screen as the forces arrayed near the ridge settled into position to command the approach of the descending *Corruptible*. At Retief's suggestion he tore himself away, and the two civilians went to the adjacent boat deck and strapped into a fast shore dinghy.

"What shall we do?" Magnan whined.

"Nothing, yet, Ben," Retief replied.

"But they'll be face to face in a moment!" Magnan protested, studying the small screen, where the two gangs were closing fast.

They made a fast descent through scattered puffs of ack-ack, and came to ground in a small park a few blocks from the Embassy. In the purple twilight, the city seemed curiously still, the streets deserted, except for a few Irish-washerwoman types left over from Ladies' Day.

"They're all away at the war," Magnan commented gloomily. "We'll have to find Gad Buy or something. Actually Bam Slang would be better: Gad's only a chief of one hundred. But where are we to find Slang?" he challenged his own proposal.

"As Minister of Internal Chaos," Retief pointed out, "he may be out of a job now that the city's quiet."

"But there's a full-scale war going on just outside the city limits!" Magnan protested. "Still, I suppose the scamp is holed up, waiting to see which way it goes, eh?"

"Maybe Gad Buy and his Cub Scouts would be the best idea," Retief suggested. "His group wouldn't be involved."

"Capital notion," Magnan agreed. "Let's see, we

might find him at the Ministry of Stuff, arranging an issue of camping gear to the lads."

"Nothing there but ruins," Retief pointed out as they came abreast of the site of the Ministry. A lone figure was poking morosely in the rubble.

"Oh, look!" Magnan cried. "There's a lone figure poking morosely in the rubble!

"Oh, sir," he caroled as he came up to the tall cadaverous local, then, to Retief: "Why, it's Mr. Buy, just as we'd hoped!"

"So what's it to you?" Gad growled, backing away. "It was you Terries started alla trouble inna first place! We was having a nice, orderly riot until you fellers came along wit' yer big giveaways! Got ever'body upset! Now look!" Gad motioned morosely at the rubble all around. "What you want from *me*?"

"Nothing," Magnan hastened to assure the suspicious fellow. "Nothing except, ah, perhaps a trifle of assistance in defusing the present situation before it's too late."

" 'Too late'?" Gad echoed. " 'Defuse'? You must be nuts, Mister. The city's been bombed to rubble, the like populace has fled, and six enemy fleets are invading sacred Bloorian soil, just outside the city limits, and Wim Dit's lawless gangs are advancing to the attack—on both sides, mind you—and you babble of 'defusing the sitooation!' "

"It's true," Magnan's voice was intermittently audible through Gad's tirade, "that the situation has gotten a trifle out of hand, pacification-wise. But," he added slyly, "there are still the GFU awards to be made as soon as calm prevails."

"Well," Buy temporized, "I did kinda have a idear I might be up fer the Yout' Prize: my work wit the Scouts and all, you know."

"It is precisely your Cub Pack on which I wish to

confer the honor of assisting in the negotiations!" Magnan cried.

"That one went over my head," Buy complained. "You expect a bunch o' kids to rake yer fat outa the fire, is that it? Which the poor little guys ain't got a chanct up against Brag Gab, not to say something about Buck Promo and that Colonel Switchback miscreant he's chasing. And then there's that Cee Dee of Eff bunch, and . . ."

"I do not propose," Magnan stated coldly, "to pit the lads in actual combat against those conscienceless rogues, but merely to allow them to participate in a jolly charade, to confuse and thus confute the warring factions."

Buy looked appealing at Retief. "Can you get this windbag to say something a feller can unnerstan'?" he pled. "Something about some kinda 'jolly cheroot' or something," he concluded gloomily. "I don't let the kids smoke no stogies."

"He's asking you to make your Cubs available to run errands and the like while he attempts to con the combatants into laying down their arms," Retief translated.

"How's he gonna do that?" Buy demanded.

"He's going to make all of them think there's a big payoff in it," Retief specified.

"Oh, I got it," Buy replied brightly. "The suckers'll prob'ly go for it, too. By the way, what's the cash honorarium wit duh Yout' Prize?"

"A few million guck," Magnan supplied. "A trifle, merely symbolic. The true prize lies in the esteem of your fellow beings."

"Yeah, I got plenty o' that esteem already," Gad Buy dismissed the idea. "I'm not just a mere Cub leader! I'm Minister of Internal Chaos, too! How many million?"

"Seven, I think," Magnan sniffed. "But to get back

to my plan, only after the success of which the awards ceremony can eventuate—"

"Ye'r doing it again," Gad complained. "OK, so I gotta go along with yer scheme, or no Yout' Prize, that about it?"

"Succinctly put, Mr. Minister," Magnan confirmed. "Consider: not only will the boys' participation make peace, and make the award banquets possible, but their contribution, under your tutelage, will go far toward qualifying you for the prize."

"Look, Mister," Buy said earnestly. "You can count on the little bassers to do whatever you want done! So what if a few of 'em get squashed inna process, I say! Right, sir?"

"By no means!" Magnan yelled. "The children will be as safe as if clasped in their mothers' arms!"

"Safer," Gad corrected. "Some o' them broads takes a while to come down offa Ladies' Day. Clobber anything that moves. Good job most of 'em is onna march to the port, to kick some rump wid their men which they're likely to get their selfs kilt inna battle!"

"Very well," Magnan agreed. "Anyway, I have no intention of risking the lads' safety. Now here's what I want you to do . . ."

Three-quarters of an hour later, Ben Magnan, Retief, and Gad Buy guided his forty-five gaping pre-adolescents down from three battered school buses with HERNANDO COUNTY SCHOOL SYSTEM in faded black letters on their sides. Each boy carried a Daisy air rifle, artfully shaped to resemble an issue stunner, plus a hastily requisitioned kitchen knife stuck in his belt.

"Jeez!" George the reluctantly drafted Embassy driver exclaimed from his high perch as Magnan herded the last of the Cubs down the narrow steps of the vehicle. "They got a war going on here! I shunt of drove youse out here! Ferd and Ralphie, too; right, boys?" he called to his colleagues who were deep in confab between the parked buses.

They *shush!*ed him and crept forward to peek around their respective front fenders to catch a glimpse of the ground action. The fringes of the mob from the city were just skirting the intrusive vehicles.

Someone saw the drivers and yelled, "Spies!" At once a vigilante mob broke away from the main body to gather round the stationary buses. One fellow, a burly eight-footer, prodded Magnan and demanded, "Who ya working for, nosy? What are they paying ya?" He shoved Magnan behind the bus, out of sight of the rest. "They need a good boy onna inside?" he persisted. "I'm Cram Dook, and I'm looking to better my lot in life here. Whattaya say, before I and the boys string youse up?"

"I'm not," Magnan croaked. "That is, there's no, I mean, I can make it worth your while if you'd just direct attention from me—*and* my associates, of course."

"Whattaya tryna spy on?" Dook asked wonderingly. "Nothing here but us Objectionables and a few stray Reprehensibles maybe, where they fell in inna wrong squad—and o' course our traditional enemies the Viles; happens they was going on a, like, picnic. Old Gad Buy here, he invited us, ain't that right Mr. Minister?"

"The oaf lies in his decayed teeth!" Buy snapped. "Now, boys," he turned to his charges. "Let's put on our beards now, eh? What fun, don't you agree?"

Each boy produced a shabby set of false whiskers Gad had thoughtfully requisitioned from a theatrical supply house on the way to BBS Headquarters. In a trice, the children took on the appearance of an army of gnomes, an impression heightened when they obediently fell into ranks.

"Hey, Mr. Minister," one of the taller lads called. "You told that bum we're going on a picnic! You told *us* we was gonna get a close-up view o' the war and all! And I'm not wearing no crummy whiskers, neither! The hair gets in my mouth!" He ripped the offending disguise from his pink-cheeked face and threw it down, spitting the offending hairs after it. Many of his fellow Cubs followed suit.

"Here, Jimmy!" Buy yelled, attempting in vain to quell the rebellion. "I have to return them beards in good order by tonight! Bobby, you stop that!" He grabbed the arm of another tall kid who was stomping on his fire-red facial hair. Bobby kicked him below the knee, and at once a free-for-all ensued, led by Jimmy. Cram Dook fled, losing himself in the passing throng, who were armed, Magnan noticed, with agricultural implements.

"Stolen, no doubt from the peaceful B-9's," he muttered to Retief, who replied, "The boys did a good job in the dress rehearsal. I hope they've saved some stuff for the main performance."

"Don't worry," Bobby, the self-appointed straw-boss, reassured Magnan. "That was lots o' fun. I seen where old Cram Dook went. Let's go get him, fellers!" He dashed off in the direction taken by the misguided fellow, followed by the entire pack, with the exception of Jimmy and a few troublemakers who had rallied to his demand for obedience. Both groups charged, all yelling, "Get 'em!" at the top of their treble voices.

The two Cub groups began shooting BBs at each other as they pushed through the townsfolk, precipitating a stampede among the rabble in arms, who overran the command car from which Slum Dob was yelling orders: "Fall in, there! Get back in ranks! We got to hit 'em onna flank, in a orderly fashion—"

His voice choked off as the car was overturned, almost rolling on him. Back on his feet, he sprinted

for town, his impromptu army dissolved into a shouting mob which slowly coalesced and began pushing its
way townwards against the press of those still advancing, while the Cubs, waving improvised fixed bayonets,
spurred them on their way with well-aimed jabs.

"Oh, dear me," Magnan twittered. "Jim! Look
there! Thrash's crews have noticed the confusion in
the ranks here, and are preparing to take advantage
of the chaos by leading an attack on the poor, unex-
pecting townsfolk! Unless . . ." His gaze went to Admiral Promo's small detachment advancing on Thrash's
gang from the rear. Meanwhile, Colonel Switchback's
uniformed crew were forming up smartly directly in
Promo's path. Another gang, under Lieutenant Ape,
(who had somehow survived the attack on his ship)
was gathering on Switchback's flank. Skunky was trying in vain to recruit fellows from both gangs, thereby
setting off small secondary riots.

"Excuse me a moment, sir," Retief said quietly. "I
think we'd better get back in our boat."

"Yes, of course," Magnan agreed hastily. "From
there we can address these ruffians, and direct them
to disperse. And we can use the deck gun to put a
round across their bows, so to speak."

Once aboard the landing craft, Retief called Chief
Blatski.

"Stan," he said sternly, "I want you to suggest quietly to Captain Muldoon that he maneuver *Ruppy* into
a position fifty feet directly over the ridge and go to
standby. Both factions down here are converging on
the high ground, and he needs to be in position to
command the situation from above."

"Just what *I* was thinking, Mr. Retief," Blatski came
back heartily. "Hey, Captain, sir!" His voice was audible as he set off to deliver the message.

A moment later the capital ship had moved, silently
for all its bulk, into a spot whence it cast a shadow

across the just-colliding factions, both of which hesitated, then raised fists and shook them at the mighty vessel hovering above them.

"Uh-oh," Magnan blurted. "They're taking it badly, Jim! What if—?"

Bobby jostled Jimmy aside and made hand-and-arm gestures to the disorganized crowd of Cubs. Jimmy was haranguing his splinter bunch.

"Good job," Magnan groaned. "Bobby is using the secret Cub signals to order the boys to retreat! Wise move! But look! Wim Dit's requisitioned space-vessels are settling in now!"

"Not quite," Retief corrected Magnan's assumption about Bobby's semaphoring as the lads renewed their bayonet charge.

"Actually," Gad muttered, "I'm not sure *what* those gestures signify. It's a system the boys have worked out for themselves."

Above, just under the rocky crest of the ridge, Bobby's lads were busily adjusting their steak-knife bayonets on their Daisies. They proceeded to form a line abreast, three rank deep, and advanced up the steep rise. The first of Wim Dit's irregulars, topping the ridge, paused to stare in horror at the array of midgets, some still bearded, threatening them with glinting steel blades affixed to their stunners. They fell back, wildly yelling to their compatriots to flee, a suggestion eagerly accepted, with the result that Buck Promo's troop, just reaching the rocky crest, were abruptly assaulted by a charging mob of yelling townsfolk bent on escape. Quarrels had broken out here and there between Objectionables who objected to being jostled by Unmentionables, and Viles who resented Filthies blocking their way. Promo's men joined in enthusiastically, while Wim Dit's grounded space-detachment waded in with nightsticks to protect the interests of their ground-based compatriots.

The harsh rattle of a cleared throat from the S-to-G talker reminded the diplomats of Chief Inspector Snail's watchful eye above.

"It appears I'd best take a hand personally," he barked. "Since you fellows have blotted your copybooks so egregiously, I'll have to step in to restore order. I'm ordering Captain Muldoon to set her down just off to the west, there."

"Jim!" Magnan bleated, grabbing at his subordinate's arm. "We have to stop him! He'll be torn to pieces! Or, on the other hand, if Chief Blatski gets impatient with the intransigence of these undisciplined mobsters, he'll open fire, and all our hopes of a halcyon future for both locals and the Chief Inspector will be dashed! So—what shall we do?"

"Nothing, sir," Retief proposed, "except record it all for the amusement of the vast Tri-D viewing public of the Arm."

"But—Pokey won't give an inch!" Magnan protested. "He'll exact exorbitant fines, which will not only bankrupt the planetary economy, but will enrage every man-jack on Bloor, of whatever allegiance, even the few who've remained relatively calm until now! Pokey will order thousands jailed, and—and write a report that will render all Bloor inadmissable forever to GFU's distribution rolls. As for Pokey, he'll be in a rest home for years, recovering from the shock of not only having his authority flaunted, but being physically manhandled by these ruffians! What are we to do to avert this confrontation?"

"Not a thing, Mr. Magnan," Retief repeated. "Let's just watch. Think about it. Don't they really deserve each other?"

FALLEN ANGELS

Two refugees from one of the last remaining orbital space stations are trapped on the North American icecap, and only science fiction fans can rescue them! Here's an excerpt from *Fallen Angels*, the bestselling new novel by Larry Niven, Jerry Pournelle, and Michael Flynn.

* * *

She opened the door on the first knock and stood out of the way. The wind was whipping the ground snow in swirling circles. Some of it blew in the door as Bob entered. She slammed the door behind him. The snow on the floor decided to wait a while before melting. "Okay. You're here," she snapped. "There's no fire and no place to sit. The bed's the only warm place and you know it. I didn't know you were this hard up. And, by the way, I don't have any company, thanks for asking." If Bob couldn't figure out from that speech that she was pissed, he'd never win the prize as Mr. Perception.

"I am that hard up," he said, moving closer. "Let's get it on."

"Say what?" Bob had never been one for subtle technique, but this was pushing it. She tried to step back but his hands gripped her arms. They were cold as ice, even through the housecoat. "Bob!" He pulled her to him and buried his face in her hair.

"It's not what you think," he whispered. "We don't have time for this, worse luck."

"Bob!"

"No, just bear with me. Let's go to your bedroom. I don't want you to freeze."

He led her to the back of the house and she slid under the covers without inviting him in. He lay on top, still wearing his thick leather coat. Whatever he had in mind, she realized, it wasn't sex. Not with her housecoat, the comforter and his greatcoat playing chaperone.

He kissed her hard and was whispering hoarsely in her ear before she had a chance to react. "Angels down. A scoopship. It crashed."

"Angels?" Was he crazy?

He kissed her neck. "Not so loud. I don't think the 'danes are listening, but why take chances? Angels. Spacemen. *Peace* and *Freedom*."

She'd been away too long. She'd never heard spacemen called *Angels*. And— "Crashed?" She kept it to a whisper. "Where?"

"Just over the border in North Dakota. Near Mapleton."

"Great Ghu, Bob. That's on the Ice!"

He whispered, "Yeah. But they're not too far in."

"How do you know about it?"

He snuggled closer and kissed her on the neck again. Maybe sex made a great cover for his visit, but she didn't think he had to lay it on so thick. "We know."

"We?"

"The Worldcon's in Minneapolis-St. Paul this year—"

The World Science Fiction Convention. "I got the invitation, but I didn't dare go. If anyone saw me—"

"—And it was just getting started when the call came down from *Freedom*. Sherrine, they couldn't have picked a better time or place to crash their scoopship. That's why I came to you. Your grandparents live near the crash site."

She wondered if there was a good time for crashing scoopships. "So?"

"We're going to rescue them."

"We? Who's we?"

"The Con Committee, some of the fans—"

"But why tell me, Bob? I'm fafiated. It's been years since I've dared associate with fen."

Too many years, she thought. She had discovered science fiction in childhood, at her neighborhood branch library. She still remembered that first book: *Star Man's Son*, by Andre Norton. Fors had been persecuted because he was different; but he nurtured a secret, a mutant power. Just the sort of hero to appeal to an ugly-duckling little girl who would not act like other little girls.

SF had opened a whole new world to her. A galaxy, a

universe of new worlds. While the other little girls had played with Barbie dolls, Sherrine played with Lummox and Poddy and Arkady and Susan Calvin. While they went to the malls, she went to Trantor and the Witch World. While they wondered what Look was In, she wondered about resource depletion and nuclear war and genetic engineering. Escape literature, they called it. She missed it terribly.

"There is always one moment in childhood," Graham Greene had written in *The Power and the Glory*, "when the door opens and lets the future in." For some people, that door never closed. She thought that Peter Pan had had the right idea all along.

"Why tell *you*? Sherrine, we want you with us. Your grandparents live near the crash site. They've got all sorts of gear we can borrow for the rescue."

"Me?" A tiny trickle of electric current ran up her spine. But . . . *Nah.* "Bob, I don't dare. If my bosses thought I was associating with fen, I'd lose my job."

He grinned. "Yeah. Me, too." And she saw that he had never considered that she might not go.

'Tis a Proud and Lonely Thing to Be a Fan, they used to say, laughing. It had become a *very* lonely thing. The Establishment had always been hard on science fiction. The government-funded Arts Councils would pass out tax money to write obscure poetry for "little" magazines, but not to write speculative fiction. "Sci-fi isn't literature." *That* wasn't censorship.

Perversely, people went on buying science fiction without grants. Writers even got rich without government funding. *They couldn't kill us that way!*

Then the Luddites and the Greens had come to power. She had watched science fiction books slowly disappear from the library shelves, beginning with the children's departments. (That wasn't censorship either. Libraries couldn't buy *every* book, now could they? So they bought "realistic" children's books funded by the National Endowment for the Arts, books about death and divorce, and really important things like being overweight or fitting in with the right school crowd.)

Then came paper shortages, and paper allocations. The science fiction sections in the chain stores grew smaller. ("You can't expect us to stock books that aren't selling." And they can't sell if you don't stock them.)

Fantasy wasn't hurt so bad. Fantasy was about wizards

and elves, and being kind to the Earth, and harmony with nature, all things the Greens loved. But science fiction was about science.

Science fiction wasn't exactly outlawed. There was still Freedom of Speech; still a Bill of Rights, even if it wasn't taught much in the schools—even if most kids graduated unable to read well enough to understand it. But a person could get into a lot of unofficial trouble for reading SF or for associating with known fen. She could lose her job, say. Not through government persecution—of course not—but because of "reduction in work force" or "poor job performance" or "uncooperative attitude" or "politically incorrect" or a hundred other phrases. And if the neighbors shunned her, and tradesmen wouldn't deal with her, and stores wouldn't give her credit, who could blame them? Science fiction involved science; and science was a conspiracy to pollute the environment, "to bring back technology."

Damn right! she thought savagely. We do conspire to bring back technology. Some of us are crazy enough to think that there are alternatives to freezing in the dark. *And some of us are even crazy enough to try to rescue marooned spacemen before they freeze, or disappear into protective custody.*

Which could be dangerous. The government might declare you mentally ill, and help you.

She shuddered at that thought. She pushed and rolled Bob aside. She sat up and pulled the comforter up tight around herself. "Do you know what it was that attracted me to science fiction?"

He raised himself on one elbow, blinked at her change of subject, and looked quickly around the room, as if suspecting bugs. "No, what?"

"Not Fandom. I was reading the true quill long before I knew about Fandom and cons and such. No, it was the feeling of hope."

"Hope?"

"Even in the most depressing dystopia, there's still the notion that the future is something we build. It doesn't just happen. You can't predict the future, but you can invent it. Build it. That is a hopeful idea, even when the building collapses."

Bob was silent for a moment. Then he nodded. "Yeah. Nobody's building the future anymore. 'We live in an Age of Limited Choices.' " He quoted the government line without cracking a smile. "Hell, you don't *take* choices off a list. You *make* choices and *add* them to the list. Speaking of which, have you made your choice?"

That electric tickle . . . "Are they even alive?"

"So far. I understand it was some kind of miracle that they landed at all. They're unconscious, but not hurt bad. They're hooked up to some sort of magical medical widgets and the Angels overhead are monitoring. But if we don't get them out soon, they'll freeze to death."

She bit her lip. "And you think we can reach them in time?"

Bob shrugged.

"You want me to risk my life on the Ice, defy the government and probably lose my job in a crazy, amateur effort to rescue two spacemen who might easily be dead by the time we reach them."

He scratched his beard. "Is that quixotic, or what?"

"Quixotic. Give me four minutes."

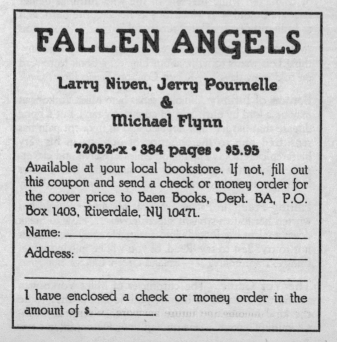

PRAISE FOR
LOIS MCMASTER BUJOLD

What the critics say:

The Warrior's Apprentice: "Now here's a fun romp through the spaceways—not so much a space opera as space ballet.... it has all the 'right stuff.' A lot of thought and thoughtfulness stand behind the all-too-human characters. Enjoy this one, and look forward to the next." —Dean Lambe, *SF Reviews*

"The pace is breathless, the characterization thoughtful and emotionally powerful, and the author's narrative technique and command of language compelling. Highly recommended." —*Booklist*

Brothers in Arms: "... she gives it a geniune depth of character, while reveling in the wild turnings of her tale. ... Bujold is as audacious as her favorite hero, and as brilliantly (if sneakily) successful." —*Locus*

"Miles Vorkosigan is such a great character that I'll read anything Lois wants to write about him. ... a book to re-read on cold rainy days." —Robert Coulson, *Comics Buyer's Guide*

Borders of Infinity: "Bujold's series hero Miles Vorkosigan may be a lord by birth and an admiral by rank, but a bone disease that has left him hobbled and in frequent pain has sensitized him to the suffering of outcasts in his very hierarchical era.... Playing off Miles's reserve and cleverness, Bujold draws outrageous and outlandish foils to color her high-minded adventures." —*Publishers Weekly*

Falling Free: "In *Falling Free* Lois McMaster Bujold has written her fourth straight superb novel. ... How to break down a talent like Bujold's into analyzable components? Best not to try. Best to say 'Read, or you will be missing something extraordinary.'" —Roland Green, *Chicago Sun-Times*

The Vor Game: "The chronicles of Miles Vorkosigan are far too witty to be literary junk food, but they rouse the kind of craving that makes popcorn magically vanish during a double feature." —Faren Miller, *Locus*

MORE PRAISE FOR
LOIS MCMASTER BUJOLD

What the readers say:

"My copy of *Shards of Honor* is falling apart I've reread it so often.... I'll read whatever you write. You've certainly proved yourself a grand storyteller."
—Liesl Kolbe, Colorado Springs, CO

"I experience the stories of Miles Vorkosigan as almost viscerally uplifting.... But certainly, even the weightiest theme would have less impact than a cinder on snow were it not for a rousing good story, and good storytelling with it. This is the second thing I want to thank you for.... I suppose if you boiled down all I've said to its simplest expression, it would be that I immensely enjoy and admire your work. I submit that, as literature, your work raises the overall level of the science fiction genre, and spiritually, your work cannot avoid positively influencing all who read it."
—Glen Stonebraker, Gaithersburg, MD

" 'The Mountains of Mourning' [in *Borders of Infinity*] was one of the best-crafted, and simply best, works I'd ever read. When I finished it, I immediately turned back to the beginning and read it again, and I can't remember the last time I did that."   —Betsy Bizot, Lisle, IL

"I can only hope that you will continue to write, so that I can continue to read (and of course buy) your books, for they make me laugh and cry and think ... rare indeed."   —Steven Knott, Major, USAF

What do you say?

Send me these books!

Shards of Honor • 72087-2 • $4.99 ____
The Warrior's Apprentice • 72066-X • $4.50 ____
Ethan of Athos • 65604-X • $4.99 ____
Falling Free • 65398-9 • $4.99 ____
Brothers in Arms • 69799-4 • $4.99 ____
Borders of Infinity • 69841-9 • $4.99 ____
The Vor Game • 72014-7 • $4.99 ____
Barrayar • 72083-X • $4.99 ____

Lois McMaster Bujold: Only from Baen Books

If these books are not available at your local bookstore, just check your choices above, fill out this coupon and send a check or money order for the cover price to Baen Books, Dept. BA, P.O. Box 1403, Riverdale, NY 10471.

NAME: _____

ADDRESS: _____

_____

I have enclosed a check or money order in the amount of $ _____.

ROGER ZELAZNY
DREAM WEAVER

"Zelazny, telling of gods and wizards, uses magical words as if he were himself a wizard. He reaches into the subconscious and invokes archetypes to make the hair rise on the back of your neck. Yet these archetypes are transmuted into a science fiction world that is as believable—and as awe-inspiring—as the world you now live in." —**Philip José Farmer**

Wizard World
Infant exile, wizard's son, Pol Detson spent his formative years in total ignorance of his heritage, trapped in the most mundane of environments: Earth. But now has come the day when his banishers must beg him to return as their savior, lest their magic kingdom become no better than Earth itself. Previously published in parts as *Changeling* and *Madwand*.
69842-7 * $3.95   ——

The Black Throne with Fred Saberhagen
One of the most remarkable exercises in the art and craft of fantasy fiction in the last decade.... As children they met and built sand castles on a beach out of space and time: Edgar Perry, little Annie, and Edgar Allan Poe.... Fifteen years later Edgar Perry has grown to manhood—and as the result of a trip through a maelstrom, he's leading a life of romantic adventure. But his alter ego, Edgar Allan, is stranded in a strange and unfriendly world where he can only write about the wonderful and mysterious reality he has lost forever....
72013-9 * $4.95   ——

The Mask of Loki with Thomas T. Thomas
It started in the 12th century when their avatars first joined in battle. On that occasion the sorcerous Hasan al Sabah, the first Assassin, won handily against Thomas Amnet, Knight Templar. There have been many duels since then, and in each the undying Arab has ended the life of Loki's avatar. The wizard thinks he's in control. The gods think that's funny.... A new novel of demigods who walk the Earth, in the tradition of *Lord of Light*.
72021-X * $4.95   ——

This Immortal
After the Three Days of War, and decades of Vegan occupation, Earth isn't doing too well. But Conrad Nimikos, if he could stop jet-setting for a minute, might just be Earth's redemption. . . . This, Zelazny's first novel, tied with *Dune* for the Hugo Award.
69848-6 * $3.95 _____

The Dream Master
When Charles Render, engineer-physician, agrees to help a blind woman learn to "see"—at least in her dreams—he is drawn into a web of powerful primal imagery. And once Render becomes one with the Dreamer, he must enter irrevocably the realm of nightmare. . . .
69874-5 * $3.50 _____

Isle of the Dead
Francis Sandow was the only non-Pei'an to complete the religious rites that allowed him to become a World-builder—and to assume the Name and Aspect of one of the Pei'an gods. And now he's one of the richest men in the galaxy. A man like that makes a lot of enemies. . . .
72011-2 * $3.50 _____

Four for Tomorrow
Featuring the Hugo winner "A Rose for Ecclesiastes" and the Nebula winner "The Doors of His Face, the Lamps of His Mouth."
72051-1 * $3.95 _____
